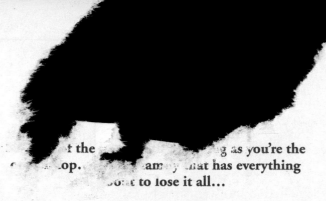

...t the ...g as you're the
...op. ...am...at has everything
...to lose it all...

The Montagues have found themselves at the centre of the
ton's rumour mill, with lords and ladies alike claiming the
family is not what it used to be.

The mysterious death of the heir to the Dukedom, and the
arrival of an unknown woman claiming he fathered her son,
is only the tip of the iceberg in a family where scandal
upstairs *and* downstairs threatens the very foundations
of their once powerful and revered dynasty...

August 2012
THE WICKED LORD MONTAGUE – Carole Mortimer

September 2012
THE HOUSEMAID'S SCANDALOUS SECRET – Helen Dickson

October 2012
THE LADY WHO BROKE THE RULES – Marguerite Kaye

November 2012
LADY OF SHAME – Ann Lethbridge

December 2012
THE ILLEGITIMATE MONTAGUE – Sarah Mallory

January 2013
UNBEFITTING A LADY – Bronwyn Scott

February 2013
REDEMPTION OF A FALLEN WOMAN – Joanna Fulford

March 2013
A STRANGER AT CASTONBURY – Amanda McCabe

D1076937

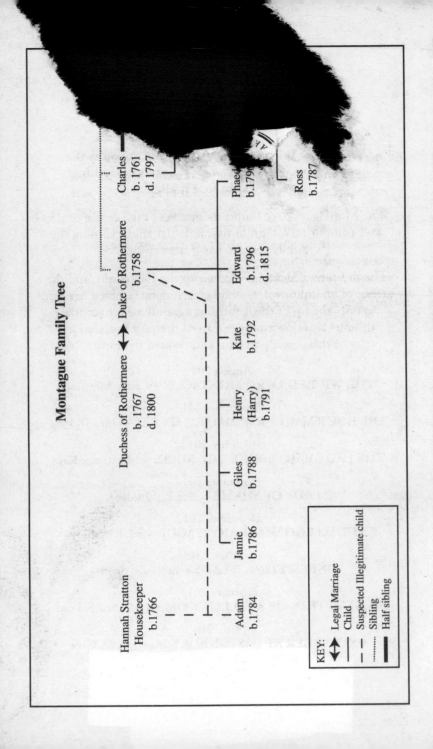

Montague Family Tree

Hannah Stratton
Housekeeper
b.1766

Duchess of Rothermere ←→ **Duke of Rothermere**
b. 1767   b.1758
d. 1800

Charles
b. 1761
d. 1797

Adam
b.1784

Jamie
b.1786

Giles
b.1788

Henry
(Harry)
b.1791

Kate
b.1792

Edward
b.1796
d. 1815

Phaed
b.179

Ross
b.1787

KEY:

←→	Legal Marriage
—	Child
¦	Suspected Illegitimate child
⋯	Sibling
▬	Half sibling

My dear Giles,

Your reluctance for responsibility, my son, has been apparent since you were a child. But under these tragic circumstances it is your duty to step into the shoes of your missing brother and hold this family together. It is what families do and, during times such as these, I will only ask you once to put your frustration aside and keep your opinions quiet. You are now, whether you like it or not, the new heir to Castonbury Park.

Your father

First published in Great Britain 2012
Mills & Boon, an imprint of Harlequin (UK) Limited,
Eton House, 18-24 Paradise Road, Richmond, Surrey TW9 1SR

© Carole Mortimer 2012

ISBN: 978 0 263 90185 6

52-0812

Harlequin (UK) policy is to use papers that are natural, renewable and recyclable products and made from wood grown in sustainable forests. The logging and manufacturing processes conform to the legal environmental regulations of the country of origin.

Printed and bound
by CPI Group (UK) Ltd, Croydon, CR0 4YY

The Wicked
Lord Montague

CAROLE MORTIMER

To the seven other lovely authors
who made writing this such fun!

Chapter One

Castonbury Park, Derbyshire, April 1816

'His Grace seems much better today, Lily, thank you for asking,' Mrs Stratton, the widowed housekeeper at Castonbury Park, assured Lily warmly as she led the way through to her private parlour situated at the back of the grand mansion house that had long been the seat of the Dukes of Rothermere. 'His Grace's valet informed me only this morning that the advent of a late spring appears to be having an advantageous effect upon the duke's spirits.' She glanced approvingly at the sun shining in through the window.

Lily wondered if it was the advent of spring which had succeeded in reviving the grief-stricken Duke of Rothermere, or the possible return of Lord Giles Montague. His homecoming was in response to the letter Lily's father said the duke had written to his son four days ago, in which he had demanded that Giles Montague return home and take up his duties as his heir. Sadly, Lord James Montague, previously the eldest son and heir of the Montague family, had died in Spain during the campaign against Napoleon. It had been a devastating blow to the long-widowed Duke of Rothermere, further exacerbated ten months ago by the death of Lord Edward, the duke's youngest son.

Being the daughter of the local vicar, and an adopted daughter at that, had put Lily in the unique position of making friends both above and below stairs at Castonbury Park, and she was friends with the two daughters of the household, Lady Phaedra and Lady Kate. But it was the late Lord Edward Montague who had been her dearest and most beloved friend. The two of them had been of an age where they had played together about the estate as children, and remained good friends as they had grown too old to play and had instead turned their attention to dancing together at the local assemblies.

Indeed, their friendship had been of such warmth and duration that Lily had been deeply shocked when Edward had succeeded in persuading his father into buying him a commission in the army a year ago, so that he might join his brother Giles in his regiment.

She couldn't bear that Edward had died in that last bloody battle at Waterloo, his life coming to an abrupt end at the point of a French bayonet in only his nineteenth year.

Edward's life.

Not Giles, the brother who was eight years older than Edward, and who had been the inspiration for Edward's desire to gain a commission in the army.

'Thank you, Agnes.' Mrs Stratton nodded approval as the maid brought in the tray of tea things.

Lily waited until she had departed before continuing the conversation. 'I have always thought this room to have a particularly lovely view of the gardens.'

'Why, thank you, Lily.' Mrs Stratton's already ample chest puffed out with pleasure as she poured their tea. 'His Grace has always been very generous in regard to the comfort of his servants.'

'I am sure his kindness is only commensurate with the care and devotion all of you have shown towards him and his family for so many years.' Lily sat forward slightly so that she might take her cup of tea from the older woman.

It was now four long days since Mr Seagrove, Lily's adoptive father, and vicar of the parish of Castonbury—and a particular friend of His Grace—had returned from dining at Castonbury Park to confide in Lily concerning the letter the duke had written to his son Giles in London, where that haughty gentleman had chosen to reside since resigning his commission in the army nine months ago.

It was a confidence which Lily had listened to with horror as she recalled the last occasion on which she and Giles Montague had spoken!

Having lived in a state of turmoil these past four days at the mere thought of Giles Montague's return, Lily had been unable to contain her restless anxiety another moment longer. She decided to walk the mile to Castonbury Park in order to pay a visit to the kindly Mrs Stratton, in the hope that the duke's housekeeper may have further news concerning the heir's return.

Presenting Mrs Stratton with a jar of Mrs Jeffries's legendary gooseberry jam on her arrival—everyone in the parish knew that the gooseberries in Mr Seagrove's garden were far superior to any other in the district— had gone a long way towards paving the way to an invitation from Mrs Stratton for Lily to join her in her parlour for afternoon tea.

Not that Mrs Stratton was one for gossip. Her loyalty to the Montague family was beyond reproach. Nevertheless, Lily hoped there would be some way in which she might steer the conversation in the direction in which she wished it would go. 'It must be somewhat lonely here for His Grace since most of the family travelled down to London for the Season?' she prompted lightly.

'Perhaps.' The housekeeper frowned a little.

Lily sipped her tea. 'Did none of them think to stay behind and keep His Grace company?'

'I believe Mrs Landes-Fraser had intended on doing so, but Lady Kate was called away on other business, and her aunt decided it prudent to accompany her.'

Lily smiled affectionately as she guessed that the eldest of the two Montague sisters, having pooh-poohed the idea of attending the London Season, was no doubt now off on another of her crusades to help the underprivileged and needy, and that her maternal aunt, Mrs Wilhelmina Landes-Fraser, had accompanied her in order to ensure she did not stray too far from the bounds of propriety.

Mrs Stratton offered Lily one of the meringues made by the duke's French chef. 'Besides which, I believe His Grace is more…settled in his manner when he is not troubled by the rush and bustle of the younger members of the family hurrying here, there and everywhere.'

Lily bit back her frustration with this unhelpful reply as she carefully helped herself to one of the delicacies. 'Perhaps there will soon be news of Lord Giles returning...?'

'None that I am aware of.' The older woman looked puzzled. 'I must say that I do not completely...understand his continued absence, given the circumstances.'

'No,' Lily prompted softly.

Indeed, she had never understood Edward's excess of affection for his brother Giles. He was a gentleman whom Lily had never found particular reason to like in the past, but for over a year now, she was ashamed to admit, she had detested him almost to the point of hatred!

Mrs Stratton gave a slightly exasperated shake of her grey head. 'And he was such an endearing scamp as a child too. I find it hard to believe—' She broke off distractedly, not one to give, or condone, any criticism of a single member of the Montague family to whom she had long devoted her time and emotions, the more so since her own son did not visit as often as she might have wished.

Lily had discovered this past year that she was not so generous of nature in regard to Lord Giles Montague. Indeed, she found it hard even to begin to imagine him as anything other than the disdainful and arrogant gentleman who, the last time they had spoken together, had so wilfully and deliberately insulted both her and the possible lowly origins of her forebears. The mere thought of his ever being 'an endearing scamp,' even as a child, seemed positively ludicrous to her!

The eight years' difference in their ages had meant that Lord Giles had already been away at boarding school by the time Lily was old enough to be allowed to play further afield than the vicarage garden, and he had not always returned home in the holidays either, often choosing to spend those times staying at the home of a friend. The occasions when he had come home for the holidays he had scornfully declined to spend any of his time with children he considered should still be in the nursery, and upon reflection, Lily had come to believe that he had only suffered Edward's company because of the young boy's obvious hero-worship of his older brother.

A hero-worship Lily firmly believed to have succeeded in bringing about Edward's early demise.

The fact that Mrs Stratton had obviously received no instructions in regard to airing Lord Giles Montague's rooms for his imminent arrival did, however, seem to be a confirmation of his continued absence. It enabled Lily to relax for the first time in days as she devoured the delicious meringue with gusto. She had always been naturally slender, and besides, this news of Lord

Giles—or lack of it!—was surely reason enough for celebration on her part.

She did feel a slight pang of guilt on behalf of the Duke of Rothermere, but ultimately believed that he, and everyone else at Castonbury Park, and the surrounding village, were far better off without the oppressive presence of Lord Giles Montague and his conceited arrogance.

Lily felt happier than she had for days as she walked back to the vicarage. She had removed and was swinging her bonnet in her gloved hand, allowing the sun to warm her ebony curls as she strolled through the dappled glade, which she invariably used as a shortcut onto the road leading back to the village.

Spring was indeed here; the sun was shining, the wildflowers were in bloom, the birds were singing in the branches of trees unfurling their leaves after the long winter. Indeed, it was the sort of pleasant early evening when one was assured of God's existence and it felt good just to be alive and in His—

'Well, well, well, if it is not Miss Seagrove once again trespassing on the Rothermere estate!'

The sun disappeared behind a cloud, the wildflowers lost their lustre and the birds ceased singing as they instead took flight from the treetops at the sound of a human voice. At the same time, the colour drained from Lily's cheeks and her heart began pounding loudly in her chest, her shoulders having stiffened defensively in instant recognition of that hatefully mocking voice. A voice which undoubtedly belonged to none other than the utterly despicable Lord Giles Montague!

'I do not remember you as being this…accommodatingly silent during the last occasion on which we spoke together, Miss Seagrove. Can it be that "the cat has finally got your tongue"?'

Lily drew in one, two, three steadying breaths, as she prepared to turn and face her nemesis; all of her earlier feelings of well-being had flown away with the birds in the face of the shocking reality that Giles Montague was returned to Castonbury Park, after all.

In the end it was the impatient snorting of that gentleman's horse which caused Lily to turn sharply, only to come face to face with the huge, glistening black and wild-eyed animal as it seemed to look down the long length of its nose at her with the same scornful disdain as its rider.

Lily took an involuntary step back before chancing a glance up at the owner of that horse, her breath catching in her throat as the late-afternoon sun shone behind the imposing and wide-shouldered figure of

Lord Giles Montague, and succeeding in casting his face into shadow beneath the brim of his tall hat.

Not that Lily needed to see that arrogantly mocking face clearly to know what he looked like; each and every one of those dark and saturnine features was etched into her memory! Cold grey eyes beneath heavy brows, a long and aristocratic nose, hard and chiselled cheeks, the wide slash of his mouth invariably thinned with scorn or disdain, the strength of his jaw tilted at a haughty angle.

She moistened her lips before choosing to answer his initial challenge rather than the second. 'It is impossible to do anything other than walk in the grounds of Castonbury Park when one has been visiting at the house, my lord.'

'Indeed?' he drawled in a bored tone, holding his skittish mount in check without apparent effort. 'And whom, might one ask, can you have been "visiting" at Castonbury Park, when most of my family are away or in London at present?'

Lily's cheeks flushed at the derision in his tone. 'I came to deliver some of last year's jam to Mrs Stratton from our own cook,' she revealed reluctantly.

'Ah.' He nodded that arrogant head, a contemptuous smile curving his lips, no doubt at the knowledge that Lily had been visiting below stairs rather than above.

Now that she could see Lord Giles's face better Lily realised that there was, after all, something slightly different about him than the last time she had seen him. 'You appear to have a smudge of dirt upon your jaw, my lord,' she told him with a feeling of inner satisfaction at his appearing less than his usual pristine self.

He made no effort to raise a hand to remove the mark. 'I believe, if you were to look a little closer, you would find that it is a bruise, and not dirt,' he dismissed in a bored voice.

Lily's brows rose. 'You have taken a tumble from your horse?' It seemed an even more unlikely explanation than the dirt, as Edward had told her years ago that the duke had placed all of his sons up on a horse before they could even walk, and Lord Giles's years in the army would only have honed his already excellent horsemanship.

'Not that it is any of your business, but I chanced to walk into a fist several days ago,' he drawled in cool dismissal. 'Mr Seagrove is well, I trust?'

Lily would much rather have heard more about the 'fist' he had 'chanced to walk into' than discuss her adoptive father's health, which had never been anything but robust. 'My father is very well, thank you, my lord,' she assured huskily, still staring curiously at the bruise upon his jaw. 'How did you—?'

'Please pass along my respects to him when next you see him.' Lord Giles nodded distantly.

Obviously the subject of that 'fist' was not for further discussion, which only increased Lily's curiosity as to who would have dared lay a fist upon the aristocratic jaw of Lord Giles Montague. Whoever he might have been, Lily knew a desire to shake the gentleman by that very same hand! 'Certainly, my lord.' Her tone was dry at the obvious omission of any of those respects being paid towards her; Giles Montague had not so much as raised his tall hat in her presence, let alone offered her polite words of greeting!

Because, as they were both only too well aware, there could be no politeness between the two of them after the frankness of their last conversation together. Not now. Or in the future. Lily disliked Giles Montague with a passion she could neither hide nor disguise, and he made no effort to hide the contempt with which he regarded her and her questionable forebears.

'You have come home to visit with your father, my lord?' She offered a challenge of her own.

Those grey eyes narrowed. 'So it would appear.'

Lily raised dark brows at his challenging tone. 'And

I am sure His Grace will be gratified to know you at last feel able to spare him time, from what I am sure has been your…busy life in London, these past months.'

Giles's expression remained unchanged at this less than subtle rebuke. A rebuke which told him all too clearly that Miss Lily Seagrove had heard something at least of his rakish behaviour in London these past nine months. 'If I had known you were counting the days of my absence perhaps I would have returned sooner…?'

Colour brightened the ivory of her cheeks even as those moss-green eyes sparkled with temper at his obvious derision. 'The only reason I would ever count the days of your absence, my lord, would be with the intention of thanking God for them!'

Giles looked down at her from between narrowed lids. As a young child Lily Seagrove had been as wild and untamed as might have been expected, given her ancestry. Her long curly black hair had seemed always to be in a loose tangle about her thin and narrow shoulders, smears of mud and berries invariably about her ruby-red mouth, her tiny hands suffering that same fate and her dresses usually having a rip or two about them where she had been crawling through the undergrowth with his brother Edward on one of their adventures.

Quite when that untamed child had become the composed and confident young lady Giles had met just over a year ago he was unsure, only knowing that he had returned home to find that his brother Edward was completely—and quite unsuitably—infatuated with the beautiful young woman Lily Seagrove had become.

The beautiful young woman she undoubtedly still was....

Her hair was just as black and abundant as it had ever been, but without her bonnet it was visibly tamed into becoming curls at her crown, with several of those shorter curls left to frame the delicate beauty of her face which boasted smooth, ivory skin, moss-green eyes surrounded by thick dark lashes, a tiny upturned nose, high cheekbones and full and sensual lips above her pointed and very determined chin.

She wore a dark brown velvet pelisse over a cream and fashionably high-waisted gown; her tall body was slender, the swell of her breasts covered by a wisp of delicate cream lace, matching lace gloves upon her hands, and tiny boots of brown leather upon her feet, the latter obviously out of deference to her walk about the countryside rather than fashion.

Yes, that wild and seemingly untameable child had grown into this beautiful and alluring woman of composure and grace. But, nevertheless, she was still one who had been, and always would be, a foundling of questionable ancestry and who was, and would ever remain, socially inferior to each and every member of the Montague family. It was an indisputable fact she still resented having heard from Giles's own lips a year ago, if the anger that now burned so brightly in Miss Lily Seagrove's moss-green eyes was any indication!

He gave a haughty inclination of his head. 'I am sure your prayers this evening will not be quite so full of gratitude on the subject.'

'I might always pray for your visit to be of short duration instead, my lord,' she returned with false sweetness.

Giles permitted himself a hard and humourless smile. 'I am sure that we both might pray for it to be so!'

She blinked up at him. 'You do not intend your visit to Castonbury Park to be of long duration…?'

In truth, Giles had no idea how long he would be able to endure being in the home where he would be reminded, on a daily basis, of all that the Montague family had lost—namely Jamie and Edward, the eldest and the youngest sons.

He quirked mocking brows. 'No doubt it would please you if that were to be the case?'

'As you made so clear to me on the last occasion we spoke, my lord, it is not for someone as lowly as I to be pleased or displeased by any of the actions of a member of a family as superior to myself as the Montagues!' Those moss-green eyes met his gaze with unflinching challenge.

She really was quite remarkably beautiful, Giles noted admiringly, as she stood there so tall and proud, with her cheeks flushed and those green eyes glittering angrily. In fact, Miss Lily Seagrove was far more beautiful than any of the numerous women Giles had known so intimately in London these past nine months.

It was a thought totally out of keeping with the strained nature of their acquaintance. 'Even you must acknowledge it really would not have done, Lily…?' Giles quirked a dark brow.

Her eyes widened incredulously. 'You would dare to talk of that again now, when Edward has been dead these past ten months, and so lost to all of us for ever?'

No, Giles would prefer never to have to speak of anything ever again which forced him to acknowledge that his brother Edward was dead. Indeed, he had spent the past nine months avoiding returning to

Castonbury Park in an attempt to do just that. Without any success, of course, but there was not a fashionable man, or willing woman, in London who could not confirm how vigorously he had attempted to achieve that oblivion, in the company of the former, in the beds of the latter.

How ironic that the first person Giles should meet upon returning to Castonbury should be the one woman guaranteed to remind him of the losses he had been trying so hard to avoid!

His mouth twisted bitterly. 'No doubt ten months has been more than long enough for you to have recovered sufficiently from your hopes regarding Edward, and to have some other unsuspecting—and, for your sake, I hope wealthy!—young man ensnared by your charms?'

Lily drew her breath in sharply, so deeply wounded by Giles Montague's dismissive scorn of the affection she had felt for Edward that for several minutes she felt completely unable to speak. She almost—almost!—pitied Giles Montague for his lack of understanding.

No—she did pity him, knowing that a man as arrogant and insensitive as Giles Montague could never appreciate or attempt to understand the love she and Edward had felt for each other, or how their friendship had been of such depth and duration that Lily had come to regard Edward as the brother she had never had, as well as being her dearest friend in all the world.

A year ago the haughty and disdainful Lord Giles Montague had been blind to the nature of that affection, and chosen instead to believe that as she was only the adopted daughter of the local vicar—her real parentage unknown—then she must necessarily be out to ensnare his rich and titled youngest brother into matrimony. It must have been a match he considered so unsuitable he had felt no qualms in arranging to talk to Lily without Edward's knowledge, so that he might inform her of such. It had been a conversation that had so stunned Lily by its forthright audacity she was ashamed to say she had felt no hesitation in returning that frankness in regard to her own less than flattering opinion of Giles Montague.

She raised her chin now. 'I will continue to love Edward until the day I die,' she stated softly and evenly, too heavy of heart to feel the least satisfaction when she saw the way Giles Montague's eyes widened upon hearing her declaration. 'Now, if you will excuse me, my lord, I believe it is past time I returned to the vicarage.' She continued to hold that guarded and icy grey gaze as she sketched the slightest of curtseys before turning on her booted heels and walking away.

Her head was held high as she refused, even for

propriety's sake, to resume wearing her bonnet. Giles
Montague already believed her to be socially inferior
to him, so why should she care if her actions now confirmed that belief.

Except Lily did care what people thought of her.
She had always cared. Not for her own sake, but for
the sake of the kindly Mr and Mrs Seagrove.

Lily had only been eight years old, and had not
understood, when one of the children from the village
had first taunted her and called her 'Gypsy.' She had
questioned Mrs Seagrove as to its meaning as soon
as she had returned to the vicarage. That dear lady
had taken Lily gently in her arms and explained that
it was merely another name for the Romany families
who stayed at the Castonbury estate during the spring
and at harvest time.

Again, having rarely bothered to waste time looking at herself in a mirror, Lily had not understood why
one of the village children should have chosen to taunt
her with such name. Until Mrs Seagrove had stroked
Lily's long and curling black hair and explained that
she was not the true child of Mr and Mrs Seagrove, but
had in fact been left, as a baby of only a few weeks,
on the doorstep of the vicarage eight years previously;
of how she and Mr Seagrove suspected that Lily's real
mother had perhaps been one of the young and unmar-

ried Gypsy girls who travelled the roads of England
with their tribe.

Gypsy.

Lord Giles Montague had made it obvious a year
ago that he was both totally aware of such a heritage,
and disapproving of its being connected with his noble
family.

Chapter Two

Giles had put aside the encounter in the glade with the beautiful Miss Lily Seagrove by the time he handed over the reins of his horse to one of the grooms at Castonbury Park. His thoughts were now on the signs of neglect, both to the outside of the house itself and other parts of the estate, which he had noted as he rode down the hillside and along the side of the lake.

Several tiles were missing from the roof at the back of the house, the stonework at the front was also in need of attention and there were weeds growing in several places about the foundations. The gardens that surrounded the house seemed to be well tended, but Giles had noted that several trees had toppled over in the woods at the back of the house, and the lake was also in need of clearing of the debris that had accumulated from the past winter. And they were only the things that Giles had noted at first glance; there were sure to be others he had not had the chance to see as yet.

They would no doubt confirm that things here were as dire as his sister Phaedra had warned they were. Something which did not please Giles at all, if it meant he would have to prolong his stay here...

Lumsden—the butler who had been with the Montague family for more years than Giles could remember—opened the front door as he reached the top step. 'Master Giles!' His mouth gaped open in surprise. 'I mean, Lord Giles,' he corrected as he obviously recovered his usual calm equilibrium. 'We had not been told to expect you.'

'I did not send word of my coming,' Giles assured as he strode past the older man and into the house.

It was almost ten months since Giles had last stepped through this doorway, on the occasion of Edward's funeral, and whilst the inside of the house was as clean and neat as it had ever been—Mrs Stratton, Giles knew, would allow nothing less from her household staff!—there was nevertheless an air of emptiness about it, of a house that no longer felt like a home.

An emptiness that Giles had expected—and so determinedly avoided these past nine months.

His mouth tightened as he turned back to hand the butler his hat and riding crop before shrugging off his outer coat. 'My father is in his rooms in the east wing?'

'Yes, my lord.' Lumsden's seriousness of tone somehow managed to convey so much more than was said in those three words. 'I will go and enquire of Smithins if he considers His Grace well enough to receive you—'

'No need, Lumsden,' Giles dismissed airily. 'I am sure I will be able to judge that for myself once I have seen my father.'

'But—'

'What is it, Lumsden?' He frowned his irritation with this further delay, anxious now to see his father for himself, so that he might best decide what needed to be done here in order that he might leave again as soon as was possible.

The butler looked uncomfortable. 'Smithins has issued orders that no one is allowed to see His Grace without his permission.'

Giles raised autocratic brows. 'Am I to understand that my father's valet now says who is and is not to visit him?' He conveyed his incredulity in his tone.

'I believe that sums up the situation very well, my lord, yes.' The butler looked even more uncomfortable.

'We shall see about that!' Giles assured determinedly. 'If you could organise a decanter of brandy brought into us, Lumsden, I would be most obliged?'

The elderly man straightened with renewed purpose. 'Certainly, my lord.'

Giles turned with that same sense of purpose, his expression grim as he strode through to his father's suite of rooms in the east wing of the house, more than ready to do battle with the man who was employed to be his father's valet and not his jailer!

'His Grace will be overjoyed, I am sure.' Mr Seagrove beamed approvingly, having just been informed by Lily that Lord Giles Montague was returned to Castonbury Park, after all.

There was no answering pleasure in Lily's face as she sat across the dinner table from her father in the small family dining room at the vicarage. 'No doubt,' she dismissed uninterestedly. 'Would you care for more potatoes, Father?' She held up the dish temptingly in the hopes of changing the conversation from the subject of the hateful Giles Montague, knowing full well that the creamy vegetable was one of her father's weaknesses.

'Thank you, Lily.' He nodded distractedly as she spooned the potatoes onto this plate before replacing the bowl on the table, a worried frown marring his usually smooth brow. 'I trust you and Lord Giles had a pleasant conversation together?'

She gave that earlier conversation some thought. 'I believe I can say that I succeeded in being as polite to Lord Giles as he was to me,' she finally replied carefully.

'That is good.' The vicar nodded, apparently unaware of the true meaning of Lily's reply. 'However, I think it best if we both call at the Park tomorrow morning to pay our formal respects.'

Lily felt her heart sink. 'Oh, must I come too? I have several calls to make in the morning, Father. Mrs Jenkins and her new baby, and the youngest Hurst boy's leg is in need of—'

'Yes, yes, I appreciate that you are very busy about the parish, Lily.' Mr Seagrove beamed his approval of the care and attention she had given to his parishioners since the death of his wife five years ago. 'But His Grace is my patron, after all, and it would seem rude if we did not both call upon his heir.'

Lily could appreciate the logic of her father's argument; Mr Seagrove's tenure in Castonbury, although of long duration, was nevertheless still dependent upon the Duke of Rothermere's goodwill. She just wished she did not have to see Lord Giles Montague again quite so soon. She had no wish to see that unpleasant man ever again, if truth be told! Though Lily knew it would never do for her father to suspect such a thing, which meant Lily had no choice but to accept she was to accompany her father to the Park tomorrow morning and make polite conversation with Lord Giles Montague.

'It is good to see you again, Mr Seagrove.' Lord Giles smiled with genuine warmth as he strode forcefully into the elegant salon where they waited.

Lily was momentarily taken aback by the change wrought on that haughty gentleman's countenance when he smiled down at her father as the two men greeted each other; those grey eyes had softened to the warmth of a dove's wing, laughter lines grooved into those hard and chiselled cheeks, his teeth appearing very white and even between the relaxed line of sculpted lips. Even the bruising on his jaw could not succeed in detracting from his pleasant demeanour.

Indeed, for those few brief moments Giles Montague looked almost…rakishly handsome, Lily realised in surprise. A rakish handsomeness, his sister Phaedra had confided to Lily, he had reputedly taken full advantage of these past months in London!

'And Miss Seagrove.' Lord Giles turned to bow, the

genuine warmth of the smile he had given her father fading to be replaced by one of mocking humour. 'I had not expected to see you again quite so soon.'

'My lord.' She met that gaze coolly as she curtseyed, her best peach-coloured bonnet covering the darkness of her curls today, a perfect match for the high-waisted gown she usually wore to church on a Sunday, her cream lace gloves upon her hands.

Mr Seagrove had been born the fourth son of a country squire, and so possessed a small private income to go with the stipend he received yearly from the Duke of Rothermere, but even so Lily possessed only half a dozen gowns, gowns she made for herself after acquiring the material from an establishment in the village. Unfortunately only three of the gowns Lily owned were fashionable enough, and of a quality, to wear out in company; including the gown Lily had been wearing yesterday, Giles Montague had already seen two of those gowns.

Which was a very strange thought for her to have— was it not?—when she had absolutely no interest in Giles Montague's opinion, either of her personally, or the gowns she wore…?

No one likes to appear wanting in front of another, she told herself firmly as she answered, 'My father, once told of your return, was of course anxious to call and pay his respects.'

Giles gave a knowing grimace as he easily discerned Lily's own lack of enthusiasm at seeing him again. He fully appreciated the reasons for her antagonism after the frankness of their conversation a year ago. It was a conversation Giles had had serious reason to regret since Edward's death; a marriage between his youngest brother and this particular young lady would still be most unsuitable. But Giles would far rather Edward had enjoyed even a few months with the woman he had declared himself to be deeply in love with, than for his brother to have died without knowing the joy of a union he so desired.

Surely Lily's words yesterday, regarding her intention of loving his brother until she died, implied her heart still yearned for the young man she had loved and lost…?

'Would you care for tea, Miss Seagrove?' Giles's voice was gentler than he usually managed when in this particular young woman's company.

'I—'

'That would be most acceptable, my lord.' Mr Seagrove warmly accepted in place of what Giles was convinced would have been Lily's refusal. 'His Grace is no doubt pleased at your return?' Mr Seagrove looked across at him pleasantly.

Giles frowned darkly. As Lumsden had warned, Smithins had stood like a guard at the door of the Duke of Rothermere's rooms the day before, his initial surprise at finding Giles walking through that doorway unannounced lasting only seconds before he informed Giles that his father was resting and not to be disturbed.

It had taken every effort on Giles's part to hold on to his temper and not bodily lift the insufferable little man out of his way. Instead he had icily informed Smithins what he would do to him if he did not step aside. The valet may be a bumptious little upstart, but he was not a stupid bumptious little upstart, and so had had the foresight to step aside immediately.

Not having seen his father for nine months, Giles had been shocked, deeply so, at his first sight of his father seated in a chair by the window, a blanket across his knees as evidence that, despite the warmer weather, his almost skeletal frame was prone to feel the cold. The duke's grief at the death of his two sons appeared to have aged him twenty years in just one, his hair having turned grey, his eyes having sunk into the thin pallor of his face whilst deep lines marked his unsmiling mouth.

His dull eyes had brightened slightly at the sight of his son, and his spirits had rallied for a short time too, but Giles could see his father's strength failing him after they had spoken together for ten minutes, and so he had made his excuses and gone to refresh himself after his journey.

'I believe so, yes,' Giles replied to Mr Seagrove; his visit to his father's rooms before breakfast this morning had led to the discovery that the Duke of Rothermere had completely forgotten his son's arrival the day before, thereby making it impossible for Giles to ascertain whether his presence back at Castonbury Park was having a positive effect upon his father or not.

The guilt Giles now felt at having neglected his father by remaining from home these past nine months was not something he intended to discuss with anyone, even the kindly Reverend Reginald Seagrove. Certainly Giles did not intend to reveal his feelings of inadequacy in front of the quietly attentive Lily Seagrove. Indeed, she was a young lady who saw far too many faults in him already than was comfortable!

'Perhaps now that you are home you will be able to see to the necessary repairs about the estate, my lord?' It was almost as if that young lady knew of at least some of Giles's thoughts as she smiled sweetly.

'Perhaps,' he dismissed stiffly.

She gave a gracious inclination of her head. 'I am sure His Grace would be most gratified. Not to mention the tenants of the estate.'

Giles's mouth tightened as Lily Seagrove's comment hit home. It was a way of pointing out his own shortcomings, he was sure. Shortcomings which Giles needed no reminding of when he had only to see the frailty of his father's health, and the neglect about the estate, to become all too aware of them himself.

'Shall I pour, my lord?' she prompted lightly as Lumsden returned with the tea tray and placed it on the low table in front of her before departing.

'Please.' Giles gave a terse inclination of his head. He suffered more than a little inner restlessness as he felt the chains of responsibility for Castonbury Park tighten even more painfully about his throat. Chains which Lily Seagrove no doubt prayed might choke him!

'Perhaps now that you are home, I might broach the subject of this year's well-dressing, and the possibility of the celebrations afterwards returning to Castonbury Park?' Mr Seagrove prompted hopefully. The Duke of Rothermere, having been in a turmoil of emotions the previous year, had requested that the garden party after the well-dressing take place on the village green rather than in the grounds of the estate as was the custom.

Although, as everyone knew, 'garden party' did not quite describe the celebrations that took place after the villagers had attended the church service and seen the three adorned wells in the village blessed. Much food was eaten, many barrels of beer consumed, with several stalls for bartering vegetables and livestock, and there was a Gypsy fortune-teller in a garishly adorned tent, and of course there would be music and dancing as the day turned to evening.

Giles was slow to turn his attention back to the older man, so intently was he watching Lily's slender, gloved hands as they deftly managed the tilting of the teapot. Good heavens, sitting there so primly, her movements gracefully elegant, it was almost possible to imagine that Lily might, after all, have made Edward a passably suitable wife!

Almost.

For one only had to look at that black and curling hair, the ivory-white of her complexion, those lively green eyes and her full and berry-red lips to be reminded that Lily Seagrove's true parentage was of much more exotic stock than the homely Mr and Mrs Seagrove.

No, as Giles had said only yesterday, it simply would

not have done. Lily Seagrove was the type of young lady that gentlemen like the Montagues took to mistress, not to wife. An opinion, if Giles remembered correctly—and he had no doubts that he did!—to which his brother Edward had taken great exception a year ago. And which, when Giles had made those same remarks to Lily Seagrove, had resulted in her landing a resounding slap upon his cheek!

Giles's mouth tightened at that memory even as he turned his attention back to Mr Seagrove. 'What exactly would that entail?'

'Oh, there is nothing for you to do personally except give your permission, my lord,' that cheerful gentleman assured him eagerly. 'Lily and Mrs Stratton usually work together on the organisation of the celebrations.' He beamed brightly.

'Indeed?' Giles's gaze was unreadable as Lily Seagrove stood up to hand him his cup of tea.

Lily kept her lashes lowered demurely as she avoided all contact with Giles's long and elegant fingers as she handed over the cup of tea into which she had placed four helpings of sugar, despite having no idea whether or not that gentleman even liked sugar in his tea. Perhaps he would understand that she believed his demeanour could do with sweetening also.

She had felt a slight uplift in her spirits as she saw

Giles Montague's discomfort at mention of the neglect currently obvious about the estate, only to have her heart sink upon hearing her father put forward the idea of the celebrations after the well-dressing once again taking place at Castonbury Park. She knew that if Giles Montague were to agree, it would necessitate her spending far more time here than she would ever have wished, now that he was back in residence.

Lily moved across the room with her father's tea. 'I am sure it is not necessary to bother either His Grace or Lord Montague with something so trivial, Father,' she dismissed evenly. 'The venue of the village green proved perfectly adequate for our purposes last year.'

'But, my dear, the garden party after the well-dressing ceremony has, by tradition, always been held at Castonbury Park—'

'Mrs Stratton informed me only yesterday that His Grace is far more comfortable when he does not have too much rush and bustle about him.' Lily could literally feel Giles Montague's gaze upon her as she resumed her seat on the chaise before taking up her own cup of tea.

'I had not thought of that…' Mr Seagrove murmured regretfully.

Lily felt a pang of guilt as she saw her father's disappointment. 'I am sure that everyone enjoyed themselves just as much last year as they have any of the years previously,' she encouraged gently.

'Yes, but—'

'Perhaps I might be allowed to offer an opinion...?' Giles Montague interjected softly.

Lily's gloved fingers tightened about the delicate handle on her teacup as she heard the deceptive mildness of his tone, to such a degree that she had to force herself to relax her grip for fear she might actually disengage the handle completely from the cup. She drew in two deep and calming breaths before turning to look at Giles Montague with polite but distant enquiry.

He was seated comfortably in an armchair, the pale blue of the material a perfect foil for the heavy darkness of his fashionably styled hair. He wore a black superfine over a pale blue waistcoat and snowy white linen, buff-coloured pantaloons tailored to long and powerful legs and black Hessians moulding the length of his calves. He looked, in fact, the epitome of the fashionable dandy about Town.

Not that Lily had ever been to Town, Mr and Mrs Seagrove never having found reason to travel so far as London. But she had often been privileged to see copies of the magazines Lady Phaedra, the younger of the two Montague sisters, had sent over, and the fashionable gentlemen depicted in the sketches inside those magazines had all looked much as Giles Montague did today.

She gave a dismissive shake of her head, as much for her own benefit as anyone else's. She simply refused to see Giles Montague as anything other than the cold and unpleasant man he had always been to her, but especially so this past year. 'I trust the tea is to your liking, my lord?' she prompted as she saw the involuntary wince he gave after taking a sip of the hot and highly sweetened brew.

Narrowed grey eyes met her more innocent gaze. 'Perfectly, thank you,' he murmured as he rested the cup back on its saucer before carefully placing both on the table.

Lily's cheeks warmed guiltily as she realised he was not going to expose her pettiness to her father. 'I believe you were about to offer us your opinion concerning the well-dressing celebrations, my lord?' she prompted huskily.

Giles, the taste of that unpleasantly syrupy tea still coating the roof of his mouth, did not believe that Miss Lily Seagrove would care to hear his 'opinion' of *her* at this particular moment! Instead he gave her a smile that did little more than bare his teeth in challenge, and was rewarded by a deepening of the blush colouring those ivory cheeks. 'I have very fond memories of the celebrations being held here when I was a boy.'

'Of course you must.' The vicar eagerly took up the conversation. 'I recall Mrs Seagrove telling me of how, before you were old enough to go to Town for the Season with the rest of the family, you and your brothers would help to put out the tables and chairs and hang up the bunting.'

Giles and his brothers... Of which there was now only one. And Harry, in his role as diplomat, currently resided in Town when not out of the country on other business.

If anyone had asked Giles if he really wanted the garden party to be held at Castonbury Park this year, his honest answer would have been no. But having now seen his father, witnessed the way in which his grief had caused him to become withdrawn, not just from his family but from the estate and village as well, and the way in which that estate had been allowed to fall into a state of gentile decay, Giles was of the opinion, no matter what his personal feelings on the matter, that the return of the annual celebrations in the grounds of Castonbury Park was exactly what was needed to bring about a return of confidence in the Montague family's interest in both the tenants and the village.

An interest which, it was becoming all too frustratingly apparent, Giles himself would have to facilitate!

As the second son, he'd had very little reason to pay heed to the running of the estate, or the other duties of the Dukes of Rothermere, and had left such matters to his father and Jamie after he had joined the army twelve years ago. Unfortunately Jamie's death, and his father's failing health, now necessitated—as Lily Seagrove had all too sweetly taken pleasure in pointing out—that Giles's disinterest in such matters could not continue.

Fortunately for Giles, his years as an officer in the army had given him an insight into the nature of people—although he thought the villagers of Castonbury would not in the least appreciate being compared to the rough and ready soldiers who had served under him for eleven years, many of them having chosen to serve only as an alternative to prison or worse!—and as such he knew that the quickest and easiest way to win a man or woman's confidence was to show an interest in them and their comfort.

In the case of the villagers, Giles had no doubts that the return of the annual celebrations to the grounds of Castonbury Park would be the perfect way of showing that interest.

'Indeed we did,' Giles answered Mr Seagrove ruefully. 'And I will be only too happy to offer assistance this year. Under Miss Seagrove's direction, of course...?' He raised a dark and challengingly brow as he turned to look across the room at her.

Lily, having lapsed into what she now realised had been a false sense of security, could only stare back at him in wide-eyed disbelief.

The thought of the well-dressing celebrations being held at Castonbury Park, and so necessitating Lily spend more time here than she might ever have wished or asked for, seemed dreadful enough, but having Giles Montague offer his personal help with the organisation of those celebrations was unthinkable!

Nor did she believe for one moment that the haughty and arrogant Lord Giles would ever agree to do anything 'under her direction.'

'I really could not ask that of you, my lord, when you obviously have so many other calls upon your time now that you are home at last.' She gave another of those sweet smiles.

Amusement—no doubt at Lily's expense!—gleamed briefly in those grey eyes. 'But you did not ask it, Miss Seagrove, it was I who offered,' Giles Montague drawled dismissively.

'But—'

'As far as I am concerned, the matter is settled, Miss

Seagrove.' He rose abruptly to his feet as an indication that their visit was also at an end.

A dismissal Mr Seagrove, his real purpose in calling having now been settled to his satisfaction, was
only too ready to accept as he rose to his feet. 'I am
sure you have made the right decision, my lord, for
both the family and village as a whole.' He beamed
his pleasure at the younger man.

For once in her young life Lily could not help but
wholeheartedly disagree with her adoptive father. Oh,
she had no doubts that the rest of the village would see
the reestablishment of the celebrations to Castonbury
Park as a positive thing, a return to normality after
almost a year of uncertainty.

But as the person who would be required to consult
with Giles Montague, Lily could not help but feel a
sense of dread....

Chapter Three

'I do believe this particular shade would complement your colouring admirably.' Mrs Hall laid out a swatch of deep pink material upon the counter top of her establishment, where several other bolts of material already lay discarded after having been rejected by Lily as not quite what she wanted.

In truth, Lily was not absolutely sure what she did want, only that she had decided to purchase some material to make up a new day gown, and Mrs Hall's establishment in the village was so much more con-venient than having to travel all the way to the nearest town of Buxton. Luckily, that lady had several new selections of material in stock, and Lily's needlework was also excellent due to Mrs Seagrove's tutelage in earlier years. Besides which, with the celebrations less than two weeks away, Lily was sorely in need of a new gown—

Lily drew her thoughts up sharply as she realised she was not only prevaricating but actually practising a deception upon herself; her reason for deciding she needed a new gown for the day of the well-dressing celebrations could be summed up in just three words— Lord Giles Montague! Which was a ridiculous vanity on Lily's part, when she had no doubts that the haughty Lord Giles would have taken absolutely no note of the gowns she had been wearing on the two occasions on which they had last met.

'Or perhaps this one…?' Mrs Hall held up another swatch, having obviously drawn a wrong conclusion as to the reason for Lily's present distraction.

'I think perhaps— Oh, how beautiful!' Lily gasped in pleasure as she focused her attention on the material which she was sure had to be a match in colour for the green of her eyes.

If styled correctly, it could be prettied up with cream lace at the neck and short sleeves to wear in the evenings. Not that Lily had attended any of the local assemblies since Edward died, but even so…

'It is perfect,' she breathed in satisfaction. 'But no doubt costly?' she added with a self-conscious grimace; she was, after all, only a vicar's adopted daughter, and as such it would not do for her to look anything other than what she was, and this material had a richness about it that was unmistakable to the eye.

As she had grown to adulthood Lily had often found herself wondering if, as so many in the village so obviously suspected, she really could be the daughter of one of the dramatically beautiful Romany women who stayed in the grounds of Castonbury Park during the summer months.

Several years ago Lily had even plucked up the courage to question one of them, a Mrs Lovell, the oldest and friendliest of the Romany women. The old lady had seemed taken aback by the question at first, and then she had chuckled as she assured Lily that the tribes took care of their own, and that no true Romany child would ever have been left behind to live with a gorjer. It had been said in such a contemptuous way that Lily had no difficulty discerning that the old lady meant a non-Romany person.

Even so, Lily had still sometimes found herself daydreaming as to how different her life would have been if, despite Mrs Lovell's denials, her mother really had been one of those lovely Romany women....

No doubt once she was grown she would have worn those same dresses in rich and gaudy colours that she had seen the Romany women wearing, with her long and wildly curling black hair loose about her shoulders as she danced about the campfire in the evenings, enticing and beguiling the swarthy-skinned Gypsy men who watched her with hot and desirous eyes.

Her daydreams had always come to an abrupt and disillusioned end at that point, as Lily acknowledged that might possibly be the exact way in which her mother had conceived the child she had abandoned on the Seagroves' doorstep twenty years ago!

'Perhaps it is not quite…suitable.' She sighed wistfully as she touched the beautiful moss-green material longingly. 'A serviceable grey would be more practical, do you not think?' Her liking for the material in front of her was so immediate and so strong, it was impossible to prevent the wistfulness from entering her tone.

The other woman laughed lightly. 'Like the gown you are wearing today, you mean?'

Lily glanced down at her gown, one of her older ones, chuckling softly as she realised the other woman was quite correct and that the gown was indeed grey, and that it was also eminently serviceable in style. 'Do forgive me.' She smiled at the other woman in rueful apology. 'My head is so filled with arrangements for the well-dressing I did not even take note of which gown I had put on this morning!'

Mrs Hall nodded. 'I have noticed that everyone in the village is excited at the prospect of the May celebrations returning to Castonbury Park this year.'

Everyone but Lily, it seemed....

How different it would have been if Lord Giles had not currently been in residence at Castonbury Park.

Ridiculous—if Lord Giles Montague was not at home, then Lily very much doubted that the May celebrations would have returned to Castonbury Park at all.

And as Mrs Hall had already stated, news that the garden party was once again to take place at Castonbury Park had quickly spread throughout the village in the two days since Giles Montague had told the vicar of his decision. Not that Mr Seagrove had spread that news himself. No, he would only have needed to mention the arrangements to Mrs Crutchley, the wife of the local butcher, for that to have occurred.

Mrs Crutchley had been in charge of arranging the flowers in the church for the Sunday services since the death of Mrs Seagrove, Lily having been considered by that lady as far too young to take on such an onerous task. As such, Mrs Crutchley also put herself in charge of orchestrating the floral decorations each year for the well-dressing ceremony.

One word from Mr Seagrove to this garrulous lady

as to the change of venue to Castonbury Park for the celebrations after the ceremony, and that knowledge had spread quickly throughout the whole village. Indeed, everyone Lily had chanced to speak with in the past two days had talked of nothing else but the prospect of an afternoon and evening enjoying the Duke of Rothermere's hospitality.

Everyone except Lily, for reasons she had not shared with anyone this past year....

But if she was to be forced to suffer a day in the company of Lord Giles—and it seemed that she was— then she really must have a new gown in which to do it! 'Yes, I believe I will take this material, after all,' she announced firmly as she stood up decisively, turning to admire the arrangement of ribbons in the window as Mrs Hall cut the appropriate amount of fabric. 'I believe I would like this also.' Lily had plucked a long length of dark green ribbon from the display and now handed it to Mrs Hall to be included in the package, knowing the ribbon would make a fine contrast to the lighter green of the material, as well as giving the gown a festive look for the well-dressing.

'Is that everything?' Mrs Hall proceeded to wrap and tie Lily's purchases in brown paper after her reassuring nod.

'You will send me the bill, as usual?' At which time

Lily would no doubt learn that there would be none of her allowance left with which to make any other purchases, either this month or the next!

It would be worth going without, if only to show Lord Giles that she could be just as elegantly dressed as any of the fashionable women he might know in London, Lily told herself as she walked briskly back to the vicarage, her parcel clutched tightly to her chest. Giles Montague enjoyed looking down his arrogant nose at her far too much—

'You are looking mightily pleased with yourself,' drawled that gentleman's superior voice. 'Can it be that you are on your way to an assignation, or have perhaps just left one…?'

Lily was frowning as she turned sharply to face Lord Giles.

'I am finding your habit of appearing out of nowhere most irritating, my lord!'

He made no reply as he raised dark brows beneath his tall hat, once again the epitome of the fashionable gentleman, the tailored black jacket and plain grey waistcoat he wore today very much in the understated elegance of the most stylish of gentlemen, like the cane he carried of black ebony tipped with silver.

Lily's chin was high as she met that mocking silver-grey gaze. 'And in answer to your question, I was neither on my way to an assignation nor leaving one, but merely visiting one of the shops in the village.'

Giles's expression was deliberately noncommittal as he looked at Lily Seagrove between narrowed lids, noting the flash of temper in those moss-green eyes and the colour in her cheeks as she answered his query. Quite why he felt the need to constantly challenge this particular young woman he had not the slightest idea, but the result, he noted—those flashing green eyes and the flush in her cheeks—was more than pleasing to a gentleman's eyes.

His mouth thinned with displeasure at the realisation that it was more than pleasing to his own eye! 'You have completed your purchases, and are now on your way back to the vicarage, perhaps?'

'I am.' She tilted her chin, as if daring him to challenge her claim.

Giles nodded tersely. 'As I am on my way to visit with your father, I shall walk along with you.'

No 'please' or 'may I,' Lily noted irritably, just that arrogant 'I shall.'

But it was an arrogance she knew from experience it would do no good to challenge. Just as she knew it would serve no purpose for her to enquire as to the reason he intended visiting with her father; it would certainly be too much to hope that Giles Montague was finding the annual celebrations at Castonbury Park too much of a bother, after all.

'By all means, my lord.' Lily nodded graciously before continuing her walk without sparing a second glance to see whether or not Giles Montague fell into step beside her.

Which was not to say she was not completely aware of his tall and dominating presence beside her as he easily matched his much longer strides to her shorter ones. Or the speculation with which several of her neighbours eyed them as they passed, even as they curtseyed or bowed in recognition of the man at her side.

Lily had no doubt those curious eyes continued to watch the two of them as they strolled along the village street towards the vicarage. 'His Grace is a little better, I trust?' After several minutes of suffering what she knew would be the avid speculation of her neighbours, Lily felt self-conscious enough to feel forced into making some sort of conversation. She turned to glance up curiously at Giles Montague when he did not immediately reply. A frown had appeared between his eyes, his mouth had become a thinned line and his jaw was tight. All of which Lily found most unreassuring. 'My lord?' she prompted uncertainly.

Lily's long friendship with Edward had resulted in

her having spent a considerable amount of time at Castonbury Park itself, and so she had often chanced to meet the Duke of Rothermere whilst in Edward's company. She had come to know His Grace as a pleasant and charming man, one who was capable of showing a fondness for his children. He had a genuine affection for Lily's father which had included Mrs Seagrove when she was alive and, as a consequence, Lily too. Certainly there had never been any sign in either His Grace's speech or demeanour towards her to imply that he considered her as anything less than the true daughter of Mr and Mrs Seagrove.

Unlike the grim-faced gentleman now striding along so confidently beside her!

But that did not infringe upon Lily's regard for the Duke of Rothermere. The poor man had suffered so these past years, losing first Lord James and then Edward, that it was no wonder he had withdrawn from the world to become but a shell of his former robust and charming self!

'You are alarming me with your delay in making a reply, my lord,' she said.

In truth, Giles was not sure what to say in answer to Lily's query. 'My father seems much the same in physical health as when I arrived three days ago.'

Which was to say his father was both frail in stature

and looking so much older than his sixty-odd years. The duke did have periods when his vagueness of purpose did not seem quite so noticeable, when he appeared to listen attentively as Giles told him of the work he had instructed to be carried out about the estate. But it had quickly become apparent to Giles that it was a feigned interest.

This was worrying enough in itself, but was made all the more so because the legalities of his father's successor were still in a state of flux. His brother Jamie had been swept away in a Spanish river, and his body never recovered. It was not an unusual occurrence admittedly—so many English soldiers had died during the years of fighting Napoleon, never to be seen or heard of again by their families. But, in the case of the heir to the Duke of Rothermere, the lack of physical evidence had resulted in a delay with regard to the naming of Giles as the duke's successor.

His father's strangeness aside, there was something not quite…right about the current state of affairs at Castonbury Park, and now that he was here Giles fully intended, before too much more time had elapsed, to find out exactly what it was.

Perhaps he would know more when he'd had a chance to thoroughly review the estate account books which Everett, the estate manager, was having delivered to him later today.

Lily frowned at Giles's reply. 'I believe my own father had hoped that your return might bring about some improvement to His Grace.'

Giles's mouth twisted humourlessly. 'No doubt you did not share Mr Seagrove's optimism?'

'I, my lord?' She raised surprised brows. 'I cannot say that I had given the subject of your return any thought whatsoever.'

Giles found himself chuckling huskily. 'I am finding your lack of a good opinion of me to be a great leveller, Miss Seagrove!' he explained as she regarded him questioningly.

Lily, finding herself once again distracted by the difference a smile made to Giles Montague's countenance, now felt the warmth of colour enter her cheeks at his drawled rebuke. 'I am sure I meant you no insult, my lord.'

He continued to smile ruefully. 'Perhaps that is what I find most telling of all!'

Lily gave a pained frown. 'I merely meant, as your return to Castonbury was in no way assured, that I tried not to—that I did not consider at any length what effect, if any,' she said, her cheeks now ablaze, 'it might have upon His Grace's health or the people here.' Only, she recalled guiltily, in regard to how self-ish it was of her to wish that Giles Montague might never return at all!

This, she now accepted, had been a childish hope on her part; Lord Giles Montague was now, to all intents and purposes, the future Duke of Rothermere, so it was only to be expected that he would come back to Castonbury Park, if only for the purpose of ensuring that his future inheritance continued to flourish.

'I believe you have instructed a great deal of work to be done about the estate...?' Indeed, village gossip had been rife with nothing else but the 'doings of Lord Giles' these past two days.

He raised dark brows. 'Work, I might remind you, which you yourself pointed out to me only days ago, was in need of my immediate attention.'

'I was not criticising, my lord—'

'No?' He looked down at her.

'Certainly not.' Lily had absolutely no doubt that Giles Montague would make a very capable Duke of Rothermere when that time came, his years as an officer in the army having given him an air of authority totally in keeping with the lofty position. Yes, the arrogantly disdainful Giles Montague was more than suited to becoming the future Duke of

Rothermere. Lily simply could not see herself remaining in Castonbury once that dreadful day came.

Quite where she would go, or what she would do, or how she would explain her departure to Mr Seagrove if he was still with them—and she prayed that he would be—Lily had no idea. She only knew that she would find remaining in Castonbury, under the charitable auspices of the hateful Giles Montague, absolutely intolerable!

'I am gratified to hear it,' the infuriating man drawled. He paused beside the gate into the vicarage garden.

Lily frowned her irritation as she was also forced to pause. 'I do not believe I care to continue this conversation, my lord.'

His mouth quirked with derision. 'And I do not believe it is really necessary for you to do so, when I already know, after our conversation a year ago, with what horror you must have viewed the thought of my returning for even a short visit.'

'Then why did you bother to ask?' Lily eyed him impatiently.

He shrugged those broad shoulders. 'I thought to amuse myself, perhaps.'

'Indeed, my lord? And did you not find enough "amusements" in London these past nine months?'

His eyes narrowed. 'And what would you know of my movements these past months?'

Lily felt the warmth of colour in her cheeks. 'No matter what you might consider to the contrary, my lord, Castonbury is not completely cut off from civilisation!' And besides, it was his sister Phaedra who had confided, in a whisper, that her brother was reputed to be enjoying the favours of many beautiful women, as well as frequenting the gambling and drinking dens!

The present Duke of Rothermere was rumoured to have once been a man who enjoyed all of the... amusements London had to offer, as well as some of the more local ones, so perhaps his second son was taking after him in enjoying those often less than respectable pursuits?

He gave an exasperated shake of his head. 'Unless you have forgotten, I spent my early years growing up here.'

Lily tilted her chin proudly. 'I have not forgotten anything about you, my lord.'

His mouth thinned. 'Including, no doubt, my words to you a year ago!'

'Most especially I will never forget those, my lord,' she assured him before turning to push open the gate for herself as Giles Montague made no effort to do so.

'Never is a very long time, Lily.'

'You— Oh, bother!' Lily had turned sharply back to face him, catching her parcel on the gatepost as she did so, and succeeding in knocking it from her arms and to the ground. She huffed at her own clumsiness even as she bent down to retrieve the parcel.

Giles, having intended on doing the same, instead found himself wincing as their two heads met painfully together, Lily's brow coming into sharp contact with the hardness of his chin. Unfortunately it was in the exact same spot as his friend Milburn's fist had landed six days previously!

'Oh, my word!' The dropped parcel forgotten, Lily now raised a gloved hand to her obviously painful brow, those moss-green eyes having filled with tears.

Giles pushed aside his own discomfort to quickly discard his cane and reach out to grasp the tops of her arms as he looked down at her anxiously. 'Let me see!' He pushed her hand aside, a frown darkening his own brow as he saw the bump that was already forming under her delicate skin. 'Do not poke and prod at it!' he instructed sternly as he clasped her gloved fingers firmly in his own even as they crept to the painful spot.

Giles tensed as he became aware of the warmth of Lily's fingers through the thin lace of her glove, the rapid rise and fall of her breasts against the bodice of her grey gown, her pulse beating rapidly at the base of her slender neck, and when Giles raised his gaze it was to see Lily catch the full redness of her bottom lip between tiny white teeth.

Because of the painful bump to her forehead? Or something else...?

Green eyes now looked up at him in questioning confusion from between long and silky black lashes. 'My lord...?' she breathed huskily.

The very air about them seemed to have stilled, even the birds in the trees seemed to have ceased their singing to look down, watchful, expectant, upon the two people standing in a frozen tableau beneath them.

Giles drew a ragged breath into his starved lungs, aware as he did so of his own rapidly beating heart pounding in his ears. Because he could feel the warmth of Lily's hand against his own? Look down upon the rapid rise and fall of her creamy breasts above the curved neckline of her gown? Smell the lightness of her floral perfume on her smooth, ivory skin?

Giles's nostrils flared at this sudden, unwelcome awareness as he released her before stepping back abruptly. 'We should go in now, your brow will need the application of a cold compress to stop the worst of the swelling,' he told her grimly.

'My parcel...!' She attempted to retrieve it.

'Hang your parcel—'

Glistening green eyes glared up at Giles as he would have prevented her from reaching for the parcel. 'It is the material for my new gown, and I do not intend to leave it outside for the birds to peck at or the rain to fall upon—'

'Oh, very well.' Giles made no effort to hide his impatience as he bent down to gather up the parcel before handing it to her. 'Now can we go inside?' he prompted harshly as he picked up his ebony cane, his expression grim.

Lily had absolutely no idea what had happened, only knowing that something most assuredly had.

Giles Montague had looked at her just now as if seeing her for the first time, his eyes no longer that cold silver-grey but instead burning a deep and un-fathomable colour of pewter. They were eyes that had swept across the swell of her breasts, the pale column of her throat, before coming to rest on the fullness of her lips. The intensity of his gaze had caused Lily to catch at her bottom lip with her teeth.

Even more puzzling had been her own response to the intensity of that gaze....

For several moments it had seemed as if they might be the only two people in the world, even breathing had been too much of an effort; the blood in Lily's veins had seemed to burn, her breasts had felt full and sensitive inside her gown.

She had taken note of every hard plane of his aristocratic face—the intelligent brow, those heated grey eyes, a long slash of a nose between high cheekbones, those firm and sculptured lips slightly parted above the square strength of his jaw. Considering all of these attributes, Lily found herself acknowledging Giles Montague as being a breathtakingly handsome man!

Giles Montague.

The arrogant and disdainful Giles Montague.

The hated and despised Lord Giles Montague.

It was unbelievable, unacceptable, that Lily should have such thoughts about a man who had never made any effort to hide the contempt he felt towards her.

She clutched her parcel tightly to her breasts as she turned and walked the small distance down the pathway before opening the door and entering the vicarage. 'My father is no doubt in his study writing his sermon for Sunday,' she dismissed with a complete lack of manners as she stared at the top button of Giles Montague's waistcoat rather than at the hard planes of his face.

'You will see to putting a cold compress on your forehead immediately.' Again there was no question or suggestion from Giles Montague, only that cold inflexibility of will that Lily had come to expect from him.

Her chin rose as she looked up at him. 'I will decide what I will or will not do, my lord!'

His grey eyes narrowed to silver slits. 'You already have a bump on your forehead half the size of a hen's egg. Do not make it any worse out of stubborn defiance of me!'

Lily drew her breath in sharply. 'You are arrogant, sir, to assume your opinion on anything would ever affect my own behaviour one way or the other!'

'Arrogant? Possibly,' Giles acknowledged with a derisive inclination of his head. 'But, in this particular case, I have no doubt I am necessarily so,' he added drily, heartily relieved to realise that he and Lily Seagrove had returned to the natural state of affairs between them.

Her cheeks flushed with irritation and her eyes flashed. 'You—'

'What on earth is— Oh, Lord Giles?' Mr Seagrove looked slightly perplexed as he stood in the now-open doorway to the family parlour and recognised the gentleman standing in the darkness of his hallway. 'And Lily…' The vicar looked even more puzzled as he saw his daughter standing slightly behind Lord Giles.

'Lord Montague and I met outside, Father,' Lily spoke up firmly before 'Lord Montague' had any opportunity to say anything that might add to her father's air of confusion.

Once seated at the kitchen table in order to allow the clucking Mrs Jeffries to apply a cold compress to the bump on her forehead—not because Giles Montague had instructed that she do so but because it was the right and sensible thing to do!—Lily could not help but think again of those few minutes of awareness as she stood outside the vicarage with Giles Montague....

Chapter Four

'So exciting! I am sure Monsieur André is beside himself at the thought of baking all those delicious cakes for the garden party! And Mrs Stratton has us all polishing and cleaning the silver until we can see our faces in it,' Daisy, a plump and pretty housemaid at Castonbury Park, chattered on excitedly. 'Do you think the old Gypsy woman will be there again this year to tell our fortunes? Oh, I do hope so! Last year she said a tall, dark and handsome stranger would sweep me off my feet. I haven't chanced to meet him yet, but I live in hopes—'

It was now two days since Lily had literally clashed heads with Giles Montague outside the vicarage, and having already made several calls in the village on her way to Castonbury Park today, she was now only half listening to Daisy as the maid chattered non-stop on the walk down the hallway in the direction of Mrs Stratton's parlour.

'She prefers to be called a Romany. And her name is Mrs Lovell,' Lily supplied, the making of her new gown and the well-dressing celebrations having taken up more of her own thoughts and time than she would have believed possible, as she dealt with the wealth of arrangements to be put in place before the ceremony next week.

She had also, after more enquiries from curious neighbours than she cared to answer, found a style for her hair which managed to cover the discolouration which still remained upon her brow despite the swelling having disappeared.

Daisy's 'tall, dark and handsome stranger' could easily be a description of Giles Montague. Lily's own dislike of that gentleman did not appear to have prevented her from acknowledging that he was indeed tall, dark and very handsome. After twelve years away from home, with only infrequent visits back to Derbyshire, he could also be considered something of a 'stranger' to most of the people in Castonbury. Daisy was certainly young enough not to have too many recollections of him.

Giles Montague's return had now resulted in the whole of the estate and household staff being 'swept off their feet,' as he began to issue orders and instructions for the work he considered needed to be done before Castonbury Park opened its gates to the village for the well-dressing celebrations the following week.

'Oh, I hope I did not cause offence, Lily!' Daisy's embarrassed expression revealed that she was aware of the things said in the village concerning Lily's true parents. 'It's just that Agnes said she saw one of the pretty Gypsy caravans on the other side of the lake yesterday. And the Gypsy—the Romany, Mrs Lovell,' she corrected with a self-conscious giggle, 'is so wonderful at telling fortunes, that I hoped it was her. It's my afternoon off today, so maybe I'll take a walk over that way and see for myself—'

Lily also wondered if the caravan might belong to Mrs Lovell, that elderly lady usually arriving at Castonbury several weeks ahead of her tribe, and so giving her the opportunity to go about the village selling the clothes pegs and baskets she had made through the winter months. Her fortune-telling had also been a feature of the well-dressing celebrations ever since Lily could remember. Whether or not those fortunes ever came true did not seem to matter to the people in the village, as they, like Daisy, simply enjoyed the possibility that they might—

Lily's wandering thoughts came to an abrupt end

as she heard the sound of raised voices from down the hallway. Or rather, a single raised voice....

'—do not say I did not warn you all! And do not come crying to me when he succeeds in killing His Grace!' There was the sound of a door being forcibly slammed.

'Uh-oh, it's Mr Smithins, and he sounds as if he's on the warpath again!' Daisy whispered in alarm as she clutched Lily's arm. 'I'd better get back to me polishing!' She beat a hasty retreat back to the kitchen just as Smithins appeared at the end of the hallway, the scowl on his face evidence of his bad temper.

A short, thin and balding man, he possessed an elegance of style about his demeanour and dress that some might consider foppish. Lily had observed that he was also something of a despot in regard to the other household servants at Castonbury Park, considering himself far above them in his position as personal valet to the Duke of Rothermere. Hence Daisy's hurried departure back to her work in the kitchen; Smithins was perfectly capable of boxing the young maid's ears if he felt so inclined!

His scowl deepened as he strode down the hallway and caught sight of Lily watching him.

She grimaced self-consciously as she felt herself forced into speech. 'Is anything amiss, Mr Smithins?'

His eyes narrowed. 'Mark my words, it will all end in tears!' he muttered as he pushed past her before continuing on his way without apology.

Lily felt slightly unnerved as she turned to look at the valet, but more by his angry claim of some unnamed person 'killing His Grace' than his rude behaviour to her just now. What on earth could have happened for Smithins to—

'Ah, Lily,' Mrs Stratton sighed wearily as she appeared in the doorway of her parlour and saw Lily standing outside in the hallway. 'Do please come in,' she invited softly.

Lily hesitated. 'I have obviously called at a bad time....'

'Not at all,' the older woman assured wryly. 'Smithins is volatile of temperament, I am afraid,' she continued as Lily slowly entered the cosy parlour.

'But...he seemed so vehement...?'

Mrs Stratton shook her head. 'He is merely annoyed because Lord Giles refuses to heed his advice concerning His Grace.'

Lord Giles? Smithins's warning just now had been a reference to Giles Montague's behaviour in regard to his father?

The housekeeper sighed. 'His latest concern seems

to be the carriage ride His Grace is to take with Lord Giles this afternoon.'

Lily's eyes widened. 'Is His Grace well enough for a carriage ride?'

'He has seemed much improved this past day or so,' Mrs Stratton assured. 'I am sure that a change of scenery will be far more beneficial to him than sitting alone in his rooms day after day, and allowing his nerves to get the better of him.'

Possibly, but it was only the end of April, and the chill wind blew off the Derbyshire hills still. 'My father has been invited to dine with His Grace and Lord Giles this evening.' Indeed, the invitation to dine at Castonbury Park this evening had been the only thing Mr Seagrove had been willing to impart to Lily concerning Giles Montague's visit to him two days ago!

The older woman frowned slightly. 'I understood the invitation was for both you and Mr Seagrove....'

It had been. It still was. But as Lily could not imagine Giles Montague really wanting to spend an evening in her company—as she had no desire to spend an evening in his—she had been sure that her inclusion in the invitation had only been made out of politeness to her father, and as such she had intended making the excuse of having a headache this evening when it came time to leave for Castonbury Park.

But having heard Smithins's warning just now, perhaps she should reconsider that decision?

'I really should pay no mind to Smithins if I were you, Lily.' Mrs Stratton gave a rueful grimace as she seemed to read Lily's hesitation, even if she had misunderstood the reason for it. 'I am afraid he has been allowed to become far too overbearingly protective this past year where His Grace is concerned.' She gave a weary sigh. 'I have long been forced to listen to his ravings for one reason or another.'

That may be so, but Lily seriously doubted that those 'ravings' had ever been about Lord Giles Montague before this week, or involved an accusation of him 'succeeding in killing' his own father. 'Do you think there is any basis for truth in Mr Smithins's concerns for His Grace?'

'None at all,' the housekeeper dismissed briskly. 'Lord Giles has always been the most dutiful of sons.'

Had it been 'dutiful' of Giles Montague to remain in London these past nine months when he had been needed here at Castonbury Park? Was it 'dutiful' of him, now that he had at last returned, to be seen to take his father, a man who was obviously fragile in health, out on a carriage ride? Admittedly, he now seemed to be taking a belated interest in the estate, but—

'Besides, you will see for yourself this evening how His Grace fares.' Mrs Stratton smiled. 'And I know that Monsieur André is greatly looking forward to preparing some more of the meringues after I told him how much you enjoyed them when you were here last,' she added with a twinkle in her eye.

Lily felt the colour warm her cheeks at Mrs Stratton's more than obvious attempt at matchmaking. She had only seen the new French chef once or twice since his arrival at Castonbury Park, although she had noticed on those occasions that he was handsome. Even so, Lily very much doubted that even a French chef would be willing to overlook her questionable pedigree.

'But I am sure you did not come here to discuss this evening's menu with me...?' Mrs Stratton prompted lightly.

Lily gave herself a mental shake as she was reminded of her reason for calling. 'I was in the village and was waylaid by Mr Crutchley as I passed the butcher's shop. He said he has not yet received an order from you for the traditional pig to roast.' The ladies of the village would no doubt enjoy partaking of the delicacies provided by Monsieur André, but the men were all of hardy farming stock, and as such required a heartier repast for their tea than the sandwiches and cakes the French chef would be providing.

The housekeeper looked slightly perplexed. 'I understood from Lord Giles that he intended to talk to Mr Crutchley personally.'

'Lord Giles?' Lily repeated slowly. 'But…I do not understand.'

Mrs Stratton smiled indulgently. 'I believe the pig roast is to be his own gift to the celebrations.'

'I— Well. That is very generous of him.' Lily still frowned her puzzlement.

'Indeed,' the housekeeper agreed warmly. 'He has stated that he also intends to provide the liquid refreshment for the gentlemen.'

To say Lily was surprised at Giles Montague's personal largesse would be putting it mildly; as far as she was aware, he had not shown any interest before now in the welfare and happiness of the people living in the village of Castonbury.

But he had not become his father's heir until Lord Jamie's demise either.

Was she being completely fair to Giles Montague, Lily wondered as she walked back to the vicarage, or was she perhaps allowing her own prejudice of feelings towards that gentleman to colour her thoughts and emotions?

Thankfully she had not seen Giles Montague again in the past two days, but he had been the subject of much discussion in the village.

She had heard from several of the women how their eldest sons had been taken on for the summer months so that the fallow fields at the Park might be prepared for a winter crop. Another had commented that her carpenter husband had been employed to effect repairs upon several of the barns to ready them for the storing of the harvest to come. A builder had been seen up on the roof of Castonbury Park itself to repair several tiles that had fallen off in the severe winter storms.

All of it was work that Giles Montague had apparently instructed to be carried out.

Perhaps her criticisms of him had had some effect, after all—

No, a more likely explanation was that Giles Montague already considered himself master here!

Could there, after all, be some truth in Smithins's earlier warning to Mrs Stratton regarding the Duke of Rothermere? Was Giles Montague deliberately endangering his father's already precarious health, in the hopes that he might become the presumptive Duke of Rothermere sooner rather than later?

Lily had no answer to those questions. One thing she was certain of, however; she no longer intended suffering so much as the twinge of a headache to prevent her from dining at Castonbury Park this evening!

'I must thank you for sending John and the carriage for us, Lord Giles.' Mr Seagrove beamed as Lumsden showed the vicar and his daughter into the formal salon that evening. He was wearing his usual clerical black, his daughter looking slender and graceful in a gown of deep blue. 'I am afraid my open carriage is not at all suitable for going out in the evenings, and our horse now so old that he is not inclined to go out after dark either.'

'Not at all,' Giles drawled dismissively. 'I could not risk Miss Seagrove suffering a chill.'

A chill which was all in those moss-green eyes, Giles discovered with a frown as he bent formally over Lily's gloved hand before glancing up to see her looking back at him with icy coldness. Not a particularly good omen for what Giles had hoped would be an evening free of the tensions he had been forced to suffer earlier today whilst out visiting with his father!

'Besides which,' he added dismissively as he stepped back from the immediate glare of those chilling green eyes, 'my father and I took the carriage out earlier today, so it was no bother for John to set out again this evening.'

'And how did your father enjoy his carriage ride, my lord?' Lily prompted evenly, the curls arranged on her brow in such a way as to cover the discolouration of skin Giles was sure she would have suffered from their clashing of heads two days ago, although he could see no sign of a bump still being there, indicating she may—but only may!—have taken his advice, after all, and applied the cold compress.

'You appear to be very well informed of the movements at Castonbury Park, Miss Seagrove.' Giles regarded her through narrowed lids, his own jaw having ached for several hours after coming into contact with her brow, but thankfully having suffered no further visible bruising.

She shrugged creamy shoulders. 'Mrs Stratton happened to mention the outing when I called on her earlier today.'

'Indeed?' Giles murmured drily.

'Yes.' Lily's cheeks became slightly flushed at the derision she heard in Giles Montague's tone at hearing she had once again called upon the housekeeper at Castonbury Park. 'You omitted to answer my query concerning your father's enjoyment of his carriage ride, my lord…' she reminded determinedly.

He looked down at her with shrewd grey eyes. 'Did I?' he drawled.

'Yes.' Lily glared her frustration, feeling at that moment much like a mouse must when being played with by a cat. In the case of Giles Montague, a large and arrogant cat!

'How remiss of me.' He turned away to look at Mr Seagrove.

'Would you care for a glass of claret before dinner, sir?'

'I would, thank you, Lord Giles.' Her father beamed at the younger man, as usual seeming unaware of the tension that existed between Giles Montague and his daughter.

'May I get you a glass of sherry, or perhaps lemonade, Miss Seagrove?' Giles Montague raised dark and mocking brows as he glanced in her direction.

He was a very large and arrogant cat whom Lily was nevertheless forced to acknowledge looked extremely handsome in black evening clothes and snowy white linen! 'No, thank you,' Lily refused stiffly, more than slightly annoyed with herself for having noticed how handsome Giles Montague looked this evening.

Giles turned to dismiss Lumsden with a terse nod before crossing the room himself to pour the claret into two crystal glasses, a frown low on his brow as his thoughts turned once again to the events of this afternoon. Not the most enjoyable time he had spent in his father's company since his return, and Lord knows those previous visits to his father's rooms had not been conducive to Giles sleeping comfortably at night!

Calling to talk with the family lawyers in Buxton earlier today had succeeded in helping Giles to slowly, very slowly, unravel the tangle his father appeared to have made of things since Jamie had perished. A tangle that the duke had only made worse during that last battle with Napoleon at Waterloo, when it had seemed as if Wellington might not prevail. Indeed, the Duke of Rothermere's actions at that time had been so extreme that Giles was still uncertain, even with the help of the lawyers, as to whether or not he would ever be able to set things to rights.

Wise investments of his own over the past ten years had enabled Giles to accrue his own personal fortune, and it was these finances which were currently allowing the estate and other Montague households to run with their usual smoothness and largesse. Although how long that could continue would depend upon how long Giles's money lasted....

Making it doubly infuriating that he now had to suffer the irritating Lily Seagrove prodding and poking at him as if he were an unfeeling son who had dragged his frail and ailing father out on a needless carriage ride. All the more so when the visit to the family lawyers had been made at his father's insistence!

'My lord—'

'I believe my father is about to join us now,' Giles bit out as he heard voices out in the hallway. 'Perhaps you would care to ask him yourself as to how he enjoyed his outing this afternoon?' He looked expectantly towards the door.

Lily's eyes widened as the Duke of Rothermere entered the room. She had seen His Grace rarely these past six months but had noted his increasing frailness on each of those occasions, but it was possible to see that there was colour in his cheeks this evening, and a faint sparkle of life in his eyes.

'Ah, the pretty Miss Seagrove!' he greeted her with obvious pleasure as he slowly crossed the room to bend gallantly over her gloved hand. 'And Reginald!' He turned to greet his old friend warmly.

'Your Grace.' Mr Seagrove beamed. 'May I say how well you are looking this evening!'

'I am feeling well.' The duke nodded. 'So much so that I hope you are feeling up to the possibility of a game of chess after dinner?'

'I should enjoy that very much.' Mr Seagrove accepted

one of the glasses of claret from Giles Montague whilst the duke accepted the other, the two older gentlemen continuing their conversation as he returned to pour a third glass for himself.

'You are positive I cannot provide you with refreshment, Miss Seagrove?' He quirked a brow as he moved to stand beside her, glass of claret in hand.

It was a mockery Lily knew she justly deserved, when the Duke of Rothermere had so obviously suffered no ill effects from going out into the countryside earlier. Indeed, appearances would seem to imply the opposite! 'No, thank you, my lord,' she said stiffly.

'I believe you wished to enquire of my father as to whether or not he enjoyed his outing today…?' he reminded softly.

Lily frowned. 'There is obviously no need when His Grace is in such good spirits.'

'Much to your disappointment?' Giles Montague prompted softly.

Her cheeks warmed as she gave him a startled glance. 'Why on earth should you think that?'

'Perhaps because earlier you all but accused me of putting my father's health in danger by taking him out for a carriage ride.' Giles knew one only had to look at the Duke of Rothermere to see that the outing had been beneficial. Indeed, his father, having had the direness of the family's financial situation revealed to Giles by the family lawyers, now seemed like a man who had had a heavy weight removed from his frail shoulders!

A heavy weight which now pressed upon Giles's shoulders instead.

'I— You— I did no such thing!' Lily spluttered even as the guilty colour deepened in her cheeks.

Giles grimaced, knowing his conversation was not at all polite to a guest in his family home, but he found it impossible to resist challenging Lily when she seemed so set on seeking reasons to dislike him. More reasons… The frankness of their conversation a year ago had undoubtedly already ensured that dislike!

It was an animosity of feelings Giles could well do without when he already had so many other problems to deal with. 'Perhaps it was I who misunderstood the reason for your concern,' he dismissed curtly.

Lily knew that Giles Montague had not misunderstood her in the slightest, and that she had, with the aid of the bad-tempered Smithins, drawn a completely wrong conclusion. But there was no way Giles Montague could have known that when he—

Stop it, Lily, she instructed herself sternly. There were no two ways about it—she was guilty of listening to gossip, and of drawing a hasty conclusion as to

Giles Montague's motivations for the afternoon outing with his father. Worse than that, she had all but
made a false accusation of heartlessness towards him
because of it!

'I apologise if I seemed…overconcerned earlier, in
regard to His Grace's health,' she spoke stiffly, her
gaze fixed upon the buttons on Giles's waistcoat as
she found herself unable to look up and meet what
she suspected would be chilling displeasure in those
icy grey eyes.

Giles scowled as he looked down at that bent head,
irritated beyond measure that he should once again
note the fineness of Lily Seagrove's looks—the dark
silkiness of her curls, that delicate nape, the long dark
lashes downcast against cheeks of ivory-white, those
full and ruby-red lips. As for the creamy swell of her
breasts just visible above the low neckline of her blue
gown…!

Damn it, was his life not complicated enough at
present without his noting the attractions of a young
woman whose position in life, and questionable antecedents, rendered her unsuitable as being anything
more to him than a gentleman's mistress? At the same
time, Giles's acquaintance with her adoptive parents
made the offer of such a role in his own life impossible.

And where that particular idea had come from Giles had absolutely no idea. Nor, having thought of it, did he wish to pursue it!

Chapter Five

'As it is a warm evening, Miss Seagrove, perhaps you would care to take a walk on the terrace whilst our fathers retire to play their game of chess?'

Lily looked up at Giles Montague from beneath thick black lashes as he walked over to where she was still seated at the dinner table, his arm extended in silent invitation as he waited for her to rise.

As could be expected of the duke's French chef, it had been a magnificent dinner—made more enjoyable for Lily by the fact that Giles Montague, seated at the opposite end of the table to his father, had remained broodingly silent for most of it!—but Lily's pleasure in the evening could no longer continue now that her father and the Duke of Rothermere had decided to retire to the duke's rooms and enjoy their brandy and cigars over the promised game of chess. And so leaving Lily, and Lord Giles, one presumed, to find their own amusement….

'Would you not prefer to remain here and enjoy your own brandy and cigar?' she prompted restlessly, her father and the Duke of Rothermere having already made their excuses and left the dining room together.

'Only if you will agree to remain also…?' Giles Montague arched dark brows.

Lily smiled dismissively. 'I am afraid I do not drink brandy or enjoy cigars!'

He gave a tight smile at her irony. 'And I could not possibly be so rude as to enjoy them either when to do so would abandon you to your own amusements.'

Perhaps a walk outside would be preferable to the two of them retiring to the salon for the next hour or so and attempting to make polite conversation.

'Then I believe I should enjoy taking a walk outside in the fresh air, thank you.' Lily gave a gracious nod of her head before standing as Giles Montague moved to pull back her chair, ignoring the arm he offered to instead turn and walk alone to where Lumsden had opened the French doors in anticipation of their stepping outside onto the terrace.

Giles regretted his suggestion as he realised—too late!—that it may not be altogether wise to venture outside in the moonlight with Lily so soon after his earlier acknowledgement of her physical attributes.

Moonlight…?

Damn it, he had never considered himself to be a romantic man, and in the past had only ever taken a woman to his bed when he felt a physical need to do so, and always in the clear understanding that the encounter meant no more to him than a passing fancy.

Whether he 'fancied' Lily Seagrove or not, her position as the adopted daughter of the local vicar meant she was not a woman Giles could ever seriously consider taking to his bed. Not the ideal circumstances under which he should follow her as she strolled outside into the moonlight, before crossing to stand beside the balustrade of the terrace and gaze out across the parklands. Her dark blue gown and ebony hair allowed her to meld into the darkness, and so made a stark contrast to the ivory paleness of her skin. Soft and silky skin dappled in moonlight, and which surely begged to be touched and caressed—

'Everything looks so much more beautiful in the moonlight, does it not?' she remarked on a wistful sigh.

'What?' Giles scowled darkly as he tried to force any idea of intimacy with this young woman, either now or in the future, firmly from his thoughts.

Lily turned to glance across at where Giles Montague stood so tense and still in the shadows of the house, her breath catching in her throat as the moonlight caught the sharp angles of his face to give him an almost satanic appearance, and making a pale glitter of those silver-grey eyes. She moistened her lips before speaking. 'I was remarking on how much more beautiful everything looks at night, my lord.'

'Yes...' Those grey eyes glittered more brightly than ever as he stepped out of the shadows; the darkness of his clothing added to his dark and predatory appearance.

Lily quickly turned away, feeling herself tremble slightly even as she reached out to tightly grip the balustrade before her, totally aware of Giles Montague as he crossed the terrace in sure but soft strides until she sensed he stood just behind her. Indeed, he was standing so close to her that Lily was sure she could feel the warmth of his breath against her nape!

'Is it too cold for you out here, after all?' he prompted huskily. He obviously saw her tremble and mistook the reason for it.

Cold? Lily had never felt warmer!

But it was the sort of warmth that came from within, a deep and compelling heat as the blood seemed to rush more quickly through her veins, and her breasts felt suddenly constricted beneath the fitted bodice of her gown, and so making breathing even more difficult.

Was she ill?

Perhaps coming down with a cold or the influenza?

Certainly her limbs felt aching and trembling, her palms damp inside the lace of her gloves and her cheeks warm as if with a fever. 'Perhaps a little,' she acknowledged softly, resisting the urge to turn and look at Giles Montague as she caught a rustle of movement behind her. She could not prevent her gasp as she felt the warmth of his evening jacket being placed about her shoulders. 'Oh, please, I could not possibly—'

'Oh, but you must.' His hands came to rest on her now-covered shoulders in a light and yet compelling grip as she would have attempted to remove his jacket, his breath now every bit as warm against her nape as Lily had imagined it might be.

She stood tense and stiff as she knew herself completely aware of Giles Montague's touch, from the tips of her toes to the top of her ebony head. As she was aware of how the heat of Giles Montague's body had been absorbed into the material of the jacket that now warmed her. Just as she was also aware of inhaling the lightness of his cologne—sandalwood and lime?—

every time she attempted to draw breath. It invaded her senses, and caused Lily's trembling to intensify as she now felt uncomfortably hot inside the confines of his jacket. It was a heat and discomfort she was sure would only deepen if she were to turn and actually look at Giles Montague!

'Better?' he breathed huskily.

Heavens, no, it was much worse to be so aware of everything about Giles Montague, of all men, and yet seemingly unable to break the spell of that awareness!

She must, after all, be suffering from a malaise, a life-threatening fever, one that made it impossible for her to breathe, and would surely carry her off completely if she did not soon find some relief from lack of breath and the heat that coursed through her veins!

'Lily...?'

'I—' She halted her protest as she heard how husky her voice sounded, her breasts quickly rising and falling as she once again attempted to breathe. 'Perhaps we should go back inside....' She finally chanced a glance over her left shoulder at him. And instantly wished that she had not!

Giles Montague's face was lean and shadowed beneath dark hair ruffled onto his forehead by the gentle brush of the breeze, his shoulders appearing very broad in the white evening shirt, his stomach taut and flat beneath his waistcoat.

Lily quickly averted her gaze. 'I think perhaps I will not wait for my father to finish his game of chess, after all, but rather I will leave now.... My lord?' she prompted sharply, as instead of releasing her, she felt his hands tighten their grip upon her shoulders. 'You are hurting me, my lord,' she protested softly as she tried to extricate herself from his clasp.

For several long seconds it seemed as if Giles Montague would not allow her to be released, and then just as suddenly the heat of his hands was removed, allowing Lily to slip away before taking the jacket from her shoulders, resisting the slight shiver at the loss of its warmth as she turned to hold the garment out to him. 'My lord?' she prompted firmly when he made no effort to take it from her but continued to scowl down at her broodingly in the moonlight.

Giles's hands were clenched at his sides, a nerve pulsing in his tensed jaw as he fought an inner battle with himself not to give in to the demand that he take Lily in his arms and—

And what?

If he should kiss Lily Seagrove, even once, then he would be openly acknowledging his desire for her. An unwanted desire, and one which Giles had no reason to believe Lily returned. In fact, her every word and gesture towards him implied the opposite!

He stepped back abruptly. 'I will instruct John to bring the carriage round,' he bit out tersely, a frown darkening his brow as he reached out and took his jacket from Lily's gloved fingers before shrugging his shoulders into its tailored perfection, determinedly straightening his cuffs in an effort not to look at her again.

'That will not be necessary—'

'It is very necessary,' Giles assured firmly as he turned to stride across the terrace and open the door for her to enter. 'Not only do I insist you return home in the carriage, but I shall accompany you.'

Her chin was raised in challenge as she joined him at the open door. 'You perhaps fear that if I were to walk home alone at night I might be set upon by the Gypsies?'

Giles's jaw was tightly clenched at her deliberate challenge towards what most—what he, certainly— believed to be her antecedents. 'The elderly Mrs Lovell is the only one of the Romany to have arrived so far, and I somehow doubt you have anything to fear from her!'

Lily raised dark brows. 'I am surprised you were even aware of her presence....'

He gave a tight and humourless smile. 'Since my return a week ago I have made it my business to know all that transpires on the Rothermere estate.'

'So many have remarked,' Lily acknowledged ruefully as she swept past him to enter the warmth of the dining room.

'You sound disapproving, when only days ago I believe you urged me to take an interest.'

'I, my lord?' Lily raised her brows as he stepped into the dining room. 'You are mistaken.'

'I do not believe so, no,' he bit out tightly.

Lily frowned. 'It must be somewhat...tedious for you that the law does not as yet allow you to officially claim the title of Marquis of Hatherton.'

'Tedious?' Giles Montague echoed softly as he carefully closed the door behind him before turning, the grey of his eyes now like shards of opaque glass as he looked down the lean length of his nose at her. 'You believe I must consider the death of my elder brother as being tedious?'

Lily had spoken hastily, still totally unnerved by the strange turmoil of her feelings towards Giles Montague. 'I meant no disrespect to Lord James's memory.'

'No?'

'Certainly not,' she insisted sharply.

Giles Montague gave a haughty acknowledgement of his head. 'In that case I must consider any intended disrespect to have been directed towards me. And if so, then I believe I should warn you that the last person to accuse me of wishing my brother James dead, so that I might inherit his title, no doubt still has the bruises about his throat to show for it!'

Lily's startled gaze instantly moved to that spot on the arrogant, square jaw where Giles Montague had sported a bruise the week before.

'Yes,' he confirmed as he saw her glance. 'That very same gentleman,' he drawled self-derisively.

'Oh,' she breathed softly.

He raised mocking brows. 'You had perhaps imagined, having heard of my exploits in London, that I received my injury for a…less respectable reason?'

Having given some thought to that bruise after their initial meeting in the woods, Lily had thought exactly that, she now acknowledged guiltily. In fact, she knew she had quite enjoyed imagining the arrogant Giles Montague to have perhaps been struck on the chin by a jealous husband or lover shortly before leaving London!

Except…

It now transpired that Giles Montague had received

that blow whilst defending the affection he had for his dead brother.

That Lord James had died far away in Spain, swept away in the torrent of a fast-flowing river, his body never recovered, had, Lily knew, been a painful blow to the members of the Montague family residing in Derbyshire. Her own prejudice of feelings towards Giles Montague had not allowed her to see that, although he had been away from home when the news arrived, he must have been just as wounded, if not more so, by the loss of his older brother.

'I apologise,' she spoke huskily. 'I meant you no insult. I—' She gave a self-disgusted shake of her head. 'I spoke out of turn, and I apologise.'

Giles slowly allowed the tension to ease from his shoulders. 'One apology would have sufficed,' he assured drily. 'Now, if you are quite ready to leave, I will ring for Lumsden and have the carriage brought round.'

'I really do not want to be any trouble—'

'My dear Lily, it is now my belief that you have been nothing but trouble since the moment your baby basket was left upon the Seagroves' doorstep twenty years ago!'

Green eyes opened wide with shock at the unexpectedness of his attack. 'I— You— That was completely uncalled for!' she gasped faintly.

Yes, it was, Giles acknowledged wearily. Uncalled for, and deliberately cruel. But, in truth, he was feeling cruel. A combination of physical frustration and inner turmoil had most definitely rendered him cruel!

He grimaced. 'It would seem that it is my turn to apologise to you.' He gave a self-disgusted shake of his head. 'Obviously the carriage ride earlier today was not as beneficial to my own temperament as it was to my father's!'

Lily looked up at Giles searchingly, but saw only that hard implacability about the firmness of his mouth, and the icy disgust in his eyes. Whether that disgust was directed towards her or himself Lily was unsure. 'No doubt you have noticed, my lord, that we do not seem able to converse for two minutes at a time without insulting each other.'

He gave a humourless smile. 'Then might I suggest that the answer would seem to be for us not to converse at all?'

Lily could find no argument with that suggestion; in fact, after the strangeness of her feelings whilst outside on the terrace just now, she would welcome never having to see or speak with Giles Montague ever again....

* * *

'So you've come to see me at last, have ye?'

Mrs Lovell ceased stirring the coals of the fire, over which her cast-iron cooking pot was suspended by a shepherd's crook. She turned to look across to where Lily stood at the edge of the small clearing situated between the lake and the river, the place where the elderly Romany usually made her camp. Lily took absolutely no offence at the elderly lady's accusing tone, knowing from years of making such visits that it was merely Mrs Lovell's way. 'I thought to give you a few days to settle before calling.' She smiled as she stepped further into the clearing, wearing one of her older gowns of serviceable blue cotton, with a straw bonnet over her curls.

'Did ye now?' The elderly Romany straightened. She was a small and wizened lady of indeterminate years, her complexion weathered by years of suffering the extremes of either the heat of the sun or the bitterness of the cold. Her eyes were hazel, a strange mixture of brown, blue and green, and her mouth slightly folded in on itself where she had lost most of her front teeth. Her greying black hair was secured beneath its usual black scarf; her gown was also black, but covered from waist to toe by a white pinafore. 'You've grown even taller than when I saw ye last year,' she added bluntly.

Lily laughed softly. 'I fear that I have, yes.'

'Why be afeared?' Mrs Lovell began to drop the ingredients for her stew into the pot as the water began to boil—several diced carrots and a parsnip or two, some potatoes, a few herbs, followed by what looked to be a skinned and boned rabbit.

'It would seem that the fashion is for the fair and delicate this Season,' Lily explained ruefully as she sat down on one of the logs of wood the other woman had gathered and would no doubt place upon the fire later.

'Fair and delicate!' Mrs Lovell's snort of disgust was indicative of exactly what she thought of that insipidness. 'Ask any man and he'll tell ye he prefers to be able to feel a bit of shape to the woman as warms his bed at night.'

Lily knew she would never ask any gentleman such a thing! And the colour that now warmed her cheek owed nothing to the flames of the fire but to memories of the liquid heat that had consumed her on the terrace yesterday evening, as Giles Montague had stood so close to her that for several moments she had imagined he might actually be about to kiss her!

Which, in the light of day, Lily could clearly see as being fanciful nonsense; Giles Montague disliked her far too much even to think about kissing her let alone attempting to do so!

True to his word, last night he had ordered one of the Rothermere carriages be brought round before accompanying her on the short drive back to the vicarage. It had been a carriage ride that had seemed excruciatingly long as, abiding by his suggestion, neither of them had spoken so much as a word to the other until they made their goodbyes at the vicarage door. It had turned into a tense and stiffly polite parting, during which Lily's gaze had remained firmly fixed upon Giles Montague's neck cloth rather than risk another glance at his face.

To now be so vividly reminded of that time alone with him on the terrace at Castonbury Park, when Lily had been trying so hard all morning not to think of him at all, caused her to speak hastily lest Mrs Lovell see her blushes and attempt to tease the reason for them from her. 'I see that Samson is still with you.' She looked admiringly at the piebald horse tethered a short distance from the brightly coloured caravan which Mrs Lovell called a vardo and which he had pulled faithfully these past ten years.

'No doubt he'll see me out,' the elderly Romany dismissed practically, her shrewd gaze still focused on Lily. 'Have you found yourself a young man yet?'

'No,' Lily dismissed lightly—nor was she ever likely to do so when she stood so uncertainly between one world and another, neither Quality nor peasant, fish nor fowl.

'Are all the men blind in these parts, then?' Mrs Lovell gave the stew a last stir before resuming her seat on the small stool that stood to one side of the fire.

'I do not believe so, no,' Lily laughed softly. 'Mrs Jeffries sent you this.' She held out the apple pie she had brought with her wrapped in muslin.

'Kind of her.' The elderly Romany nodded as she accepted the gift, sniffing appreciatively. 'Mmm, cinnamon,' she murmured with satisfaction before placing it carefully to one side. 'If the men here are not blind, then they must surely be senile,' she continued with her usual asperity.

'No, I do not believe they are senile either,' Lily dismissed patiently when her attempt at diversion obviously failed. 'I am merely—I am afraid my lack of position in Society does not encourage many suitors,' she finally explained with a sigh, knowing of old that Mrs Lovell was too direct in manner to tolerate any attempt at prevarication from others.

'What does that mean, your "lack of position in Society"?' the old lady repeated with obvious scorn.

'Exactly as it sounds.' Lily smiled ruefully. 'It is

well known in these parts that I am a foundling. It is not what a gentleman might expect of his wife and the future mother of his children.' She shrugged without rancour.

'I never heard of such a thing!' Mrs Lovell gave another dismissive snort. 'In my day a pretty face and child-bearing hips was all as was required to be a wife and mother!'

Lily held back another smile with effort, knowing that the old lady had not intended to cause amusement with the bluntness of her remark. 'Do you have children of your own, Mrs Lovell?' The old lady had been a widow for as long as Lily had known her, nor did she recall ever having been introduced to any children from that marriage.

'I did.' The other woman busied herself stirring more herbs into her stew pot. 'As fine a son as any woman ever had.'

Lily sensed sadness beneath the statement. 'He is not with you any more…?' she prompted gently.

'He died right here in Castonbury almost twenty-one years ago,' Mrs Lovell revealed gruffly.

A pained frown appeared on Lily's brow. 'I had no idea— Oh!' She gave a breathless gasp as memory stirred; she had heard tales of a young Romany man who had met with an accident in the woods here twenty or so years ago, believed to have been shot by mistake by the then Rothermere gamekeeper, and buried in the churchyard across the lane from the vicarage. She had never seen the grave, nor the name carved upon it, but it seemed too much of a coincidence for it not to have been Mrs Lovell's son.

'It will be exactly twenty-one years in two days' time.' The old lady's gaze met hers unflinchingly.

Lily's eyes were wide. 'Is that the reason you always arrive here some days or weeks ahead of your tribe?'

'Maybe,' the other woman conceded gruffly.

She gave a pained wince. 'I am so sorry for your loss—'

'It was long ago and a different time.' Mrs Lovell straightened with brisk dismissal. 'But I don't recall him as being stupid enough not to marry the pretty woman he fell in love with, no matter what her breeding,' she added caustically.

Lily smiled gently, moved by the things Mrs Lovell had not said, able to see the pain of the loss of her only child still raw in that lady's expressive hazel eyes. 'I am afraid that a gentleman requires a little more than prettiness and child-bearing hips in his wife.'

'There ye go again with that "I am afraid."' Mrs Lovell frowned her disapproval. 'What is there for one as beautiful as you to be afraid of, except the stupidity of men?'

This time Lily could not hold back her laughter. 'You are very good for my self-esteem, Mrs Lovell.' She chuckled merrily.

'Self-esteem, is it?' The elderly woman gave a disgusted shake of her head. 'The men in these parts must be stupid, as well as blind and senile, is all I can say!'

'Your assessment appears to be harsh, Mrs Lovell, but quite possibly a correct one!'

Lily turned so sharply in the direction of that familiar, mocking voice that she was in danger of falling off the log on which she sat, only just managing to catch herself in time, and feeling the colour drain from her cheeks as she stared wide-eyed at where Giles Montague stood on the edge of the clearing, his tall hat once again throwing his face into shadow.

But Lily was more concerned about how long he had been standing there, rather than how he looked. And exactly how much of the frankness of Mrs Lovell's conversation he may have overheard....

Chapter Six

Lily gathered her wits enough to stand up awkwardly before making an abrupt curtsey. 'My lord.'

Giles nodded briefly in response, his smile humourless as he easily discerned the emotions that had flickered across Lily's expressive face at the unexpectedness of his appearance at Mrs Lovell's fireside—alarm, quickly followed by surprise. The former could be—and no doubt was!—attributed to seeing him again so soon after their stilted parting yesterday evening, and the surprise was no doubt due to finding Giles visiting Mrs Lovell at all, when Lily made no secret of the fact that she considered him to be not only arrogant but toplofty.

He quirked his brow before turning his attention to the elderly Romany as he stepped forward into the clearing. 'I brought over some tea and honey for you, Mrs Lovell, and Tom Anderson also sent over some of the liniment for your horse that he says you covet.' He presented her with the sack he carried.

'Kind of ye both, I'm sure.' The elderly woman nodded her thanks as she checked the contents of the sack. 'Perhaps the two of ye would like to join me in a cup of the tea?' she prompted even as she sat forward to hook the stew pot from over the fire and replace it with a blackened kettle.

'I believe my father will be expecting me back at the vicarage.' Lily instantly refused the invitation, having no real wish to cut short her visit with Mrs Lovell but also having no desire to spend any more time in Giles's unpleasant—and unsettling—company.

'Nonsense.' Mrs Lovell briskly dismissed her excuses. 'I am sure Mr Seagrove enjoys yer company enough that he can spare ye for the short time it will take to drink some tea with me.'

How could Lily refuse when Mrs Lovell put forward her argument in such reproving tones! 'Well, of course, if you insist…' she agreed weakly.

'I do,' the old lady said firmly.

Lily sank back down upon the log, keeping her gaze averted from Giles…even if she was completely aware of his presence only feet away from her!

Giles had walked over from the house, checking to make sure the work he had ordered to be done at the lake was in progress on the way, only realising that his approach to Rosa Lovell's camp must have been masked by the undergrowth as he heard the two ladies in candid conversation.

And he had not particularly liked what he had overheard, knowing that in all probability he was responsible for the opinion Lily obviously now had of herself. A less than flattering opinion, which Giles had expressed a year ago when he had told Lily of all the reasons she was unsuited to being the wife of his brother Edward, or any other gentleman of Quality....

'Sit ye down beside the yag, lad, and stop making the place look untidy!' Mrs Lovell's eyes twinkled merrily as she gave Giles a gap-toothed smile and drew up another log with the obvious intention of having him sit down upon it. 'And afterwards I'll do a little dukkering, if'n it pleases ye both,' she added with a sly glance at first Lily and then Giles.

The elderly lady looked so mischievous that Giles could not help but chuckle. 'Do we have to "cross your palm with silver" first?'

'Gold would be better,' Mrs Lovell came back cheekily.

'No doubt.' Giles smiled ruefully.

'Unless Miss Lily thinks that Mr Seagrove would

not approve of her indulging in such pagan practices as fortune-telling...' the elderly lady added teasingly.

Lily gave a rueful smile. 'I am sure my father's clerical profession dictates that he should not approve, at the same time as he would admit that his innate curiosity makes him eager for any and all knowledge!' she conceded affectionately.

Giles's gaze was guarded as he turned to her. 'You would not consider it an intrusion if I were to join the two of you?'

She barely glanced at him from beneath her straw bonnet as she shrugged dismissively. 'I believe we decided some time ago that I am the intruder here, and that it is your property to stay or go as you see fit.'

Giles should have expected to receive such a reproof after all that had passed between them, but even so his mouth firmed at the flat disinterest in Lily's tone. 'It would only please me to join the two of you if you were to assure me I am welcome to stay.'

Then go, Lily wished to tell him, *and go now.* Her nerves were already frayed to breaking at this unexpected encounter with the man whose very presence now caused her discomfort, and moreover a man who had made it more than obvious he could not abide to be in her company for any length of time either.

But she could not speak so bluntly to the future

Duke of Rothermere with the ever-curious Mrs Lovell as watchful witness to the exchange. 'Mrs Lovell made the invitation, not I,' she answered huskily.

'Even so…'

'Will you stop dithering, lad, and sit ye down!' Mrs Lovell lost all patience with their stilted politeness. 'The tea's made now, and I'll not have it go to waste. I'll not be a minute finding the mugs.' She left the two of them alone as she disappeared off to her brightly coloured caravan.

Lily smiled at hearing the haughty Giles Montague referred to as 'lad'—anyone less like a lad she could not imagine! But no doubt it was how Mrs Lovell thought of him, having been coming to stay at Castonbury Park since before he'd been born. No doubt the elderly Romany probably also remembered him as being the 'mischievous scamp' Mrs Stratton had referred to some days ago.

It led Lily to question how long he had been in the habit of visiting Mrs Lovell's fireside; Lily would never have believed it of the disdainful Giles Montague if she had not witnessed it with her own eyes. Perhaps she did not know the haughty Giles Montague as well as she had thought.…

Giles knew that he really should not have intruded once he became aware of Lily's presence at Rosa Lovell's fireside, and instead returned later in the day when he was sure the elderly lady was alone. Except, having heard the husky warmth in Lily's voice as she chatted so easily and warmly with Mrs Lovell, he had been unable to resist joining them. In the hopes, perhaps, that some of that warmth might spill over onto him.

Even wearing that unfashionable gown of faded blue cotton and an unbecoming straw bonnet that had also seen better days, Giles knew he could not look at Lily without feeling the same stirrings of desire that had kept him awake long into the previous night, stirrings which now resulted in him shifting restlessly upon the log as he sought a more comfortable position that would not expose the direction of his thoughts.

'Here ye are!' Mrs Lovell returned triumphant with three mismatched metal mugs before proceeding to pour the tea, all in apparent ignorance of the strained silence between her two guests. 'Drink it all down, my chivvies,' she encouraged gleefully as she handed them their steaming mugs of honey-sweetened tea. 'And then I'll look at your palms and see what the future holds in store for the both of you!'

Giles did not need a crystal ball to 'see' that his immediate future held a soaking in the coldness of either the lake or bath in order to cool his thoughts.

'One of my reasons for visiting was to ask if you will kindly do the fortune-telling at the well-dressing again this year.' Lily concentrated all of her attention on Mrs Lovell.

Which was not to say she was not still entirely aware of Giles sitting on the log beside her own. Or immune to that faint hint of sandalwood and lime of his cologne, that same masculine smell which had surrounded her the evening before when he had wrapped his jacket about her for warmth. A warmth which, seconds later, and for totally different reasons, Lily had found almost unbearable!

She had every reason to dislike the man intensely, and yet still she could not deny the heat and trembling she had felt at his close proximity yesterday evening, or that sudden sensitivity of her breasts pressing against the bodice of her gown. An aching sensitivity that still made Lily blush to think of it!

'Of course.' Mrs Lovell nodded in answer to her request. 'Some of the tribe have decided to resume the pilgrimage to Saintes-Maries-de-la-Mer this year, now that the fighting is over and we can travel across to France again, but I'm too old for such things.' She grimaced dismissively.

And, Lily realised after their earlier conversation, if the elderly lady had gone on the pilgrimage to France with the rest of her tribe, then she would not have been able to visit her son's grave on the anniversary of his death.

'I am sure we will appreciate your company all the more because of it.' Lily smiled warmly at the older woman, determined to visit the grave of Mrs Lovell's son herself, and place some wildflowers upon it, now that she was aware of its existence.

'Get on with you!' Mrs Lovell snorted at the compliment. 'Put aside your tea now, my chivvy, and let me take a look at your palm and tell ye what the future holds.'

Lily had a certain reluctance to know what was in store for her—she would much rather have had foreknowledge of Giles arriving at Mrs Lovell's fireside today than anything that may or may not be about to happen in her distant future!

A surreptitious glance at Giles beneath lowered lashes revealed that he did not seem in the least put out that he was not sipping tea from his usual fine china. Instead that silver-grey gaze rested on her broodingly, and in doing so made Lily even more aware of how her old blue serge gown had become a little tight about the breasts from constant washing, and how the shortness of the hem revealed her ankles in scuffed and muddied brown boots.

Her less than fashionable appearance prompted her

into hurried speech. 'Your father has suffered no ill effects from his late evening?' It had been almost midnight when she heard her father arrive back at the vicarage.

Giles frowned darkly as the question forced him to recall the visit to his father's rooms this morning. The duke was indeed suffering from exhaustion after his carriage ride yesterday afternoon and the burst of social largesse in the evening, resulting in the over-attentive Smithins treating Giles with more than his usual coolness. The valet was merely an irritant Giles had no trouble ignoring, but he could not dismiss his father's obvious lack of physical stamina with the same disinterest.

'If he did I am sure he will be fully recovered by tomorrow,' he assured her.

'I have a sarsaparilla tonic you might take for your father when you leave. Very good for cleansing the blood.' Mrs Lovell nodded sagely.

'Thank you.' Giles accepted gracefully, already knowing that Rosa Lovell's tonic would suffer the same fate as the doctor's appeared to have done— placed on the shelf beside his father's bedside before being completely ignored.

Mrs Lovell seemed satisfied with his answer, however, as she turned briskly to Lily. 'Time to remove yer glove and let me take a look at yer palm.'

'Perhaps His Lordship might like to be first...?' she prompted with a cool glance in Giles's direction.

His gaze narrowed as he easily guessed that Lily believed he would refuse to be a part of such nonsense as fortune-telling. 'By all means...' He held out his left hand for Mrs Lovell's inspection.

'The other's yer dominant hand.' The elderly lady chuckled dismissively and waited while Giles replaced his left hand with his right. 'And I don't really need to look too closely to know as your square finger-tips indicate an orderly and methodical nature. That the length of your index finger says ye are a leader and maker of decisions.' She turned his hand over. 'Or that these—' she chuckled again as she touched the dark hair on the back of his hand '—show ye to have a passionate nature, for all ye would rather not.' She bent over his palm once again. 'Your love line is strong and true—'

'Perhaps you should take a look at Miss Seagrove's hand now,' he suggested lightly as he firmly removed his hand from further perusal.

His parents' marriage had, as far as Giles was aware, been one of mutual respect and liking, and as content as any of the arranged marriages of the *ton*.

But even so, he did not believe that contentment to have prevented his father from occasionally enjoying the company of other women, and so giving Giles the rather jaundiced view that a wife was taken in order to provide the necessary heirs, a mistress for physical enjoyment, and the two were never to be found with the same woman.

Mrs Lovell gave him one of those piercing looks that saw far too much before turning to look at Lily. 'Let me take a look,' she prompted eagerly.

Giles could not remember having seen Lily's hands bare since she had reached adulthood, and now found himself looking on interestedly as she slowly removed her glove to reveal long and slender fingers, the nails kept short, no doubt in deference to the work she did about the parish. Nevertheless, her skin appeared pale and delicate in contrast to Rosa Lovell's brown and work-roughened hands as the old lady gazed down at Lily's palm.

'A long and uninterrupted lifeline, which is good,' Mrs Lovell said softly. 'A determination of nature. A yearning for travel…' She looked up as Lily's breath caught in her throat. 'A well-hidden yearning for travel,' she amended lightly. 'Again, a passionate nature,' she murmured distractedly as she touched the mound at the base of Lily's thumb. 'No man is going to be left wanting in your bed, that's for su—'

'I believe I really must be going now!' Lily's cheeks burned as she snatched her hand from the elderly lady's grasp before standing up abruptly, only to give a grimace of dismay as she realised she had accidentally knocked her booted foot against the metal mug she had previously placed upon the ground, and succeeding in tipping out the last of the tea.

The ever-watchful Mrs Lovell instantly scooped up the mug to look at the contents. 'What do we have here...?' she murmured softly.

'I thought the Romany considered the reading of tea leaves to be beneath them?' Giles Montague prompted drily.

'Not at all, there's just no money to be had from it!' the old lady dismissed scornfully. 'No one's going to part with their silver, let alone gold, to have the tea leaves read! There is something here, though....' Her frowning attention returned to the contents of the mug.

Lily gave a firm shake of her head. 'I really do not think—'

'I see a darkness in your future,' the elderly Romany said slowly.

'A man of darkness. One who means to do you harm—' Mrs Lovell broke off her dire predictions as Lily lightly lifted the mug from her fingers. 'I was nowhere near finished.' She scowled her disapproval as Lily emptied the last of the tea dregs into the grass.

'I am sure it is better if we do not know too much about what the future may bring, Mrs Lovell, else we should all go mad with worrying about it,' Lily dismissed lightly as she set down the mug before replacing her glove, sure that she already knew which gentleman that 'darkness' referred to! 'I may rely on your presence at the well-dressing celebrations next week, Mrs Lovell?' she added briskly.

'I have said ye may....' The elderly lady still looked troubled as she rose less spryly to her feet. 'Ye will take care, Lily—'

'You must not worry about me, my dear Mrs Lovell.' She laughed dismissively as she bent instinctively to kiss one leathered brown cheek. 'I am perfectly capable of ensuring that no harm comes to me. From any gentleman,' she added firmly.

'I do not recall saying as it would be a gentleman—'

'Gentleman or otherwise, there is no one in Castonbury who wishes me harm, I do assure you,' Lily repeated before turning coolly to Giles Montague. 'My lord.' She nodded dismissively before turning quickly on her booted heel and hurrying away.

Nevertheless she felt the weight of that gentleman's

gaze following her with the same heaviness as she might feel a rain cloud over her head.

'Well, laddie…?'

Giles had stood up the moment Lily fled. Now he turned to look down enquiringly at the much shorter Rosa Lovell. '"Well," Mrs Lovell…?'

Hazel-coloured eyes glittered up at him mockingly. 'I trust you have sense enough to chase a pretty lass ye desire when the opportunity arises?'

He gave a rueful shake of his head. 'I assure you I have no wish to chase Lily Seagrove, or any other "pretty lass"!' Mrs Lovell raised sceptical brows. 'You really are an outrageous rogue, Mrs Lovell!'

She gave a wry chuckle. 'I'm not so old yet as I can't see when a handsome man desires a pretty woman. Go after her, laddie. If only to see that she comes to no harm,' she added worriedly. 'The tea leaves are never wrong, my lord. Someone means to do Lily harm. And soon, if I'm not mistaken.' A frown darkened her furrowed brow.

'And what if Lily believes that "someone" to be me?' Giles prompted drily.

Shrewd dark eyes gazed searchingly up into his before Mrs Lovell gave a slow shake of her head. 'Then she would be wrong.'

He gave a mocking acknowledgement of his head. 'I doubt Miss Seagrove would agree with you!'

'She's too young as yet to realise that a man's passion all too often leads him to behave like a fool,' the old Romany dismissed bluntly.

Giles gave a rueful burst of laughter. 'I have no idea why it is I continue to like you, Mrs Lovell!'

She eyed him teasingly. 'No?'

'No,' he confirmed drily. 'But I will do as you ask, and follow Lily. If only to set your mind at rest concerning her safe arrival back at the vicarage.'

'You tell yourself that's the reason, by all means, laddie.' Mrs Lovell gave him a condescending pat on the arm.

Giles gave another self-derisive laugh before setting out to follow Lily through the woods.

'Lily? Lily, wait!'

Lily's instinct was to increase her pace rather than reduce it as she heard Giles calling after her. She had no desire to engage in further conversation with him.

'Lily, I asked you to wait, damn it!'

Hearing that customary arrogance in Giles Montague's voice only succeeded in making Lily all the more determined that he should not catch her, as she all but ran through the dense woodland. But she was aware of the increasingly loud crackle of the dry undergrowth as indication that Giles's much longer strides meant he was gaining on her with every step.

Giles's gaze was narrowed on his quarry as he hurried after Lily's lithe form flitting between the trees with a familiarity which spoke of her having done so many times before. As indeed she no doubt had, when she and Edward were children.

The haste needed to catch his quarry gave him sharp cause to remember the injuries he had sustained in battle as his thigh began to ache from a deep sabre wound he had received at Talavera, the scars upon his chest from Salamanca unsightly, but no longer as painful. 'Lily!' His fingers finally curled about her arm as he pulled her to a halt, glowering down at her as he swung her about to face him. 'Running away will not—'

'I am not "running away"!' She glared her indignation. 'I have merely tarried too long at Mrs Lovell's fireside and now must hurry if I am to return to the vicarage in time for lunch.' She gave a pained wince. 'You are hurting me—'

'And you were running away,' Giles repeated grimly even as he relaxed his grip on her arm.

Those green eyes flashed her displeasure as she gazed up at him challengingly. 'That would seem to imply that there is something I feel the need to run away from.'

He shrugged. 'Is there not?'

A frown appeared between those magnificent eyes. 'You think far too much of yourself, sir.'

'Perhaps that is because you choose to think far too little of me!' Giles bit out harshly.

Lily did not want to think of this gentleman at all. In any way. At any time. Ever again. She had spent far too many hours the previous night doing exactly that as she lay awake in her bed. And had succeeded in finding very few answers to the unsettling questions such thoughts had posed.

She tilted her chin. 'What is it you want from me, my lord?'

What did Giles want from Lily Seagrove?

All and everything that the astute and blunt Mrs Lovell had minutes ago stated that he did!

Chapter Seven

Giles's total awareness of Lily the evening before, and again today, now told—warned!—him that he desired nothing more at this moment than to lay her down on the soft green moss on the forest floor, an exact match in colour to her eyes, before slowly removing every article of her clothing until she lay pale and naked before him. After which he wished to remove all the pins from her hair before releasing that long cascade of ebony silk down onto her shoulders and draping it across her breasts, leaving those rosy-red tips peaking temptingly through that darkness as he lowered his head—

Oh, good heavens!

Giles's hands began to shake as he desperately tried to resist that temptation, but it was a battle he lost, as rather than releasing her and moving away, he instead began to pull Lily towards him with a determination which far surpassed any and all warnings of inner caution.

Lily's eyes widened in alarm as Giles Montague pulled her ever closer. 'What are you about…?' she managed to gasp breathlessly even as his heat once again enveloped and drew her closer.

He gave a grim smile. 'Madness,' he bit out harshly. 'Complete and utter madness!'

'Giles—'

'Say it again!' Those silver-grey eyes burned down at her with an intensity that was frightening.

'What…?' Lily could no longer think as she was pulled against the hard heat of Giles's muscled chest and the flatness of his stomach, before his arms moved about her with the implacability of steel bands.

'Say my name again, Lily!' he encouraged gruffly. 'Say it!' he repeated fiercely, his eyes now glowing with that same fervour of emotion.

This was indeed madness. But of a kind Lily had never encountered before. A madness which robbed her of all will, as she knew she could no more resist the allure of Giles Montague than he seemed to be able to resist her.

The stiffness drained from her as her body softened intimately into and against his much harder one.

'Giles,' she murmured softly.

'Again!'

'Giles,' she repeated breathlessly.

'Oh, dear God…!' Giles groaned achingly even as he lowered his head towards hers.

Her lips were soft, and she tasted of the honey she had taken in her tea, Giles very quickly discovered. He kissed her fiercely, urgently, his lips and tongue exploring the moist heat of her mouth, even as he revelled in the softness of her curves arched against him, her hands clasped onto the lapels of his jacket, as if she feared she might fall if they did not.

Giles was hungry for her. Hungry for the taste of her. The feel of her. And it was a hunger that he knew had begun that first day they had met here in the woods, and it had only grown deeper with each subsequent meeting, until Giles knew he could no longer deny that aching hunger.

He held her tightly against him, groaning low in his throat as he moved his hands down to cup the firmness of her bottom before pulling her up and into him, her lush and slightly parted thighs becoming a tortuous friction against him.

The blood began to pump hotly, feverishly, through Giles's body, and he dragged his mouth from hers to bury his face against her throat, tasting her there even as one of his hands moved up to cup the lushness of her breast, the material of her cotton gown thin enough that he could feel the tight nipple pressing into his palm. He tasted the lobe of her ear, her cheek, before his mouth was once again on Lily's to claim her soft gasps of pleasure as the soft pad of his thumb laid siege to her breast.

Lily became lost in that same madness as Giles kissed her deeply, feverishly. Burning, consuming heat. And pleasure. An aching, pulling pleasure as Giles grasped the tip of her breast between finger and thumb, the heat building between her thighs as his lips and tongue explored the deep recesses of her mouth, evoking feelings, sensations, unlike anything she had ever known or experienced before. An aching burning heat that consumed even as it begged, pleaded, for—

For she knew not what!

Lily only knew that this pleasure was so intense, so all-consuming, that she wanted…something more. Needed…something more.

She felt she might truly go mad if she did not find relief from the pressures building ever higher inside her hot and aching body.

She gasped as she felt Giles's fingers against her flesh as he deftly unfastened the buttons at the front of her gown to pull the chemise aside and bare her breasts to his ministrations, her nipple captured between thumb and finger as he began to tug gently, rhythmically, causing a hot pool of moisture to flood between Lily's thighs.

She drew in a ragged breath as Giles wrenched his mouth from hers to once again bury the heat of his lips against her throat before moving slowly downwards, his lips and tongue a fiery caress against the slope of her other breast before she felt that heat close over the aching tip to suck deeply, the drawing, pulling sensation on her breast causing Lily's knees to buckle.

Giles followed as Lily sank to the forest floor, laying his long length down beside her on the soft moss as he continued to taste the fullness of her nipple even as his other hand moved down the slope of her slender waist, across the full curve of her hips and lower still as he gently pulled up her gown to discover she wore stockings held up with ribbons, and soft cotton drawers.

'Giles…?' She gave a strangled gasp as his hand nudged her legs apart to allow him to cup her there, that gasp turning to a groan—of pleasure, Giles hoped—as he pulled fiercely on her nipple with his lips even as he sought her silken folds amongst the fabric of her drawers.

Those silken folds parted to the caress of his fingers, a deep well of moisture dampening him as he began to stroke her, lingering as he felt her pulse and swell to his ministrations, and heard Lily's panting breaths as her pleasure deepened and grew, her hips now moving up to meet those caresses.

Giles parted those wet folds to plunge one moist finger inside her opening even as his thumb continued to stroke the bud above. He drew hungrily on her nipple, thrusting his finger, and then two, deep into her as he felt the inner walls quiver in a way which he knew signalled she was hurtling towards climax.

'Giles…!' Lily gazed up at him in alarm as she felt herself overwhelmed by unimaginable pleasure.

'Let go, damn it!' he demanded fiercely. 'Now, Lily!'

As if the encouragement was all she had needed, Lily felt as if a dam suddenly burst inside her, pulsing inward and then outward, her breath coming in aching sobs as wave after wave of that pleasure engulfed her before ripping her apart and then slowly putting her back together again.

She buried her face against Giles's chest as those waves slowly, oh-so-slowly, subsided. She felt overwhelmed and her body shook as those tremors continued to quiver through her body.

'Would you touch me now, Lily?' Giles encouraged throatily even as he grasped one of her hands in his and began to move it slowly down between their two bodies.

Lily, still weak and gasping from that overwhelming pleasure, now gasped anew as Giles cupped her hand against the lengthy bulge beneath his breeches. A living, pulsing bulge, which moved enticingly against her fingers....

A burning curiosity to know more overcame her own feelings of uncertainty as she heard Giles groan low in his throat at her touch, his head resting against her breasts as she continued to move caressing fingers against him to feel its insistent throbbing in response to her actions.

'Oh, God, again, Lily!' he pleaded gutturally as he fell back onto the mossy ground, his eyes closed, his cheeks flushed, lips slightly parted, his breathing becoming increasingly laboured.

Lily sat up, unconcerned by her bared breasts as she caressed that hard and throbbing length from root to tip, slowly, tenderly, and was rewarded by Giles's groans of pleasure. She had never dreamed, never even guessed at the pleasure Giles had just shown her, let alone realised that she might be able to give him that same pleasure....

'Touch me, Lily!' Silver eyes blazed fiercely into her own.

Lily hesitated only briefly, her curiosity once again winning out over embarrassment, her hands shaking slightly as she unfastened the buttons at the sides of his breeches to reveal white drawers beneath, her eyes opening wide as she looked down upon that pulsing hardness she had so recently caressed as it jutted through the opening at the front.

Lily found herself watching in fascination as it seemed to grow even longer and thicker under her regard, as if in silent invitation.

Giles groaned low in this throat as he watched Lily's tongue move moistly over the parted plumpness of her lips, and easily imagined how that hot little tongue might feel against him. His hot gaze moved to her bared and pert breasts, the nipples red as berries as they stood firm and puckered.

Aching, unable to resist, Giles reached up to cup one of those tempting globes, watching Lily's flushed face as he took the nipple between his thumb and finger, squeezing gently, and was instantly rewarded by her sharp intake of breath as she began to tremble and shake. 'Place your other breast in my mouth, Lily,' he encouraged throatily as he lay back against the mossy ground.

Her eyes were wide green orbs as she slowly bent over him, her breast now hanging temptingly above his mouth as he continued to caress its twin, watching the pleasure that lit her eyes and flushed her cheeks as he parted his lips to draw the plump nipple into the heat of his mouth. He continued to hold her heated gaze as he caressed, gently at first, and then deeper, harder, as he felt the fingers of her gloved hand close about him, and the rasp of those lace-covered fingers moving up and down.

'Grip me tighter, Lily.' He released her breast to groan, 'Oh, God…!' His head fell back against the moss, eyes closed, back arching, knowing he was close to reaching his own climax—

He froze, his eyes opening wide as he felt a hot, moist caress and looked down to find Lily bent over him. He was about to lose control from simply watching her tongue caressing him. 'You have to stop now, Lily!' he pleaded fiercely, but he knew his plea came too late as he felt himself pulse and release.

Lily pulled back slightly and with a hoarse cry Giles reached out to hold her gloved hand firmly in place.

Giles's throat was dry and he felt completely spent after the deepest and most satisfying climax he had ever known in his life. It was an intensity of pleasure he owed completely to Lily's ministrations and this strange and deep attraction they had for each other.

Lily's heart thundered in her chest, not breathing at all as she knew herself completely mortified by what had just transpired, as she recalled—in shocking detail!—the intimacies the two of them had just indulged in together.

'Lily...?'

She could not even look at Giles again as she drew back sharply, turning her face away to stand up and turn her back towards him with the intention of refastening her gown, only to give a low groan as she saw the state of her lace glove.

Had her actions been purely instinctive? A desire to please Giles, as he had undoubtedly pleased her? Or was her behaviour due to something else, something much more fundamental, and inherited from the mother who had given birth to her before abandoning her?

'Lily?'

She kept her back turned towards Giles as she peeled off her glove and dropped it to the ground before attempting to refasten her gown with fingers that shook uncontrollably as they refused to do her bidding.

'Here, let me,' Giles prompted huskily, his own

clothing straightened to decency as he stepped forward to push Lily's hands aside so that he might refasten the buttons at the front of her gown. Her head was bent so that he could not see her features, but he was nevertheless able to feel the way she had stiffened as his fingers brushed lightly against her breasts. 'Lily?' He raised a hand with the intention of lifting her chin so that he might see her expression.

'Please…do not touch me.' She flinched before stepping away from him, her face deathly pale as she continued to stare down at the ground.

Giles gave a pained frown as his hands dropped back to his sides. 'We did nothing wrong—'

'Nothing wrong!' she repeated incredulously as she finally looked up at him, those moss-coloured eyes glittering brightly.

Whether with tears or anger, Giles was as yet unsure…

She gave a jerky shake of her head and groaned. 'If our shocking behaviour just now were ever to become public knowledge…!'

'I have no intention of telling anyone,' he said quietly. 'Have you?'

She began to pace agitatedly. 'The Duke of Rothermere has always made these woods available for the use of the people in the village, and as such any one of them could have…could have—'

'Chanced to walk by whilst we were lost to the throes of passion?' Giles supplied evenly, wishing to know for certain this conversation was going in the direction he believed it was before he gave suitable reaction to it.

'Exactly!' Lily groaned.

His mouth twisted derisively. 'The chances of that are minimal.'

'But not impossible!'

'No…' he accepted abruptly.

She gave a low and keening wail as she continued to pace. 'What little standing I have in the village will be destroyed—destroyed!—if our indiscretion should ever become known!'

Giles drew himself up warily. 'Exactly what is it that you require of me, Lily?'

Lily ceased her pacing to look across at him as she heard the chill in his tone, not in the least encouraged by the ice she also detected in his gaze, or the firm set of his jaw and thinned lips. Those very same lips which had kissed and known her so intimately only minutes ago….

She gave a slow and wary shake of her head. 'I do not remember saying that I required anything of you.'

Those sculptured lips twisted derisively. 'But I sense that you do, nevertheless.'

'I—' She swallowed, her throat having gone dry. 'I cannot think what to do or say at this moment.' She could only feel! And her feelings were ones of humiliation and regret.

Humiliation that she had succumbed so quickly and so completely to Giles's seduction.

Regret that her actions, if they should become known, would reflect badly on the kind and gentle Mr and Mrs Seagrove, for having taken one such as her into their hearts and home.

'Enlighten me, Lily,' Giles bit out harshly. 'Can this possibly be the same manner in which you persuaded the more gullible Edward into offering you marriage?'

'I— What...?' Lily gave a dazed shake of her head.

'I believe my words were clear enough, Lily.' Giles's mouth had thinned as he looked disdainfully down the long length of his nose at her. 'If not, let me re-iterate that I am curious to know if this was the way in which you secured a marriage proposal from my brother Edward? By allowing him to make love to you, and afterwards suggesting a scandal?' he said coldly.

What little colour had returned to her cheeks as she paced so agitatedly now drained away completely, the only colour in her face now being those huge moss-green eyes that looked up at him in disbelief. 'How dare you? How could you even suggest such a thing?' she finally gasped. 'You think that I—? You believe that I have behaved in that shameless manner before today? With Edward, of all people!' she added incredulously. 'And that I did so in order to entrap him into marriage?'

What else was Giles to think, when Lily's first concern had been for her own good reputation if their indiscretion today should ever be realised? A reputation which Giles already had serious reasons to doubt.

His jaw tightened. 'I believe I asked if that was the manner in which his marriage proposal came about.'

Her chin rose challengingly as she informed him, 'I received no marriage proposal from Edward!'

If that had indeed been the case, Giles thought, then the omission had only been because Edward had had the foresight to first inform Giles of his intentions towards Lily. Intentions Giles had spoken firmly against, advising Edward, if he must, to make the woman his mistress but never his wife. The heated manner of their own lovemaking just now, and Lily's less than virginal responses—surely no virgin could have touched him as Lily had?—would seem to indicate that Edward had taken that advice, after all.

At least Edward had had carnal knowledge of the

woman he had claimed to love before he died, but at the same time that put Giles in the position of having made love to his brother's lover! A young and beautiful woman who now seemed intent upon using her sensual charms to ensnare yet another Montague into marriage, this time the heir presumptive to the dukedom!

'Nor will you receive one from me,' Giles informed her coldly. 'But the position as my mistress may be available if you are at all interested in taking up that role.'

And if she said yes, what would he do then? Would he take her to mistress, after all, or do the sensible thing and turn away from the temptation she so obviously represented to him?

With his body still satiated from the pleasure he had known at Lily's touch, Giles had no immediate answer.

Lily recoiled as if she had been struck. Indeed, she felt as if she had. This man, a man whom she had allowed to make love to her and whom she had made love to, dared to insult her still further by offering her a position as his mistress!

'You are sensual enough.' Giles seemed to take her silence as indication she was considering his suggestion. 'And with a little tutoring as to my personal preferences, I am sure that we would deal very well together in the bedchamber. Your adoptive father's friendship with mine poses something of a problem, of course, but as long as we are both discreet I see no reason why either of them needs ever know of the arrangement. There are several empty cottages on the estate in which we might meet—'

'Stop!' Lily managed to gasp when she finally recovered her breath enough to speak, her emotions in turmoil. 'I do not— You—' She gave a protesting shake of her head. 'How dare you even suggest such a demeaning arrangement to me!' she accused. 'How dare you!'

He shrugged those broad shoulders. 'It is all you will ever receive from me. My wife, when I choose to take one, will certainly not have been used by my brother first, nor be the illegitimate offspring of a Gypsy!' His top lip curled back disdainfully.

Lily felt as if she might faint. Or scream. Or hit something. Preferably Giles Montague, for daring to stand there looking at her so contemptuously as he offered her the position as his mistress!

'I do not think so!' Giles reached out and grasped Lily's slender wrist as her hand swung upwards with the obvious intention of slapping him on the cheek, just as she had done a year ago. 'Shall I take it from your response that your answer is no?' He looked down at her with hard mockery as he continued to hold her immobile.

'You may—because my answer is most certainly no!' She wrenched her arm out of his grasp, and no doubt bruised her delicate flesh in the process.

'Then there would appear to be nothing further for the two of us to discuss.' Giles gave an abrupt inclination of his head before bending down to pick up his hat from where he had dropped it earlier, and then turned on his heel to stride away in the direction of home.

But in full knowledge that it had been Lily, rather he, who had been the one to turn down the role as his mistress.

Chapter Eight

'You have seemed very quiet these past few days, my dear.…' Mr Seagrove looked across the luncheon table at Lily. 'The arrangements for the well-dressing are not proving too much for you, I hope, on top of all the other work you do about the parish?'

It was that very work about the parish which Lily believed to have kept her sane these past three days!

Ordinarily she would have shared her confused feelings by speaking, or writing of them, to her friend Lady Phaedra, but as Phaedra was Giles's sister, Lily had no one in whom she might confide.

Instead she had kept herself too busy to think during the day, and too tired to do anything other than fall straight to sleep in her bedchamber at night. Because she dare not allow herself the time to think, refused to think, about Giles Montague, or the things that had transpired between them the last time they had been alone together. Something which had proved some-what difficult the day following their lovemaking, when the tips of her breasts had felt sensitive, and between her thighs had suffered a similar soreness.

She had seen Giles several times whilst she was out and about in the village, but thankfully always at a distance, either riding about the estate on his black steed, or in one of the ducal carriages, no doubt on his way to Buxton in pursuit of business, or possibly pleasure. And each time she had chanced to see him Lily had inwardly shrivelled with mortification as she was once again reminded of their lovemaking, and the humiliating conversation which had followed.

'Not at all, Father,' she now answered her adoptive father evenly. 'Indeed, once Mrs Stratton and I have discussed the last details this evening all arrangements for the well-dressing celebrations should be well in hand.'

Mr Seagrove nodded. 'Then perhaps there is some other reason for the air of…melancholy I have sensed in you these past three days?'

The fact that her adoptive father was aware of exactly how long Lily had been less than her cheer-ful self was cause for concern; his curiosity would certainly be piqued if he were ever to learn that it was the same day upon which she had last visited with Mrs Lovell, and Giles Montague had joined the two women shortly thereafter!

'I believe there has been thunder in the air as a precursor to the storm, and I have merely suffered a headache because of it,' she dismissed lightly. 'I am sure I shall be completely recovered now that the weather has broken.' The unseasonal rain was currently lashing down outside their cottage, with the occasional flash of lightning, quickly followed by a crash of thunder.

'Let us hope that there will not be too much damage to crops or property,' the vicar remarked ruefully as he glanced out of the window at the storm raging outside. 'No doubt Sir Nathan will enjoy regaling me with news of it over dinner this evening, if that should prove to be the case,' he added with less than his usual forebearance.

Lily could not help but smile at Mr Seagrove's obvious lack of enthusiasm for the dinner he was to take this evening at the home of Sir Nathan Samuelson, a single and eligible gentleman of forty or so years who owned a small estate in the area, but also a man who was known to be rather a dull, dour character.

Indeed, Sir Nathan was twice Lily's age at least, and had such an unappealing nature, she had felt less than enthusiastic when several times during the past year

Sir Nathan had appeared to show a preference for her company. She had certainly been relieved to have the excuse of her previous engagement with Mrs Stratton this evening, as a polite way of refusing Sir Nathan's invitation for her to join her father and him for dinner!

Sir Nathan did possibly have one thing in his favour, however, in that he made no secret of the fact that he was no more enamoured of the male members of the Montague family than she now was—in Lily's case, one member of that family in particular!

'No doubt,' Lily agreed softly. 'And now, if you will excuse me, Father, I believe the rain is lessening at last, and I should perhaps call upon Mrs Lovell to ensure all is well with her.'

Aware of Mrs Lovell's shrewdness of nature, and wishing to avoid any questions that elderly lady might have in regard to Lily's previous visit, she had avoided returning to the Romany camp, but knew she could delay no longer, knowing that whilst the elderly lady stayed here Mr Seagrove considered her as much one of his parishioners as any who lived in the village.

Besides which, yesterday had been the anniversary of the death of Mrs Lovell's son, and Lily wished to reassure herself that the elderly lady had not suffered any ill effects from that sad day. Out of respect for her grief Lily had herself visited the graveyard beside the church yesterday and placed daffodils on the grave of Matthew Lovell, presuming the wildflowers already arranged there to be from Mrs Lovell.

She stood up now, somewhat relieved they were at the end of their meal rather than the beginning of it; she had no wish for her father to delve further into the reasons for her preoccupation. 'I believe I will take Mrs Lovell some fresh milk and eggs.'

'I am sure she and her nephew will appreciate your thoughtfulness.' Mr Seagrove smiled his approval of the suggestion.

'Her nephew…?' Lily raised surprised brows as she recalled the elderly Romany telling her that the rest of her tribe had travelled on a pilgrimage to France, and would not be joining her for several weeks.

'Judah Lovell.' The vicar nodded. 'I chanced to meet him in the village yesterday. He informed me it is many years since he returned to Castonbury, so you perhaps will not remember him. A very friendly and cheerful young man. He is the son of Mrs Lovell's deceased brother-in-law, I believe.'

'No, I cannot say I ever remember meeting a Judah Lovell… But it is very kind of him to join his aunt,' Lily approved warmly, pleased to know that Judah Lovell had arrived in time to be with his aunt on the anniversary of her son's death. 'I will take some extra eggs and milk, in that case.' She nodded decisively; hopefully the presence of Mrs Lovell's nephew would also help to discourage that lady from asking Lily any personal questions concerning her abrupt departure three days ago and Giles Montague's pursuit of her only minutes later!

The rain had stopped falling some time ago. Giles's gaze narrowed as he sat atop his horse and looked in satisfaction at the men preparing the fields for the winter crop, having found himself drawn into matters about the estate in spite of himself. Indeed, he had been kept very busy about the estate over the past few days, and had also made another visit alone to the family lawyers in Buxton, so that he might further discuss the Montague family's financial situation with them without his father being present.

The news Giles had received from those gentlemen was every bit as dire as he had initially feared it to be, with his father having made the same mistake as so many other members of the *ton* the previous year, when news had reached London that Wellington was in retreat in Brussels and may possibly lose the battle completely. Fearing large government expenditure on a continuing war, or possibly even a French invasion of England itself, many—including Giles's father, it now transpired—had sold off their investments in 'consols,' and at a tremendous loss.

It was these very investments which had provided the Montague family with its twice-yearly income, the loss of which had now left the estate almost bankrupt, and also accounted for the money not being available for work to be carried out about the estate as usual.

There was still the considerable inheritance left to Jamie by their mother, as the eldest son, of course, but the same law governed the retrieval of that as it did the inheritance of the title of Marquis of Hatherton; neither one could be claimed until irrefutable proof of Jamie's death could be produced.

And through all of these worries, Giles also had the added burden of the memory of that last encounter with Lily Seagrove....

Just to think of what he now believed to have been her machinations and manipulations was enough to bring about a return of those feelings of revulsion Giles had experienced upon realising they had not been indulging a shared passion, as he had believed at the time, but that he had been deliberately and shamelessly manoeuvred into a position where Lily Seagrove had believed he would have no choice but to make her an offer of marriage or risk possible exposure as her seducer.

His prompt and cold response to those less than subtle hints had put paid to any such idea of blackmail, he hoped!

Certainly Giles had so far not received a visit from a shocked and distressed Mr Seagrove, with that gentleman demanding Giles make suitable amends—namely by an offer of marriage—for having brought possible disgrace upon his adopted daughter.

Neither, surprisingly, had Giles heard anything further from that young woman herself.

Which he had quite expected to at any moment during the past three days. After all, there were only two of the Montague sons left alive and unmarried, and Harry's responsibilities in London meant that for the main part he remained well out of range of Miss Seagrove's reach. Giles could only wish that he had remained so too!

Instead of which he was here and available at Castonbury, and circumstances now dictated he had no choice but to remain here for some time to come. Quite how he and Lily Seagrove were to conduct themselves towards each other for the duration of that time Giles could not even begin to guess, most especially when they were in the presence of the amiable Mr Seagrove. He—

A flash of colour—grey or possibly blue?—to the

right of his vision, caught and held his attention, his gaze frosting over, mouth thinning, jaw tightening, as he recognised Lily Seagrove walking along the lane which edged the Castonbury woods.

And looking for all intents and purposes as if, following the rain, she were on a pleasurable stroll and enjoying the beauty of the freshened countryside!

Lily avoided going through the woods at Castonbury Park and instead took the much longer way along the still-dampened lane to the Romany encampment, carrying in a basket the eggs and pitcher of milk intended for Mrs Lovell and her nephew; Lily had no wish to ever again enter those woods, let alone see or visit the place of her seduction and humiliation.

Just to think of Giles's coldness when he had insulted her was enough to make Lily shudder and tremble in mortification.

She was still unsure as to why he should believe she had seduced Edward, but his disparaging reference to her supposed Romany heritage had been unmistakable. And how she hated him for it! Indeed, Lily now wondered what demon could possibly have taken possession of her for her ever to have behaved in such a shameless fashion in Giles's arms three days ago. She—

'And what's a pretty maid like you doing wandering about the countryside all on yer lonesome?'

Lily's expression was curious rather than alarmed as she turned to face the owner of that cheerfully teasing voice, finding herself looking at a young man dressed in a shabby brown jacket, a collarless white shirt and thick black trousers over heavy, worn boots. His over-long hair glinted in the sunshine that had appeared after the rain and his dark eyes twinkled merrily in his boyishly handsome face as he stepped out of the woods directly in front of her.

The fact that Lily did not recognise him, or he her, would seem to imply he was a stranger to these parts. Mrs Lovell's nephew, perhaps? 'Good day to you, sir,' she returned politely. 'Do I have the pleasure of addressing Mrs Lovell's nephew?'

'Ye do, indeed,' he confirmed lightly, the slightest hint of an Irish accent in his tone. 'Judah Lovell's the name. And who might you be, my lovely?'

Such familiarity would certainly not be acceptable in a gentleman, but Lily took no offence, used as she was to Mrs Lovell's often less than respectful manner. 'Miss Lily Seagrove, daughter of the Reverend Mr Seagrove, whom I believe you met yesterday,' she supplied softly. 'And I am on my way to visit with your aunt.'

'Then it's fortuitous that the two of us chanced to meet, so it is,' Judah Lovell came back cheerfully. 'Would ye care to take my arm so that I might ensure you don't trip over any tree roots on the way there?' The sleeve of his shabby jacket looked less than clean as he offered her his arm.

It placed Lily in something of a quandary. It was not really seemly for her to be alone with this handsome young Romany, but Mr Seagrove had mentioned meeting Mr Lovell yesterday, and had seemed to find him acceptable. And as they were both on their way to Mrs Lovell's camp it would surely be rude of Lily to refuse to accompany him.... 'That is very kind of you, Mr Lovell, thank you.' She maintained a suitable distance as she tucked her hand lightly into the crook of his arm.

Giles instinctively urged Genghis forward as he saw a brawny man step out of the woods in front of Lily Seagrove, only to then check his restless mount as he belatedly recognised the young man as Mrs Lovell's nephew Judah, who Giles had encountered yesterday when that young man came to enquire about work on the estate, employment the young Romany should be about at the present moment.

Giles continued to watch as the two appeared to

converse pleasantly together for a minute or two, before Lily took that young gentleman's arm and happily accompanied him into the darkness of the woods.

Indicating, perhaps, that the meeting between the handsome young Romany and Lily Seagrove was an arranged one?

A case of like calling to like?

Certainly, if Lily Seagrove's true heritage was indeed that of the Romany, then the young and roguishly handsome Judah Lovell was far more suited to being her lover than Giles could ever be.

A realisation which left a surprisingly sour taste in Giles's mouth.

Lily was disappointed to find Mrs Lovell was not in her usual place beside the fire when she and Judah entered the encampment a short time later. Disappointed, and not a little uncomfortable. Walking alone through the woods with Judah would no doubt be considered improper by some, but remaining alone with him here, when his aunt was not present, was entirely unacceptable.

'Aunt Rosa has no doubt gone to gather some herbs for her medicines and potions while the stew cooks,' Judah said. 'Would you care for some tea while we wait for her return?'

The stew bubbling in a pot over the fire seemed to suggest that Judah's assertion was correct, but even so... 'I—'

'What are you doing back here so soon?'

Lily's relief at Mrs Lovell's return, which spared her from the embarrassment of explaining to Judah that she could not stay, was tempered somewhat by the harshness she detected in the old lady's tone. She had always welcomed Lily's visits in the past.

Did she know something of what had transpired between Giles and Lily following her last visit?

Her cheeks were ablaze with those memories as she turned to face the elderly Romany, her guilty expression turning to one of puzzlement as she saw that Mrs Lovell was looking accusingly at her nephew rather than at Lily.

'I thought you said as His Lordship had given you work in the fields today,' the elderly woman added sharply.

'I came back for some of yer stew for me lunch.' Judah shrugged unconcernedly. 'And 'ad the good fortune to meet the beautiful Miss Seagrove on the way,' he added flirtatiously, that merry twinkle once again in his dark eyes as he looked at her admiringly.

Mrs Lovell's gaze narrowed disapprovingly. 'See

about your lunch, lad, and leave Miss Seagrove to me,'
she instructed gruffly.

Her nephew gave a shrug. 'The fields'll still be there
whether I return in ten minutes or an hour.'

'Lord Giles may not see it in quite the same way,'
his aunt said drily.

Judah Lovell grinned unabashedly. 'What Lord
Giles don't know ain't gonna hurt him!'

'It's that attitude that gets us a bad name!' Mrs
Lovell gave an exasperated shake of her head as she
moved to ladle some of the delicious-smelling stew
into a wooden bowl. 'Take that with you and get along
back to work!' She thrust the bowl into her nephew's
work-roughened hands.

'Da always said ye were a terrible slave-driver!'
Judah grinned unrepentantly as he easily ducked the
swipe his aunt took at him with the ladle from the
stew. 'No doubt I'll be seeing ye again soon, Miss
Seagrove,' he added cheekily, before turning to whis-
tle a merry tune as he went on his way.

Lily had not known what to think as she listened to
the exchange between aunt and nephew, never having
heard Mrs Lovell speak quite that harshly to anyone
before, although Judah had not seemed at all abashed
by it.

She turned to look curiously at Mrs Lovell, who

muttered to herself as she banged and clashed pots together for what seemed no apparent reason. 'You seem somewhat…agitated today, Mrs Lovell,' Lily prompted after several minutes of this pointless exercise.

'I seems agitated because it's what I am!' Piercing eyes, which appeared more brown today than blue or green, glared across the fire at Lily. 'What do you think the Reverend Seagrove would have to say to me if'n he was to learn I returned to me fireside to find his daughter alone here with me nephew?'

Lily could not even pretend not to be taken aback by the force of the elderly lady's accusing tone. She gave a pained frown as she answered calmly. 'My father knows and trusts me well enough to realise that the circumstances of our being together were perfectly innocent.'

'Your father, mebbe.' Mrs Lovell nodded impatiently. 'But what of others in the village? What sort of scandal do ye think there'd be if'n it became known you've been alone here with my young rogue of a nephew?' She gave an exasperated shake of her head.

Lily blinked. 'I assure you that nothing untoward happened—'

'It's not me as needs reassuring.' Mrs Lovell gave an exasperated sigh. 'Gossip is gossip, and it's been known in the past to bring disgrace upon a lovely lass such as yourself.'

Lily sat down abruptly on one of the logs placed about the fireside. They were much as they had been three days ago when Giles had sat down beside her, before the two of them had indulged in exactly the sort of scandalous behaviour Mrs Lovell was now saying that people might suspect had occurred between her nephew and Lily, if their time here alone together were ever to become known!

'Now there's no need to look so downhearted.' Mrs Lovell obviously regretted her earlier sharpness as she reached over to pat Lily's clenched hands together upon her knees. 'It's yourself as I'm thinking of, and no one else. Judah has been across the sea in Ireland with his da since he was a boy, and I has no doubts as there's a bairn or two over there with his yellow hair and wicked black eyes!'

'Mrs Lovell!' Lily felt the warmth of colour enter her cheeks.

'Just promise me you'll stay well away from the likes of him,' the older woman pressured firmly.

'As Mr Lovell has already stated, the two of us only met today by chance,' Lily assured huskily.

Mrs Lovell nodded. 'Promise me it won't happen again.'

Lily grimaced. 'Good manners would prevent me from being rude to Mr Lovell if we were to meet again by chance.'

'Hmmph!' The elderly Romany gave a dismissive snort. 'With Black Jack Lovell as a father Judah's got no more idea of what's mannerly than the cows in the fields!'

Lily smiled ruefully. 'But Mr and Mrs Seagrove have ensured that I do.'

'Now just ye take heed of me, young lady!' Mrs Lovell gave a firm shake of her head. 'Good manners or no, ye must stay away from him, or I has no doubts as you'll live to regret it, the same as a lot of other beautiful young women have likely had reason to!'

Lily gave a surprised laugh. 'That is not a particularly... familial warning, Mrs Lovell.'

'Familial, be dem—!' The elderly Romany's mouth tightened as she broke off abruptly. 'If'n ye won't give me your promise, then I'll have to insist ye don't come visiting me no more.'

'Mrs Lovell!' Lily straightened in shock at the other woman's obvious vehemence of purpose. 'If it bothers you so much, then yes, of course I must give you my promise, my dear Mrs Lovell.'

Those shrewd eyes brightened. 'As you'll stay away from Judah.'

She gave a gracious inclination of her head. 'I promise I will do everything I may to avoid finding myself alone in the company of your nephew, yes.'

The older woman visibly relaxed. 'I don't mean to be—' She gave a shake of her head. 'It's just—he's a young rogue, and too much like his father to be trusted alone with any pretty maid, you understand?'

'I believe so…' Lily nodded slowly.

Just thinking of the intimacies she had shared in the woods three days ago with Giles Montague was more than enough reason for Lily to understand the dangers Mrs Lovell alluded to.

If that occurrence was anything to go by, Lily could not be trusted at all. She would do well to mind Mrs Lovell's advice with respect to *all* men, whether gentleman or not!

Chapter Nine

'Would you care to explain exactly what it is you are doing here alone and so late at night?'

Lily halted as if frozen. Which it felt as if she truly might be, in blood as well as in body and spirit, as she easily recognised Giles Montague's voice speaking to her in the darkness.

Her meeting with Mrs Stratton having passed satisfactorily, it had indeed been Lily's intention to now walk back to the vicarage alone, just as she had walked here earlier, Mr Seagrove having required their ancient carriage this evening to take him to Sir Nathan's home for dinner.

But Lily had not realised quite how late it was, or how dark it had become, whilst she and Mrs Stratton talked so amiably together. She would certainly have hoped, as she left quietly and unobtrusively through the servants' entrance at the back of Castonbury Park, before hurrying in the direction of the path and gate opening out to the lane, not to find herself face to face with Giles Montague, of all people!

Although 'face to face' was not an accurate description as yet, when Lily had still to turn in order to look at that gentleman!

'Well?' Giles prompted harshly as Lily Seagrove kept her back firmly turned towards him, her shoulders appearing stiff beneath the darkness of her cloak, with a pale bonnet covering her dark curls.

He had decided to take a stroll towards the stables as he smoked his cigar after enjoying an early dinner with his father, lingering there to chat with head groom Tom Anderson before walking back to the house, only to come to an abrupt halt in the shadows as he had spied Lily Seagrove leaving by the back of the house, her movements appearing almost furtive as she looked first one way and then the other, before dashing across the yard towards the pathway leading down to the lane. A lane which was so dark and shadowed it was impossible to distinguish from the surrounding trees!

Giles's mouth tightened ominously. 'I swear, Lily, if you do not soon answer me—'

'I have every intention of answering you, my lord.'

She turned abruptly, her face appearing very pale in the moonlight, lashes downcast rather than turned up at him, although her chin was raised at its usual stubborn angle. 'I am here because I have called on Mrs Stratton and now intend to walk back to the vicarage.'

'In the dark and alone?'

She shrugged dismissively. 'My father had need of the carriage this evening, and it is no hardship at all for me to walk down a lane I have known for the whole of my life.'

'A lane which at this moment is very dark and deserted,' Giles bit out impatiently. 'But perhaps it will not remain the latter for long if you have arranged to meet someone along the way...' he added scornfully.

Those dark lashes rose as Lily Seagrove gave him a startled look. 'And why might I have done that?'

Giles looked down at her coldly as he resisted the hurt reproach in her pale eyes, knowing his anger was directed towards himself as much as Lily. He had fallen as much into a tangle over this particular young woman as his brother Edward had a year ago.

Unlike Edward, Giles did not believe there to be anything more than desires involved in his intentions towards Lily, but there was no denying that he did desire her. Still. Even after discovering her pretty performance yesterday was an act, and seeing her with Judah Lovell earlier today…

There was just something too appealing about the wild passion he knew burned beneath the innocent beauty of Lily's eyes and the fineness of her features. A passion which had resulted in her reaching a physical climax in his arms, and which Giles had answered in kind beneath the caress of her fingers. Those same caresses which Giles had recalled and relived ever since in an effort to rid himself of this ridiculous desire he felt to possess her completely!

He had no intention of becoming involved with any of the local women whilst he was here, although he could perhaps have sought release by riding over to Buxton and seeking out some willing woman there. But somehow the thought of making love to any woman but Lily Seagrove had not appealed.

And still did not, if the tightening in his breeches, just at sight and smell of her light and floral perfume as she shook those dark curls, was any indication!

He eyed her impatiently. 'It is quite useless for you to attempt to deny the possibility of such a tryst, Lily, when earlier today I saw you enter the woods with Judah Lovell!'

She gasped. 'I— You—' She gave another shake of her head, those dark curls caressing the paleness of her cheeks. 'I am sure there was nothing for you to see, my lord.' Her voice was low and husky when she finally managed to speak.

'No?' He raised dark brows. 'The two of you seemed to be…well acquainted.'

A frown appeared between her eyes. 'I had never met him before today, and no doubt when you saw the two of us together he was merely offering to accompany me on my visit to his aunt.'

'Indeed?'

'Yes—indeed!' Lily felt stung into snapping indignantly, irritated beyond words that it should have been Giles Montague, of all people, to see her at that moment. He had clearly drawn his own condemning conclusions, which she already knew he would have been only too pleased to make where she was concerned.

'At a time when Mr Lovell should, by rights, have been at work in the fields at Castonbury Park,' he added impatiently.

'Your arrangement with Mr Lovell is not my concern,' Lily dismissed. 'I only know that he behaved the perfect gentleman throughout our own meeting earlier today.'

'As opposed to…?' Giles's voice was dangerously soft.

A danger Lily chose not to heed. 'As opposed to

those who should, but obviously choose not to, be-have as such!'

His mouth thinned with displeasure. 'You are refer-ring to me, no doubt?'

'No doubt,' she confirmed coldly.

A derisive smile curved those sculptured lips, the darkness of his clothing and the snowy white linen seeming to indicate he was dressed for dinner. 'Oh, I assure you, Lily, I have no difficulty whatsoever in behaving the gentleman—when I believe the lady to whom I am talking warrants such niceties!'

Lily's eyes widened indignantly. 'You—'

'I believe I have advised against repeating this once before,' Giles warned between gritted teeth even as he reached out and grasped the wrist of the hand Lily Seagrove had once again raised with the obvious intention of striking him. 'Unless you are goading me into retaliating?'

She gasped. 'You would strike a woman?'

'No,' he assured softly, eyes narrowed. 'But if you were to strike me, I should very much enjoy putting you over my shoulder before carrying you into the stables, throwing you down upon the straw in one of the stalls before making love to you with all the en-thusiasm the stallion shows the mare!'

Lily had felt herself go deathly pale as each successive—and shocking!—word left Giles Montague's scornful lips, so much so that her own lips now felt numb, and her mouth and throat so dry that she could not have spoken even if she had been able to think of anything she might say in answer to such deliberate crudeness of speech.

A crudeness which had nevertheless caused a rush of liquid heat between her thighs, and also rendered her breasts hot and aching.

'Nothing to say?' Giles Montague raised one arrogantly mocking brow. 'Perhaps that is because you find the idea of such a...wild coupling to be arousing?'

To her everlasting shame, Lily knew that was exactly how his words had affected her!

To a degree that her breasts now felt so swollen and aching she could barely breathe, and the hot dampness between her thighs had become a veritable flood as she began to throb and ache with a desire to know the same completion she had experienced once before under the expert attentions of this gentleman's caressing fingers.

Lily attempted to swallow and then moisten the dryness of her lips, and instead shook her head in denial as her tongue refused to do her bidding.

Grey eyes glittered down at her knowingly and hard lips smiled in satisfaction at her silence. 'Indeed, I assure you I would be only too happy to oblige, Miss Seagrove—' he managed to invest a wealth of insult into the formality '—but having just come from the stables myself, I am fully aware that Tom Anderson is still there tending to one of the horses. Unless, of course, you would find having Old Tom as audience to our lovemaking to be even more...stimulating?'

'You are being both disgusting and crude!' Lily finally managed to gasp her outrage.

Yes, that was exactly what he was being, Giles acknowledged, disgusted with himself. Just as he was also aware that it had been Lily's disparaging remarks to him that were responsible, in part, for goading him into being so drawn into the problems now besetting the Castonbury estate, when his initial intention had been to visit briefly before leaving again for the entertainments of London.

He drew himself up to his full height. 'I apologise, Miss Seagrove,' he bit out curtly. 'A single...taste of your passions does not entitle me to insult and abuse you simply because I do not approve of the next man upon whom you choose to bestow those same favours.'

She released an incredulous gasp. 'Only you could possibly contrive to make an apology sound even more insulting than the original slight!'

He gave a humourless smile. 'Perhaps that is because only I know of your true nature, Miss Seagrove?'

She gave a slow shake of her head. 'And perhaps you do not know me at all, my lord,' she spoke quietly. 'Now, if you will excuse me—'

'I asked if it is your intention to meet with Judah Lovell on your way home?' he demanded harshly as he reached out and clasped her arm.

'Not that it is any of your business, but no, it is not!' Her eyes flashed in the darkness before she looked down at that restraining hand. 'Now release me, sir, before I am forced to scream and alert Tom Anderson, and no doubt others of your household staff, to my imminent danger.' She glared up at him in challenge.

Giles's hand dropped slowly back to his side as he looked down at her in grudging admiration. 'You are in no danger from me, I assure you. Of a repeat of our time together three days ago, or anything else. Which is not to say,' he continued firmly, 'that you would not find yourself in such danger from others if you are allowed to walk home alone in the dark. Did you not heed anything of what Mrs Lovell told you with regard to the "dark and dangerous man" who means to "do you harm"?' he added derisively.

'Why should I, when it is clear the only person who

is a danger to me stands before me right now?' Lily came back challengingly.

'I am?' Giles's mouth was tight with displeasure.

'Do not look so surprised by my deductions, my lord,' she taunted. 'Your crudeness this evening is but another example of how much you enjoy hurting me. As such,' she continued over his protestations, 'Mrs Lovell's dire predictions or otherwise, I would still prefer to face alone whatever dangers may lie in wait in the darkness for me, than be forced to suffer your insulting company another moment longer!' She turned firmly on her heel before marching away.

Admiration gleamed grudgingly in Giles's eyes and he continued to watch Lily until she had disappeared into the darkness. A totally futile gesture of defiance, of course, when his own father's friendship with Mr Seagrove at least dictated that Giles could not allow that gentleman's daughter to roam about the darkness of the countryside alone.

Nor did he like the idea that Lily had so obviously decided that he was a danger to her safety.

As to Giles enjoying hurting her—he knew he would far rather pleasure Lily than hurt her....

Lily barely had time to stumble blindly along the pathway and out onto the lane, as hot tears tracked down her cheeks, before she heard the sound of something moving stealthily through the forest beside her, accompanied by the sound of loud and laboured breathing.

One of the deer allowed to roam the Park, perhaps?

Or possibly a fox, or a badger?

Or perhaps one of the cows had escaped from the field?

Whatever it was it appeared to be coming ever closer!

Lily's tears ceased and she stumbled slightly as she continued walking whilst turning to look nervously into the depths of the woodland that now seemed so much darker and more menacing than it had in daylight. She wished she had not so rashly refused Giles Montague's offer to accompany her home; she may have every reason to consider him the most obnoxious gentleman she had ever met, but she had no doubt that his presence would have ensured that no harm came to her. From anyone but himself, at least!

None of which was at all comforting when Lily was now so obviously alone and vulnerable to whatever might be chasing her…

She gasped, unable to move, even her heart seeming to stop beating, as she saw a pair of glittering eyes fast approaching before a huge black beast rushed out of the forest towards her, snorting loudly, and slathering at the mouth, before it rose up on its back legs and—

'Down, Genghis!'

Lily's eyes widened even further at the harsh sound of Giles Montague's voice in the darkness, and she stumbled back as she realised that voice was coming from the back of that huge and glittery-eyed black beast.

But she had no time to think further, even to attempt to turn and run, as hands reached down to painfully grasp the tops of her arms and she was lifted up to sit sideways on the back of that huge black beast as it began to heave and buck beneath her!

'Easy, Genghis,' Giles softly soothed his mount again. 'Genghis only eats stubbornly unaccompanied young ladies on Fridays, and today is Thursday, I believe,' he drawled tauntingly as he now easily held the skittish Genghis in check with one hand on the reins whilst holding the warmth of Lily Seagrove against his chest with the other.

Lily only seemed to cling to the lapels of Giles's jacket all the tighter as she turned her face into his waistcoat. 'Please put me down at once...' she instructed shakily, her voice barely more than a whisper.

Giles scowled in the darkness. 'Stop being ridiculous, Lily—'

'It is not ridiculous when I have never learnt to ride!' She raised her head to glare up at him, her eyes large in the pale oval of her face.

'Then that is clearly an oversight in your education which is about to be remedied.' Giles ignored her protest, his arm tightening about her slender waist as he turned Genghis in the direction of the village. The muscles in his thigh began to ache from the effort of controlling Genghis and the old sabre wound he had sustained on the Continent.

'I insist you return me to the ground, at once!' Lily repeated fiercely as she began to struggle in his arms, only to still again as the horse beneath her showed his displeasure by tossing back his head, and causing the heavy black mane to whip lightly across her cheek. 'Giles, please…!' She looked up at him in appeal.

He scowled down at her, his face appearing all hard planes and angles in the moonlight. 'You are completely mistaken if you think I intend to walk to the village when I might ride. As it is I had to leave the stables so quickly I am without benefit of the comfort of a saddle!'

'I did not ask that you accompany me to the village.'

'And yet here I am,' he pointed out as he looked grimly ahead.

Lily gave an impatient shake of her head. 'If you insist on accompanying me—'

'I do.'

She heaved a shaky sigh. 'Then by all means you must ride. I shall walk beside you.'

'That is utterly preposterous when we have a perfectly good horse we might both ride!' he bit out scathingly as he urged the mount into a slow trot.

It was a move which instantly prompted Lily to cling all the tighter to Giles's lapels as that heated horseflesh surged and dipped precariously beneath her thighs. 'I…admire horses tremendously,' she spoke huskily. 'Have always believed them to be splendid, beautiful creatures—'

'I am sure Genghis will be pleased to hear it!'

'—but I have never wished, have no wish still, ever to be upon the back of one,' she continued raggedly. 'Edward tried several times to encourage me to learn to ride, but I—I could not…cannot…bring myself to do so. The truth is…' She drew in a deep breath. 'The truth is I have always been rather nervous of being too close to all that—that uncontrolled power!' she admitted huskily, at the same time aware that she was now just as nervous of being near Giles Montague's uncontrolled power! Her sudden embarrassment caused her to rush into further speech. 'Mabel is the only horse I have ever been able to dare approach—'

'Mabel...?'

'My father's old mare.'

Giles easily recalled the nondescript brown mare which he had seen in front of the vicar's equally as decrepit carriage. 'There is no comparison between a docile nag of that kind and a fine hunter like Genghis!' he snorted dismissively.

'Which is why I have asked that you put me down—'

'We will arrive back at the vicarage in less time than it would take me to halt and lower you to the ground.'

'Please...!'

A frown darkened Giles's brow as he felt Lily trembling in his arms, her face turned pleadingly up to his as he glanced down at her in the moonlight. 'You truly are frightened...' he realised slowly.

'Yes.' She gave an involuntary shudder.

That the normally indomitable Lily was willing to admit as much to him was, Giles knew, a testament to the depth of that fear. Just as he knew that his displeasure earlier at being thought the 'dark and dangerous' man Mrs Lovell had predicted in Lily's future had rendered him less than understanding in regard to that fear. 'I was always taught that the best way to overcome fear is to face it—'

'And I am sure that for you that is true,' she acknowledged softly. 'I am obviously made of poorer stuff!'

Giles knew that to be untrue, in as much as he had learnt these past ten days that Lily was more than a match for him, both in obstinacy and determination. Nor—no matter what Lily may think to the contrary!—was he a deliberately cruel man. He remembered now that as a small child one of his sisters—he did not recall now which of them it had been, Kate or Phaedra—had had an irrational fear of spiders, and he or Jamie had always been only too happy to rid their sister of the offending arachnid. His upbringing now demanded that he could not be less considerate of Lily's nervousness in regard to Genghis.

'If that truly is the case...' He halted Genghis before gathering Lily more firmly against him, her face once again turned into his chest as he kept one arm behind her back and placed the other beneath her thighs as he swung his uninjured leg over the hunter's sleek back before sliding them both down onto the ground. 'You may look now, Lily,' he drawled, as she kept her face buried against his chest.

Lily raised her head tentatively before looking around, relieved to see that she was no longer up on the back of that fierce-looking horse. Although she was not sure she considered her present position as being any safer than she had been on the hunter's back!

'I am capable of walking now if you would care to release me,' she assured huskily.

He glanced down at her only briefly as he began to stride down the lane to the vicarage visible in the distance, grimly ignoring the twinges of discomfort in his thigh. 'And I am perfectly capable of continuing to carry you in my arms.'

Lily's cheeks blazed with colour. 'If someone should see us together like this—'

'Such as the baker's cat? Or Mrs Crutchley's overweight pug unexpectedly out for an evening stroll, perhaps?' he dismissed scornfully.

Admittedly, it was very late for anyone to be abroad in this part of the village, but even so… 'You are the one who earlier seemed concerned about my reputation,' Lily reminded him, her voice sharp as she recalled how offensive Giles had been in his hurtful accusations.

Not that her precarious social position rendered the young Romany as an unsuitable match for her. Perhaps the opposite. But she liked Judah Lovell no more than she did Sir Nathan Samuelson and felt no romantic interest in either man.

How could she possibly, when despite her own dislike of Giles Montague and his less than flattering opinion of her, simply being held in his arms now was enough to make her heart beat faster and her body to feel fevered?

Chapter Ten

'They do not appear to have left a candle burning in anticipation of your return,' Giles observed gruffly as he lowered Lily to the ground at the front door of the vicarage several minutes later.

She finished smoothing and straightening her cloak over her pale gown, and righting the bonnet upon her curls, before looking up at him. 'It is an unnecessary expense in a household where every penny must be accounted for,' she dismissed without complaint.

Giles had lived all of his life at Castonbury Park, the only hardships he had ever suffered being his years spent abroad fighting the French, and even then his comfort had still been far greater than that of the enlisted men. That the situation might soon change at Castonbury Park, if the family finances did not improve in some way, did not seem so important when

Giles considered that Lily had lived all of her young life with a lack of the comforts he had always taken for granted as his right.

A fact that perhaps went some way to explaining—to excusing—her wish to marry well?

It certainly rendered Lily's behaviour in regard to an advantageous marriage as no more ambitious and designing than that of the dozens of young debutantes who appeared in London each Season, having been tutored and polished for the sole purpose of finding themselves a rich or titled husband, preferably both.

'My lord...?' Lily prompted at his continued silence.

Giles gave himself a mental shake. 'I seem to remember you called me "Giles" earlier.'

'Amongst other things, yes.' Her lips twitched as she repressed a smile.

'Amongst other things,' he conceded drily. 'Such as "insufferable" and "crude." Names, which I am sure you feel no regret at having used in regard to me?' He frowned darkly.

Lily knew that at the time he had most certainly deserved them, that Giles was more inclined to judge her on what he believed to be her nature rather than attempting to see her as she truly was. 'No, I do not regret them in the least. Indeed, your manner towards me since your return to Castonbury has, for the most part, been inexcusable and offensive.' Her cheeks felt warm as she thought of that single occasion upon which his behaviour—and her own!—had been something else entirely! 'But— You said something to me...when last we met.' Lily's gaze dropped from his at the mention of their time together in the woods. 'Something which has...troubled me ever since.'

'I said many things to you that day which, as with the things I said to you earlier this evening, may perhaps have been better left unsaid,' he acknowledged harshly.

She frowned. 'But this— It is not the first time that you have said something in a similar vein.' She looked up at Giles searchingly in the darkness, but the moon was not shining brightly enough this evening for her to be able to discern his features properly. Which was perhaps part of the reason why she felt able to talk with him so frankly...? 'You implied—seem to be under the misapprehension—that I meant to marry Edward.'

Lack of light to see by or not, there was no missing the stiffening of Giles shoulders as he straightened before looking down the long length of his nose at her, a nerve visibly pulsing in his clenched jaw.

'I seem to recall we had a more than frank discussion on that very subject a year ago!'

'A conversation which, at the time and since, has left

me completely bewildered as to why you should ever have thought I might have desired to marry Edward,' she owned huskily.

'You would have been a fool not to have wished to marry him when he was the son of a duke!' he rasped harshly.

'Then I must indeed be a fool,' Lily murmured ruefully.

Giles frowned darkly. 'You are saying that you did not deliberately set out a year ago to entice my brother into offering you marriage?'

She drew in a sharp breath. 'That is exactly what I am saying, yes,' she confirmed softly.

He gave an impatient shake of his head. 'Do not make the mistake of thinking me a fool too, Lily—'

'But it is foolish to have believed I could ever have considered taking Edward as my husband,' she insisted exasperatedly.

'You told me yourself only days ago that you loved Edward.'

'But not in the way one should love a husband,' Lily denied earnestly. 'I did love Edward, I love him still, but as my brother. As he loved me as his sister.'

'In that you are completely wrong.'

'No, I am not, Giles, and I must insist you hear

me out before you make any more false accusations,' she said.

'You must insist…?' he repeated, steely soft.

'Yes.' She remained determined in the face of his haughtiness. 'Edward and I grew up together, played together as children, danced and gossiped together at the local assemblies—usually as to which of the young ladies present was attempting to attract Edward's interest!' she acknowledged ruefully. 'We were as brother and sister, always. And our affection for each other was exactly that, as one sibling for another.'

Giles stared down at her wordlessly. When he and Edward had spoken on the subject a year ago his brother had declared that he was in love with Lily Seagrove and wished to make her his wife. A marriage Giles had felt no hesitation in firmly advising his brother against.

Yet, Lily now denied there had ever been such a relationship between herself and Edward, nor had there ever been any suggestion of marriage between them. Because, she claimed, she had loved Edward as a brother, and not as her future husband.

A truth—if indeed it was the truth!—which would have rendered Giles's behaviour towards Lily a year ago as completely incomprehensible, and the depth of his lovemaking, and offer to make her his mistress three days ago, as truly scandalous!

But it could not be the truth—could it? Edward had been so certain that he was in love with Lily, that he wished to make her his wife, and surely no man could be that certain of his feelings if he had not received some sort of encouragement from the lady whom he professed to love?

Besides, Lily had returned the intimacy of Giles's lovemaking three days ago, before then talking of the scandal which would ensue if they had been seen by anyone. And Giles had certainly seen her disappearing into the woods earlier today with Judah Lovell!

No, Lily's actions proved that she was—that she had to be!—exactly the devious young woman Giles had always thought her, and that this claim of innocence on her part was just a deliberate attempt to bewitch him into believing her lies. 'It makes a very pretty story, Lily,' he acknowledged derisively. 'But it does not stand against all evidence to the contrary.'

Her eyes widened. 'What evidence?'

His mouth twisted mockingly. 'Edward himself told me of the love he felt for you—'

'I have told you—'

'—and of his intention of asking you to become his wife,' Giles continued harshly. 'A marriage proposal I advised most strongly against, I assure you,' he added scathingly.

Lily felt the colour drain from her cheeks even as she stared up at Giles, sure he could not be telling her the truth, that he must just be saying these things to further hurt and confuse her. She and Edward had only ever shared a friendship. A friendship Lily had treasured all the more for its not being in any way romantic, and so never necessitating her to be anything other than herself when in Edward's company. Edward could not have told his brother that he was in love with her and wanted to marry her. She—

She had not loved Edward in that way, certainly, but was it possible that Edward could have been in love with her? Enough, and in such a way, as he really had told Giles of his wish to make her his wife?

Giles certainly seemed convinced this was the case. Just as his disapproval of such a match, and his conviction that Lily had used her feminine wiles in order to ensnare Edward, would also explain the hateful things Giles had said to her a year ago.

It would also go a long way towards explaining his less than respectful behaviour towards her—his scandalous behaviour towards her!—since his return to Castonbury ten days ago.

Could it really be true that Edward had loved her,

not as a sister but as a woman? To the extent that he had wished to marry her and make her his wife…?

Certainly Edward had never shown any interest in the young ladies who lived locally, and who always made such a fuss of him at the assemblies or if they happened to meet in the village. But Lily had always assumed that to be because Edward preferred the more sophisticated young ladies to be found during his visits to London, and her own lack of interest in any romantic attachment between the two of them merely another reason Edward had liked to spend so much time with her whenever he was at Castonbury.

But what if she had been wrong? What if she was the one who had misunderstood, and Edward's disinterest in those other young ladies had been because he actually preferred to be with Lily for another reason entirely than mere friendship—

No!

It was not— It could not be true! It was impossible for Lily even to consider the possibility that for all of those years Edward had desired her as a man desires a woman. The very same desire Giles had shown for her three days ago…

Lily could not bear to think of indulging in those same intimacies with Edward. Nor did she want to believe that Edward had ever wanted that sort of intimacy with her.

'You are truly a cruel and hateful man to say such things to me merely in an attempt to spoil my own sweet memories of my friendship with Edward!' She glared up at Giles, her gloved hands clenched into fists at her sides as she fought back the tears, of anger as well as pain.

That frown still darkened his brow. 'Lily—'

She evaded his reaching hands. 'I— You— And I am sure I never hated anyone as much in my life before as I now hate you!' She turned to open the door to the vicarage, hurrying inside and closing the door firmly behind her before collapsing back against it. Her breathing was loud and ragged in the silence of the hallway as the hot tears fell unchecked down her cheeks for the second time that evening.

It was a lie!

Everything Giles Montague had just said to her had to have been a cruel and hateful lie, deliberately intended to hurt her.

As much of a lie as Lily's claim of hating Giles....

Giles stood unmoving outside on the doorstep for several long minutes after Lily had entered the vicarage so suddenly, too surprised at her vehemence, her obvious and genuine distress, to be able to make sense of what had just occurred. To comprehend why she had found it so upsetting for him to talk of Edward's feelings for her.

Her distress had seemed so genuine, her anger towards Giles so heated, that he was now forced at least to consider the unpleasant possibility that his conclusions of a year ago, of Lily being a designing female out to ensnare herself a rich and titled husband, may have been wrong, and that her distress, at the thought of their own discovery three days ago, had also been genuine rather than a deliberate ploy to force an offer of marriage from him.

Edward had talked to Giles of his feelings for Lily, of his desire to make her his wife, but what if Lily herself had been completely ignorant of those feelings, of that desire, as she now claimed to be?

She stated she had found Giles's conversation a year ago bewildering, his less than respectful behaviour towards her since his return to Castonbury highly offensive. Which it truly would be if Lily was as innocent in her dealings with Edward—with him!—as she now claimed to be!

Dear God, what if he had been wrong...?

'You are out and about very late this evening, Lord

Giles? There is nothing amiss with His Grace, I hope?' Mr Seagrove's voice sharpened with concern.

Giles had been so deep in thought, so lost to the possibility of Lily's complete ignorance of Edward's feelings for her—of the depth of his own insulting behaviour towards her, if that were true!—that he had been completely unaware of Mr Seagrove's return until the other gentleman spoke to him.

He drew in a deep and steadying breath before turning to face the older man. 'No, there is nothing at all amiss at Castonbury Park, Mr Seagrove,' he assured him. 'I merely escorted Miss Seagrove home after she had visited with Mrs Stratton,' he explained economically.

'That was very kind of you, my lord.' Mr Seagrove beamed up at him approvingly. 'Perhaps, if you are in no hurry to return home, you would care to come inside and join me in my study for a glass of brandy?'

Did Giles wish to sit with Mr Seagrove and enjoy a glass of brandy, aware as he did so that Lily was in one of the bedchambers overhead? To imagine how she would slowly remove all of her hairpins to release those glorious ebony curls over her shoulders and down the length of her spine, before taking off all her clothes, to stand barefoot and naked before don-

ning a sheer nightgown to slip between the warmth
of the bedcovers?

With an almost painful throb in his breeches Giles
answered a very firm no, he could not think of staying. 'It is late, Mr Seagrove,' Giles excused lightly.
'And you must be very tired after your evening out.'

'Not at all,' the other gentleman assured unhelpfully.
'Indeed, I would more than welcome your company,
after an evening spent listening to Sir Nathan talk of
his crops and the necessity of him taking a wife to
grace his estate.' He gave a delicate grimace.

Giles had no doubt that Mr Seagrove had to be referring to the less than stimulating company of Sir
Nathan Samuelson, a gentleman who owned an estate in the area, and as such was known to Giles, but
whom he had never been able to muster a partiality
for. 'I had not heard that Sir Nathan was betrothed,
let alone about to be married.'

'He is not either as yet.' Mr Seagrove sighed heavily. 'Indeed, I have noticed that the ladies of marriage-
able age in the area seem to avoid him, and he does
not care for London, apparently. I myself find him to
be— Forgive me.' The reverend waved a hand, as he
clearly realised he was being less than discreet about
one of his flock. 'I am afraid I am a little out of sorts
this evening after learning that Sir Nathan's marital

intentions may, for lack of interest elsewhere, have turned towards my darling Lily.'

Sir Nathan Samuelson and *Lily*?

Why, the man was twice her age, and a pompously self-important bore to boot.

What did it matter what the man's character was; Lily's questionable parentage rendered marriage to a man of Sir Nathan Samuelson's standing as nothing less than advantageous from her perspective. Once married to him, she would become Lady Samuelson and mistress of a modest estate, future mother to the son who would one day inherit that title and estate.

And Giles felt nauseous just thinking of Sir Nathan Samuelson going to Lily's bed each night, imagining the other man touching and caressing every inch of her smooth and silky skin, before nudging her legs apart and—

He scowled darkly. 'Would such a marriage find favour with you, Mr Seagrove?'

'It would not be for me to choose, but Lily.' The older man avoided a direct answer.

'But you think she might be willing to accept if Samuelson were to offer?' If Lily were the things Giles believed her to be, had accused her of being, surely she would be a fool not to accept such an offer of marriage.

Mr Seagrove looked pained. 'If the offer were to be

formally made it would be my duty to advise that she do so, certainly. Such a marriage would be...more than Mrs Seagrove and I could ever have hoped for, given the lack of knowledge of Lily's forebears.' He looked even more distressed. 'Indeed, Sir Nathan informed me that he would be willing to...overlook that lack once she has produced his heir.'

Giles scowled. 'And how does he intend to regard her until that day occurs?'

'He did not care to say....' Mr Seagrove looked less than happy at that omission.

As well he might not! Giles's dislike and distrust of Sir Nathan had not been made indiscriminately. As a child he had chanced to see Sir Nathan whip a disobedient horse into submission, and the other man's behaviour in regard to the people who worked on his estate was also said to be less than kind. The thoughts that Sir Nathan might privately use that same harshness on his wife—on Lily!—did not even bear thinking about!

It also posed the question—despite Lily's own opinion on the subject!—as to whether Sir Nathan Samuelson's interest in Lily might not make him that 'dark and dangerous man' Mrs Lovell had predicted in Lily's future....

'Perhaps I will join you in a glass of brandy, after

all, Mr Seagrove,' Giles rasped harshly, his expression
pained as he followed the older man inside. A pain
which he knew had very little to do with the throbbing of the muscles in his injured thigh.

'Yes...?' Lily bristled warily as she opened the door
of the vicarage the following morning to discover
Giles Montague standing outside on the doorstep.

Mrs Jeffries had gone to shop in the village this
morning, so making it necessary for Lily to answer
the brisk knocking on the door herself. But, following their conversation the previous evening, the last
person Lily would have expected to call this morning
had been Lord Giles Montague!

Especially as she had overheard him and Mr
Seagrove in muted conversation in her father's study
for half the night, and found the decanter of brandy
in there to be completely empty this morning. Her
father's headache at breakfast had testified to his having consumed his fair share of its contents! Under the
circumstances, Lily would not have expected Giles
Montague to be out and about at all this morning, let
alone looking every inch his normal arrogant self in
a tall hat, brown tailed jacket over a darker brown
waistcoat and white linen, with cream buckskin pantaloons above brown-topped black Hessians, the lat-

ter seeming to indicate that he had once again ridden his horse here.

She continued to hold the door partially closed. 'I am afraid that my father is not at home this morning.'

He looked down the length of his nose at her. 'I have not called with the intention of speaking with Mr Seagrove.'

Lily raised surprised brows. 'Oh…?'

Giles smiled bleakly as he saw her increased wariness. No doubt a perfectly justified wariness, following the abrupt end of their own conversation the previous evening. After Lily had professed to now hate him more than she had ever hated anyone in her life before! 'Your father and I talked at great length together last night,' he admitted ruefully.

Indeed, only the disgusting concoction produced by his valet—the contents of which Giles had no desire to know!—had saved him from the blinding brandy-induced hangover which, upon awakening, had threatened to incapacitate him for the rest of the day!

'So I understand.' Lily's frosty tone implied that her father had suffered that same fate, no doubt without the benefit of the same remedy. Her next comment confirmed that to have been the case. 'I am sure it is not seemly for a man of the cloth to feel so ill from overimbibing! Perhaps in future you might limit your shared libations to one or two glasses of the fine brandy which your own father provides for mine?'

Giles gave a tight smile. 'Surely it is preferable that I was present than that Mr Seagrove should have indulged alone?'

'I am sure it would have been better if he had not indulged at all!' she came back tartly. 'Which I am sure he would not have done without the encouragement of your own company.'

That may be so, although somehow Giles doubted it. Mr Seagrove had been most despondent concerning Sir Nathan's interest in Lily—no doubt some of that misery could be attributed to the thought of having the old bore as a son-in-law for the rest of his life!—and Giles had found himself to be equally as disturbed by the thought of Lily marrying Sir Nathan. Most especially at the thought of that dour and taciturn gentleman exercising his marital rights in her bed every night.

That Giles's own less than respectful behaviour towards Lily should have precluded his feeling murderous at the mere thought of Lily in Sir Nathan's bed, his to do with as he wished, whenever he wished, made absolutely no difference to Giles feeling exactly that excess of emotion!

Which, following a night lacking in restful sleep

despite imbibing a vast quantity of brandy, was the reason Giles had been quite unable to interest himself in anything else this morning other than riding over to the vicarage so that he might see and speak with Lily again, aware as he was that there were still many things left unsaid between them.

The fact that Lily looked so pale this morning, her eyes appearing dark and haunted, would seem to indicate that she had not spent a restful night either. 'I feel our conversation yesterday evening was left unfinished,' he bit out tautly. 'So much so that I feel we must talk on the subject further.'

'I do not see why.' Her chin rose proudly, the pink that had entered her cheeks a perfect match for her high-waisted gown. 'I believe I was more than clear as to my feelings towards…towards certain members of your family, as well as towards yourself!' She clenched her hands together in front of her.

Those same slender and graceful hands that only days ago had caressed Giles until he climaxed.

It was an unprecedented loss of control Giles would not have believed possible until he had experienced the excitement of having Lily's hands upon his naked flesh. An excitement he had been unable to put completely from his mind, let alone forget entirely.

'You implied yesterday evening that we may have

been speaking somewhat at odds with each other this past year, an implication I feel merits further discussion—'

'I believe I have said all I wish to say to you, on that subject, or any other!'

Giles drew in a harsh breath at her vehemence of feeling. 'If I were to ask nicely might you not reconsider, and take a short walk outside with me?'

Lily's eyes widened at the unexpectedly pleasant tone of voice. 'Why should I wish to do that?'

'After stating so frankly yesterday evening how much you hate me?' he prompted ruefully.

'Perhaps *hate* was too strong a word.' Lily gave a pained frown as she inwardly acknowledged that it was the things Giles had said to her which she had so hated and not the man who had said them, in that his comments now made her question the nature of Edward's friendship with her.

Oh, she was still angry with Giles, resented him for causing her to question the cherished memories she held of her friendship with Edward. But as she'd lain awake in her bed last night she had realised that she was more troubled by those remarks than angry.

It had not helped that she had also been aware of her body once again feeling hot and feverish just from listening to the deep tenor of Giles's voice as he and her father conversed in the room beneath her, forcing her once again to acknowledge that it was not dislike alone she felt for Giles Montague....

'Will you not reconsider, Lily?' he now prompted huskily. 'If only for the sake of the friendship and regard our fathers bear for each other?'

She gave a pained wince. 'Is it not a little unfair of you to bring that friendship into our own disagreement?'

'More than a little,' he conceded grimly. 'Which should only serve to show you how much I wish to continue our conversation.'

Lily knew she should refuse. To do anything else, aware of her attraction to this man in spite of the bad feeling between them, would not only be unwise on her part but possibly reckless too.

Why, despite everything Giles had said and done to her since returning to Castonbury, did Lily so much want to accept his invitation?

Chapter Eleven

'I would consider it a great service to me if you were to agree to take a walk with me, Lily.'

Her heart skipped a beat at the husky entreaty she now heard in Giles's tone. An entreaty she at least tried to resist. 'I have so many other things to do this morning....'

'We need not be gone long,' he encouraged softly.

'If you really feel we must talk together, then could we not just sit in the parlour here?' she prompted impatiently.

'The fact that you opened the door to me yourself just now would seem to imply that Mrs Jeffries is also away from the vicarage?' He raised dark brows.

Lily nodded in confirmation. 'She has gone to the butcher's.'

Giles felt his desire quicken just at the thought of

being alone in the vicarage with Lily. A desire which was totally inappropriate given their previous conversations. 'Then we cannot remain alone here.'

Lily hesitated only a moment longer as she looked up at him searchingly before stepping back to fully open the door. 'Perhaps you would like to wait in the parlour whilst I go upstairs and collect my gloves and bonnet.'

Giles allowed himself a brief moment of triumph at Lily's acquiescence even as he gave a shake of his head in refusal of the belated invitation to enter the vicarage; he was feeling too restless of spirit this morning, too aware of everything about Lily, if truth be told, to be able to suffer the confines of the vicarage alone with her, even for so short a time. 'I will stay out here and ensure that my horse remains securely tethered in our absence.'

'Very well.' She gave a cool nod of her head, leaving the door open as she turned away.

Giles remained standing where he was for several minutes after Lily had disappeared down the hallway to ascend the stairs, the lingering aroma of her perfume once again invading his senses, the stirring of his arousal serving as confirmation that his decision not to remain alone here in the vicarage with Lily had been the sensible one.

Which did not prevent him from pausing in the doorway, hard and aching, hands clenched at his sides, as he fought the totally inappropriate urge he felt to follow Lily up the stairs and finish what they had started four days ago.

Giles finally gathered enough control over his desire to be able to move down the pathway and step out into the lane and secure Genghis's reins to the fence, talking softly as the stallion nudged him affectionately in the shoulder. 'I agree, Genghis, this is indeed a madness, but I cannot seem to—'

'Do you speak often to your horse, my— Oh, my goodness!' Lily gave a gasp as, having locked the vicarage behind her and placed the key beneath one of the flower boxes in the window as was the family custom when everyone was out, she now reached Giles's side and saw for the first time the long scar which ran the length of the horse's long silky neck, from ear to wither. 'What on earth can have happened to him?' One lace-gloved hand was raised to her throat at the thought of what could have caused such a grievous injury to such a magnificent animal, her earlier feelings of reluctance, at the thought of spending any time alone with Giles, completely forgotten as she stared compassionately at the scarred horse.

Giles gave the beast a reassuring and affectionate

stroke down the length of that long and glistening neck. 'I will tell you as we walk, if you really care to know.'

'I should, very much.' Lily may have no inclination to learn to ride a horse but that did not prevent her from appreciating and empathising with the serious nature of an injury which could have resulted in such an horrific scar. 'I believe I have heard you call him Genghis?' She looked at the silky black horse admiringly.

'Yes.'

'Like the Mongol emperor?'

Giles smiled slightly. 'Exactly like.'

'He was with you during the battles against Napoleon's army,' Lily guessed huskily.

'Some of them, yes,' Giles confirmed grimly. 'He belonged to a fellow officer who named him that, no doubt because Genghis proved himself to be fearless in the face of the enemy.' He fell into step beside her as they walked across the lane and into the churchyard.

'And that fellow officer…?'

His jaw tightened. 'Cut down and killed.'

'I am sorry. Did you know that this is the grave of Mrs Lovell's son?' She paused beside the mound upon which the two arrangements of flowers, her own and Mrs Lovell's, had been placed two days ago.

Giles frowned as he read the inscription on the weathered gravestone: *Matthew Lovell, Beloved Son and Husband, 1768-1795.* 'Can it be that he was the Romany killed here on the estate twenty-one years ago?'

'So I am told, yes,' Lily confirmed softly.

'I was only seven at the time, but still I remember it well.' He nodded. 'The Romany were beside themselves with grief, and my father utterly distraught that one of his employees was thought to be responsible for the death.'

She raised surprised brows. 'The estate gamekeeper was only "thought to be responsible"?'

Giles shrugged broad shoulders. 'I believe the man denied that he had been anywhere near the woods that day. Nor could it be proven otherwise. His claim of innocence made no difference to my father having to dismiss him, of course,' he added grimly. 'He could not allow a possible murderer to continue to live and work on the Castonbury estate.'

Lily nodded heavily. 'I had no idea, until a few days ago, that Mrs Lovell had ever had a son.'

Giles's mouth tightened as he recalled that Mrs Lovell also had a nephew. A very handsome and flirtatious nephew whom Giles had chanced to find chatting and laughing with one of the housemaids near the stables at Castonbury Park earlier this morning! The same handsome young nephew he had seen Lily meet and enter the woods with the previous day....

'Shall we go on?' he prompted abruptly.

'Of course.' Lily nodded graciously as she continued walking through the graveyard towards the meadow on the other side. 'You were about to tell me about Genghis's injury,' she reminded him huskily.

Giles grimaced. 'Well, to answer your earlier question—yes, I can often be found speaking to my horse!'

She eyed him mischievously as she tried to shake off her earlier sadness for Mrs Lovell's loss. 'Could that possibly be because he is incapable of answering you back?'

Giles grinned appreciatively. 'I had not thought of it in quite that way before now, but perhaps you are right!' He laughed and inclined his head. 'Although I have no doubt that Genghis would find a way to let me know of his displeasure if needs be.'

'He is such a beautiful and fearsome creature!'

Giles sobered as he held open the gate so that they might walk out into the meadow. 'You would not have thought so if you had seen him shortly after he was cut down.'

'Tell me,' she invited softly as they walked down the grassy slope towards the river.

Giles's expression became grim as he thought back to that day two years ago. 'I was with my regiment, and we were preparing to go into battle against Napoleon's troops once more. Not one of the bigger battles, but what we would normally have called a skirmish.' He gave a pained grimace. 'We were wrong. It more resembled a slaughterhouse— I am sorry, Lily.' He turned to her apologetically as she gave a soft gasp. 'Perhaps it would be best if I did not tell you any of this.'

'But of course you must tell me.' She frowned crossly. 'I assure you, I am not some simpering miss who runs away from hearing the truth!'

'I never thought that you were.' In fact, the opposite; Lily had demonstrated several times—including agreeing to walk with him today—that she preferred to face unpleasant situations rather than run away from them.

She nodded briskly. 'That I am shocked is due only to my own ignorance of such things. You, on the other hand, and so many others like you, actually lived and fought your way through times so terrible that those of us at home cannot even begin to imagine the horror of it all. I wish for you to tell me, Giles,' she encouraged huskily. 'If it will not distress you....'

It was not that final plea which encouraged him to

comply with Lily's request—although goodness knew Giles had given her little or no reason this past year to feel in the least considerate towards his own feelings—but the fact that for the first time she had called him Giles without his bidding…

He straightened. 'Then I must start at the beginning of the day, and not the end. I had received word that morning that my brother Jamie had been lost to us, drowned at Salamanca.' His jaw tightened as he heard Lily's sharply indrawn breath. 'It was too immense, too sudden, for me to comprehend. I simply could not believe that Jamie was truly gone.'

Lily frowned. 'I well remember how devastated your father and other members of your family were when they received the news at Castonbury Park. But at least they had one another. I can only imagine how awful it must have been for you to be so far away from your family when news of Lord Jamie's death was brought to you.' Her eyes had darkened in sympathy.

Giles nodded grimly. 'It certainly put me in the mood to fight that day.' He scowled. 'Unfortunately we were outnumbered and outgunned, and after several bloody hours of fighting on horseback and foot we looked defeat in the face. Somehow a last rallying of the troops secured the victory. But so many of my comrades were already dead or dying, and I myself was left for dead after receiving a blow to the head which had rendered me unconscious. When I awoke some hours later it was to find all unnaturally still about me, with no noise to be heard except for the low moans of dying men and the pained whinnying of the horses as they, too, lay injured and dying.'

He had described the scene so well and so vividly that Lily was almost able to hear the guns firing, the shouts of the fighting men and the terrified snorting of the horses, to smell the lingering odour of gunpowder and the blood of so many dying men and horses.

Giles gave a grimly humourless smile as he continued. 'I lay there on the ground, numb from the waist down, all of me covered over in blood, and for several moments believed that I had only woken in order that I might die too.'

Lily instinctively reached out a hand and placed it upon his muscled forearm. 'Please…you have said enough. I insist you not talk of it any more when it is so obviously painful for you to do so!'

He gave a perplexed frown as he looked down at her. 'Should you not be rejoicing at my suffering rather than sympathising, when time and time again I have demonstrated such a lack of understanding in regard to your own feelings?'

'I could never be glad at another's suffering,' she assured him huskily.

Giles gave a pained smile. 'Even my own?'

'Even yours,' Lily conceded softly.

He gave a puzzled shake of his head. 'You are very generous of heart.'

Lily returned his gaze quizzically. 'And that surprises you?'

In truth, everything Giles had learnt about this particular young woman, since returning to Derbyshire, had succeeded in surprising him—her genuine concern for his father's deteriorating health, even if that concern had on one memorable occasion reflected so badly upon him; the care he had heard many in the village say that Lily gave so unselfishly to her father's parishioners; the affection Lily so obviously felt for the roguish Mrs Lovell, and the compassion she felt for the loss of that lady's son, a man who must have died before Lily was even born.

It was the same compassion she now felt for Genghis's injury, even though she had admitted to being somewhat afraid of horses.

And the concern she now showed for Giles, in regard to Jamie's death, and the bloody battle he had fought only hours after that terrible news had been brought to him, showed a capacity for empathy Giles believed few to be capable of, and certainly none that had been so deliberately mocked and insulted by the very object of her compassion.

'You truly are Mr Seagrove's daughter,' he acknowledged huskily.

'I only wish that were true—' She broke off abruptly to look up uncertainly at Giles as he lifted one of his hands to cover her gloved one as it rested on his forearm.

He shrugged. 'It is true, in as much as we are all surely a result of our upbringing rather than those who are physically our parents.'

Her throat moved convulsively as she swallowed before speaking. 'If you continue being kind to me, Giles, then I fear there is the distinct possibility that I may actually come to like you—an occurrence which I am sure would not be pleasing to either one of us!'

Giles looked down at her wordlessly for several stunned moments, before bursting into throaty laughter. Something he had not felt in the least inclined to do since his return to Castonbury ten days ago.

It caused Giles to acknowledge that Lily's ability to ignite his sense of humour, when onerous financial and family problems gave him very little reason to find anything in the least amusing, was yet another thing which surprised him about this young woman.

'I doubt there is any real danger of that ever happening, Lily,' he finally drawled, 'when I am just as likely to insult you—either intentionally or unintentionally—with my very next breath!'

She looked up at him from beneath long, dark lashes. 'Something you might perhaps avoid doing for more than two minutes at a time if you were to accept that my feelings for Edward were only ever that of a sister?'

Giles scowled darkly. 'And are your feelings towards Judah Lovell as innocent?'

'You were right, it was almost with your next breath!' Lily acknowledged with a snort as she purposefully removed her hand from beneath his, her face flushed as she continued to look up at him. 'As I have informed you, I only met that young man for the first time yesterday. I can honestly claim not to have any feelings whatsoever towards him beyond the politeness of acknowledging him as Mrs Lovell's nephew.'

Giles gave a disbelieving snort. 'And what of Sir Nathan?'

'Can you possibly be talking of Sir Nathan Samuelson?' She looked up at him with obvious puzzlement.

Giles nodded haughtily. 'He is a single and eligible gentleman.'

'And I barely know him!' Lily did not know whether

she should laugh or feel angry at the unlikely introduction of Sir Nathan Samuelson into their conversation.

Not only was Sir Nathan old enough to be her father, but he was also portly, red-faced and bewhiskered—and pompous and bad-tempered to boot. Lily had certainly never looked at that gentleman as being anything other than one of her father's less pleasant parishioners—

She stilled as an unpleasant idea occurred to her. 'My father dined with Sir Nathan at Grantby Manor yesterday evening.'

'So he informed me.' Giles's teeth were now so tightly clenched he could feel the throb of his own pulse in the tautness of his jaw.

'Can it be possible that he—? Could he have—? No, surely even Sir Nathan cannot have—' She broke off with a shudder. 'He cannot!'

Her distaste for even the idea of Sir Nathan as anything more than one of her father's parishioners was so obvious that Giles felt discomforted at having allowed his own feelings of distaste for the man to have prompted him to usurp Mr Seagrove's role as Lily's father. To such a degree that he had sounded like a jealous suitor himself!

Which was utterly preposterous. Admittedly, their conversations yesterday evening and again today had made Giles question his summation of Lily's character a year ago, but that did not imply he felt any romantic interest in her himself.

'Perhaps, if Mr Seagrove has not yet found opportunity to discuss the matter with you, I should not have spoken on the subject either.'

'Mr Seagrove seems to have found opportunity to discuss the subject with you—no doubt while the two of you indulged in an excess of brandy last evening!' Her eyes flashed a deep warning.

Hers was now a glittering and angry gaze which Giles found he no longer had any wish to meet. 'Perhaps we should return to discussing how Genghis suffered his injuries—'

'It can wait until you have fully explained what you meant by your remarks regarding Sir Nathan,' Lily insisted firmly.

Giles winced as he heard the anger in her voice. Even if that anger did give a sparkle to Lily's fine green eyes, and add becoming colour to the ivory perfection of her cheeks! 'I really cannot—'

'Oh, but you really can, Giles!' she assured with controlled determination.

He grimaced, finding it did not please him at all to hear Lily say his name in that angry tone. 'Mr Seagrove merely mentioned yesterday evening that

Sir Nathan had talked in a…complimentary fashion about you, over dinner.'

'And in what manner did I even enter into their conversation, let alone have Sir Nathan talk about me in a "complimentary fashion"?' she repeated with dangerous softness.

Giles shifted restlessly, wishing he had never begun this particular conversation. 'I am sure Mr Seagrove will happily explain all when next you see him.'

'But you are with me now, Giles, and so may save me the bother of the wait,' Lily reasoned sweetly.

What Lily suspected could not possibly be true, could it? That Sir Nathan Samuelson, a man of plain if not unattractive looks, of an unpleasantness of manner which Lily knew had already caused at least one lady in the county to refuse his offer of marriage, had now turned his lecherous gaze in her direction?

Lily would rather remain an old maid for the rest of her life than marry a man she could not even bring herself to like, let alone love! Indeed, given her circumstances, she had long ago decided that in all probability an old maid was exactly what she would one day become….

She breathed out shallowly. 'When you and Mr Seagrove spoke on the subject yesterday evening, did he also say whether or not he would approve of such an offer?'

Giles shifted uncomfortably. 'He…implied it would be your own decision, not his.'

'That would appear to settle the matter, then.' Lily felt some of the tension ease from her shoulders, having been aware that if Mr Seagrove had approved of the match, then she would at least have had to appear to give the matter some thought before refusing. Indeed, she would much prefer it if Sir Nathan could somehow be persuaded into not asking at all!

'It does?' Giles eyed her questioningly.

'Undoubtedly,' she dismissed briskly. 'When—if my father asks, I will simply state that I would not be willing to accept Sir Nathan as my husband if he were the very last gentleman upon this earth!' She repressed a delicate shudder of distaste.

'Poor Sir Nathan!' Giles felt as if a heavy weight had been lifted from his shoulders. But it was quickly followed by a frown appearing on his brow at his acknowledgement of those feelings of relief to be even more ridiculous than the ones he had earlier attributed to jealousy.

Lily eyed him critically. 'You do not sound very sympathetic.'

Possibly because Giles did not feel in the least sympathetic towards the gentleman who had caused him to spend the past twelve hours gnashing and grinding his teeth in frustration at the very thought of that gentleman sharing Lily's bed and body.

'Nor,' Lily continued tartly, 'do I appreciate my father having discussed this matter with you before it has even been mentioned to me!'

Giles winced at what he knew to be her perfectly justified feelings of resentment. 'Mr Seagrove did not so much discuss it with me as mention it to me casually as we enjoyed a glass of brandy together—' He broke off to catch Lily's disbelieving snort. 'A glass or six of brandy together,' he allowed drily.

She gave him a reproving glance. 'You are obviously a bad influence upon each other and should be kept apart in future!'

In truth Giles had very much enjoyed his conversation and brandy with Mr Seagrove the night before, had found that gentleman to be both learned and well informed, and he now perfectly understood his father's long and warm friendship with the man. Being a duke had long set his father apart from all but his peers, in the same way Giles would also find himself set apart were he to one day inherit the title from his father.

If he inherited the title from his father, Giles reminded himself grimly, the manner of Jamie's death, and the lack of a body as proof of that death, meaning that as a family they still had to find physical evidence before the succession could be secured, along with Jamie's considerable inheritance from their mother. It was—

'I was only jesting, Giles.'

He blinked, realising that he had allowed his thoughts to wander to the other problem which had begun to plague him day and night since his return to Castonbury.

The *other* problem?

Lily had become something of a problem to him, Giles now acknowledged, as just looking down into the exotic beauty of her face once again reminded him that she was not Mr Seagrove's daughter at all.

As such, an offer from someone of Sir Nathan's ilk was far more than Lily could ever, or should ever, have hoped for. Moreover, it was an offer Giles should be encouraging her to accept in his role as the future Duke of Rothermere.

Instead he found himself raising a hand to cup the warmth of one of Lily's ivory cheeks as he continued to gaze down into that lovely face; those green, slightly uptilted eyes, and the full and berry-red of her lips were an enticement Giles was finding more and more difficult to resist. 'You are so very beautiful, Lily.'

She looked slightly alarmed. 'Perhaps we should, after all, resume our walk whilst you continue to talk of Genghis?'

Yes, that is exactly what they should do.

Should?

Must!

And yet just the feel of Lily's silken skin beneath Giles's fingertips, her warmth, made it impossible for Giles to think of anything else but the need he felt to make love to her again.

Chapter Twelve

Lily's heart began to beat wildly in her chest as she saw the intensity of Giles's silver gaze fixed firmly, hungrily even, upon her slightly parted lips, instantly making her aware of how very alone the two of them were out here in the meadow together amongst the scented wildflowers, the only sounds their own soft and husky breathing and the twittering of the birds.

A pleasurable lethargy descended over Lily's body, an aching heaviness in her breasts, and heat between her thighs. A heat and aching heaviness that she acknowledged were becoming all too familiar when she was anywhere in the vicinity of Giles Montague!

'We really should continue our walk, Giles,' she prompted with a sharpness she was far from feeling.

He blinked as if waking from a dream, or perhaps the same sensual spell under which Lily had felt herself falling. His hand dropped away from her cheek as he straightened abruptly. 'Yes, of course.' His expression became remote as he indicated she should precede him.

Even Lily's legs felt unwieldy as she turned to walk down to where the river tripped and gurgled over rocks smoothed by years of the water's caress, at the same time completely aware of Giles as he matched his much longer strides to her own. A glance from beneath lowered lashes revealed that he now looked every inch the grimly forbidding Giles Montague, rather than the man who had made love to Lily so passionately four days ago, and touched her again so gently only moments ago whilst his eyes had sought to bore into her very soul.

She could not forget the look, no matter how hard she tried.

'I remember playing here as a child,' she remarked abruptly, having reached the riverside, in an attempt to try to ease the tension between them.

Giles nodded. 'Before we went away to school Jamie and I would often hide from our tutor beneath that willow.' He looked at the magnificent tree as its branches draped down even heavier and thicker than he remembered, creating what he remembered to be a cool and shadowed den beneath.

Lily looked up at him. 'As did Edward and I....'

His smile was tinged with sadness. 'And now there is only the two of us left to remember those happy times.'

'Yes.'

'You really did not love or wish to marry Edward, did you.' It was a statement rather than a question.

Lily turned back to look at the river. 'I loved him as my very best friend in all the world. I always will.' She had realised, as she lay unable to sleep the night before, that her friendship with Edward was not spoilt, after all, and that Edward had gone to his death with hope still alive in his heart that she might return his love. There was some comfort in knowing that.

'But never as your lover.'

She continued to stare down at the flowing water. 'No, never as a lover.'

Giles drew in a sharp breath. 'I needed to talk to you today, Lily, because I—I have realised that I owe you an apology.'

Her face remained averted. 'Just one?' She couldn't resist the taunt.

'I— You were so insistent yesterday concerning your feelings for Edward, and your father also spoke last night of your sisterly regard for Edward.'

Her profile showed the sadness of her smile. 'And

you have chosen to believe my father when you did not believe me.'

'I— It was—' Giles shook his head. 'Please understand, Edward was so firm in his declaration of love for you that I felt sure you must be aware of those feelings.'

'I was not.' Her eyes were wet with tears as she turned to look at him. 'Could you not—? Please— please do not break my heart again, by talking of a love I could never have returned!'

Giles straightened, cut to the quick by sight of those tears. Tears for which he knew he was responsible. 'Perhaps, for now, we could continue our conversation of Genghis?'

'If you please,' Lily encouraged softly.

If Giles pleased…!

His shoulders ached almost as much as that old wound to his thigh as he fought to keep his hands from once again reaching out and taking Lily into his arms before kissing her. Except Giles knew he did not want to stop at taking her in his arms and kissing her; he wanted so very much more.

Lily's fierce denial the evening before, of loving Edward as anything more than a brother, and Mr Seagrove's fond memories of his daughter and Edward's friendship since childhood, had caused Giles to think long and hard on the subject once he returned to Castonbury Park. It was hard for him to acknowledge the possibility that, no matter what Edward may have told him a year ago of his feelings for Lily, she may not have returned those feelings. Nor would she have accepted his offer of marriage if he had ever made one.

As she had today rejected the suggestion that she might ever accept such an offer from Sir Nathan Samuelson—

'Giles?'

It was now his turn to stare blindly at the river as he forced his memories back to the day two years ago rather than give in to the urge to take Lily in his arms. 'Genghis had fallen across my lower body when he was cut down, and so gave me the mistaken impression that I had lost the use of my legs. Once I realised that the blood over me was not mine but his, I was able to crawl out, inch by inch, from beneath his weight. And, as I did so, I realised that Genghis still lived.'

Giles had forgotten his own discomfort completely that day as he was instead filled with elation at seeing that slight rise and fall of Genghis's heavy barrel chest, something he would not have believed possible once he saw the extent of the stallion's injuries. A French sabre had sliced him open from ear to wither, and the blood still seeped from the wound.

'It was—' Giles shook his head, knowing that his behaviour towards Lily this past year dictated he could not be less than honest with her now concerning his own feelings and emotions in regard to the events of two years ago. 'The extent of Genghis's injuries dictated it would have been a kindness on my part to shoot him then and there. But I—I could not bring myself to do it. Jamie was gone. My fellow officers and most of my men were also slain. To allow this magnificent creature to suffer that same fate seemed beyond bearing.'

'What did you do?' Lily prompted huskily.

He sighed. 'I tried to get help for him, but the medics were far too busy dealing with the injuries of the men to bother with a mere horse.'

'You tended him yourself?'

Giles nodded abruptly. 'I did what I could for him— cleaned the wound, sewed it up as best I could with the supplies I had—and then sat down beside him and simply willed him to live.' He frowned grimly as he recalled those hours—days—during which he had sat at Genghis's side, ignoring his own wound as he ensured that the horse's wounds remained clean and free of the flies that swarmed constantly over the battle-ground soaked with blood.

Hours and days when Giles had not left the horse's side except to collect water from a nearby stream, occasionally dribbling some of that water into his own mouth once he had seen to Genghis's needs, but taking no other food or sustenance as he concentrated all of his attention on willing the fallen horse to recover.

The same hours and days when Giles had also come to accept the loss of his elder brother, and to the knowledge that there was nothing he could do or say which could ever bring Jamie back to them.

They had been the bleakest and loneliest hours and days of Giles's life, his only companion the seriously wounded horse whom he had refused to allow to die. Lonely hours and days, when the loss of Jamie and his fellow soldiers had left scars inside him which had healed but would never be forgotten....

Lily could only imagine the scene Giles described to her, but even that was horrific enough; to have lived through it was beyond her comprehension. 'You obviously succeeded.'

He smiled grimly. 'Something Genghis did not at all thank me for once he began to regain his strength, I assure you. His suffering then was immense.' The bleakness in those silver-grey eyes revealed that Giles's own suffering had been almost as severe. 'He several times tried to show his displeasure by attempting to bite me.'

Having seen the affection which now existed between this man and that fierce warrior of a horse, Lily had no doubt that Genghis had long ago forgiven Giles for the pain he had suffered because of this man's stubborn determination that he should live.

Giles grimaced. 'I think— I have come to believe since, that Genghis had somehow come to represent the whole of those bloody years of war to me, and that if he were allowed to die, then all of it—Jamie's death, the deaths of all those other brothers and sons and fathers and husbands—would be rendered utterly meaningless.'

'And yet I can tell that you now miss your life in the army.'

Lily knew with a certainty that this was so.

His jaw firmed. 'It is what I was brought up to be. What I have always known I was meant to do.'

And if not for the unexpected death of his older brother, no doubt what he would still be doing. 'And is that the reason you found it so...so difficult to come back here nine months ago after you had resigned your commission?' Lily prompted huskily.

He drew in a harsh breath. 'No. That was due to something else entirely.'

Lily looked at him enquiringly, adding nothing, just waiting silently for him to speak again.

'The thought of coming back to Castonbury,' Giles continued forcefully, 'of being here, where I knew I would feel Jamie and Edward's loss more deeply than anywhere else, was unbearable to me! Of course, I had not realised quite how my father's health had deteriorated, else I should have been here sooner, my own feelings of loss be damned!' He looked grim.

And this, Lily acknowledged achingly, was the same man for whom she had harboured such anger and resentment this past year.

Even more so in the almost eleven months since Edward had been struck down at Waterloo.

Giles was a man Lily could now see she had judged as harshly as he had judged her, in that she had chosen to see only what she had perceived to be Giles's cold and arrogant nature, rather than attempting to see him as he truly was: a man who felt emotions so strongly, and so deeply, that he must hide them beneath a veneer of cold arrogance lest he be thought weak or vulnerable.

Lily now believed he had deliberately chosen to

share his vulnerability with her today, as a way of atoning, apologising, for his previous behaviour to her.

And in doing so he allowed Lily at last to see that Giles was indeed a man who had more than deserved Edward's hero-worship. That if he bore any responsibility at all for Edward's premature death, then it was only in having been the man that he was, a man of strength and loyalty whom Edward had wished to emulate.

The anger and resentment Lily had felt towards Giles for so long melted like the winter snow in the warmth of spring, as she knew she looked up into the face of a man who was still tormented by the death of both his brothers, as well as the men who had served with and under him. Giles had now confided that torment to her in a way she doubted he had ever done with anyone else, and in doing so allowed her to see that he was not a man lacking in emotions at all.

Her face was full of compassion as she reached up to gently curve her hand about one of Giles's rigidly tensed cheeks—

'Do not, Lily!' he bit out harshly, every part of him having tensed, his eyes a glittering silver as he looked down at her.

She stilled with her fingers against that tensed cheek. 'Why should I not?'

A nerve pulsed in Giles's rigidly clenched jaw. 'I am not in full control of— You should know that our conversation has left me with few defences. I have nothing left with which to resist taking you in my arms and kissing you, as I so long to do!' He looked down at her hungrily as he fought that inner battle.

A battle which Lily's beauty would surely ensure he was destined to lose?

That nerve once again pulsed in the rigidity of his jaw. 'Lily—'

'Giles?'

His breath caught in his throat as he saw the tears glistening in those beautiful green eyes. Were those tears for him? 'I did not tell you any of those things with the intention of arousing your pity—' He broke off as she laughed softly.

She gave a gentle shake of her head. 'Giles, you are not a man for whom I or anyone else could ever feel pity,' she assured huskily.

Giles continued to look down at her searchingly but found none of the mockery in her expression that he might have expected from her words. 'It is a fact that during times of war women would…allow soldiers to make love to them, for the simple reason they believed it might be their last such memory.'

She moistened her lips with the tip of her tongue.

'And did you personally…accept many of those offers?'

His mouth tightened as he answered her honestly. 'Too many for me now to recall any of their faces!'

Lily drew her breath in sharply at the bluntness of Giles's reply, even as she knew with certainty that it had been his intention to shock her, perhaps to disgust her, in an effort, no doubt, to regain the shield over his emotions which he had lost during those minutes of baring his soul to her.

But Lily knew she was no longer capable of feeling shock and disgust where Giles was concerned.

She again ran the tip of her tongue over her full lips. 'You underestimate your…attraction, Giles, if you believe that to have been the only motivation for those women to have invited you into their beds.'

His throat moved as he swallowed before answering her harshly. 'We are venturing onto dangerous ground, Lily.'

Lily had known the moment she opened the door to Giles this morning that she should not be alone with him today, that to do so, after her longings of the night before—when just to hear the low rumble of his voice, as he talked with her father in the room beneath her bedchamber, had been enough to arouse her—would be to flirt with danger. An irresistible danger, which

Lily knew had only intensified as Giles talked of his despair and determination on the day Genghis had been so mortally injured.

She looked up at him quizzically. 'Is it so very dangerous?'

'Very.' Giles was totally aware of the light caress of Lily's fingers still resting against his cheek, of her soft floral perfume, of the swell of her breasts above the neckline of her gown, of the temptation of her red and delectable lips!

'And if I were to tell you that I am not afraid?' she prompted huskily.

His mouth thinned. 'Then I would advise you to think again!'

She shook her head in gentle reproof. 'You may try all you wish, Giles, but I can no longer be fooled by your air of coldness or arrogance.'

'But I am cold and arrogant—'

'Yes, you are,' she conceded softly. 'But you are also the man who obviously loves his family deeply. The same man who refused to allow the fearsome Genghis to die.'

He gave a pained frown. 'I am also the man who might insult you again with his very next breath,' he reminded harshly.

'And if that occurs, I shall think of our conversation just now, and refuse to take insult at anything you have said to me.'

Giles drew in a harsh breath as Lily gazed up at him with those clear and trusting green eyes, knowing that, for the moment at least, he had no defences with which to resist her. 'You are a very stubborn young woman—' He broke off as she laughed huskily.

'I believe us to be as stubborn as each other,' she explained ruefully.

He grimaced. 'Perhaps.'

'There is no "perhaps" about it.' She chuckled as she shook her head. 'If not for that stubbornness, that set opinion of each other that we refused to let go, we might have become friends much earlier than this.'

Friends? Giles pondered. Did Lily really consider them to have now become friends? In the same way that she and Edward had been friends? 'I already have two sisters, Lily,' he bit out harshly. 'I have no need of another.'

She breathed softly. 'My regard for you is not in the least sisterly!'

Giles looked searchingly into those clear and candid green eyes, knowing himself to be without armour to resist their unwavering glow. 'I am not a man deserving of your admiration, Lily,' he rasped harshly.

'Nevertheless, you have it.'

He gave an impatient shake of his head. 'And have you considered that perhaps that was my intention all along? That I may have told you these things merely as a way of persuading you into thinking more kindly of me?'

She regarded him quizzically for several long moments. 'Do you wish me to think more kindly of you?'

'What I wish is for you to remove your bonnet and release your hair!'

Those green eyes widened at the vehemence of his tone. 'Release my hair?'

He nodded abruptly. 'I have imagined—' He shook his head, knowing he could not tell Lily the amount of times he had lain on his bed aroused and throbbing, imagining the fingers about him were hers, and the silkiness of her hair was draped across the nakedness of his chest and thighs! 'I have long wondered as to its length and thickness,' he rasped throatily.

She continued to look up at him for several long seconds before raising her gloved hands to untie her bonnet, removing it completely to allow it to fall to the grassy riverbank at their feet before peeling her gloves down her arms and allowing them, too, to flutter to the ground next to her bonnet. Her slender, bare hands now moved up to seek out the pins holding her dark curls in place.

'Good heavens…!' Giles's breath caught in his throat as Lily at last shook her head and allowed her curls to fall about her shoulders and down her back, a glossy, ebony tumble so long and thick as it fell all the way down to the gentle curve of her bottom. 'Lily…!' He reached up to touch those curls wonderingly before allowing their silky softness to fall and cascade through his fingers. 'I have never seen anything so beautiful.'

Her cheeks were flushed. 'My mother always said it would be sacrilege to cut it.'

Giles could not stop touching the ebony softness. 'Mrs Seagrove was a very wise woman.'

Lily laughed softly. 'It takes hours to dry when it is washed.'

Giles's breath caught in his throat as an image of a naked Lily instantly filled his head, her hair a wet and silky curtain over that nakedness, her breasts full and pert, the rosy nipples peeping out temptingly through those dark curls. 'You must never cut it, Lily.' His fingers became entangled in the rich darkness as he pulled her unerringly towards him.

Lily could barely breathe, let alone speak, her proximity to Giles now such that she could feel the soft warmth of his breath against her cheek, and see the dark pewter ring of colour edging the paler iris of his glittering grey eyes. Piercing grey eyes which now held her own captive....

'Promise me, Lily!' His fingers tightened painfully in her curls as he tilted her head back, exposing the creamy column of her throat. At the same time, his other arm curled about her waist and pulled her against his parted thighs, making her aware of the hard length of his arousal even as the solidity of his chest pushed up the full swell of her breasts.

Lily's palms lay warmly against the waistcoat covering that muscled chest. 'If it is your wish—'

'It is!'

'Then I promise you never to cut my hair.'

His breath caught in his throat. 'Thank you.'

She looked up at him, so very aware of the throb of Giles's swollen arousal pressing into her own heat. 'Is it now your intention to kiss me again?'

Was it—?

Good heavens, Giles wanted nothing more than to kiss the wild and exotically lovely creature he held in his arms. To kiss Lily, to touch and caress her, to hold her wildness to him, if only for the short time she might allow it.

Every muscle and sinew in his body was tense with that need as he answered her gruffly. 'I will not take anything you do not give willingly, Lily.'

'I—' She broke off abruptly, tensing at the sound of someone whistling.

'Stop dawdling back there, boy!' The harsh tones of Mrs Lovell's voice were unmistakable.

The whistling stopped. 'Sure an' it's a fine day for a walk, Aunt Rosa,' Judah Lovell answered her unconcernedly.

'Carry this basket of herbs for me if ye can't be useful in any other way,' his aunt snapped her impatience as those two voices came steadily closer to where Lily and Giles stood.

Lily looked up at Giles with wide eyes, her cheeks having paled. 'We should not be found here together like this!'

A brief wave of…something washed over Giles, as he wondered if Lily's panic was thoughts of discovery by Mrs Lovell or her nephew. He quickly dismissed the emotion; there had been so many misunderstandings between him and Lily already, without his jumping to yet more.

'Come!' Giles urged softly as he released Lily to remove his hat before taking a firm hold of her hand and leading her quickly beneath the branches of the overhanging willow, the two of them at once enclosed inside its dark cavern of foliage, allowing them to hear the approach of Mrs Lovell and her nephew if not actually see them. And if Giles and Lily could not see Judah and Mrs Lovell, then hopefully the pair could not see them either....

'There's usually mushrooms hereabouts,' Mrs Lovell could be heard announcing cheerfully.

'Can't we get 'em on the way back?' her nephew grumbled.

Giles knew he should have been at work in the fields of the estate but he had obviously decided not to bother.

'You're a lazy good-for-nothing.' Mrs Lovell obviously echoed Giles's sentiments. 'Just like your father before ye.'

'And 'ow would you know what me da were like, when ye never troubled yourself to set eyes on 'im again after we left for Ireland twenty years ago?' Judah Lovell came back dismissively.

'Black Jack was a lazy good-for-nothing then, and I has no reason to believe that changed afore he died,' the elderly Gypsy returned scathingly. 'And don't look at me like that, Judah. You know as well as I what a wastrel ya da were, and from what I've seen since ye got back you're just like him,' she added remorselessly.

Her nephew gave a merry laugh. 'Why bother me-self working for something when it sits there for the taking!'

'We'll have none of your thieving ways round here, Judah-me-lad,' Mrs Lovell warned harshly. 'No, nor none of your wicked ways with the lasses neither. You'll leave no tow-headed chivvies here when ye go.'

'There's only one lassie in these parts beautiful enough to waste me time on,' her nephew informed her with youthful dismissal.

'Oh?'

'That vicar's daughter is—*ow*! What the 'ell was that for?' Judah exclaimed, following the loud sound of flesh meeting flesh.

'Keep ya trap shut about Lily Seagrove!' Mrs Lovell hissed fiercely. 'You hear me, boy?'

'I 'ears you,' her nephew confirmed disgruntledly. 'Weren't no need for ye to 'it me just because I said Lily—'

'I said as you weren't to talk of her again,' Mrs Lovell warned angrily. 'You'll stay well away from her if'n you know what's good for ye.'

'The only time I've even spoken to her was when I brought 'er to your yag yesterday.'

'Well, make sure as you don't see or speak to her again. Now pick up ya feet, boy, and get a move on before I decides I feel like hitting ye again—hello, what's this?'

'Looks like a lady's bonnet and gloves to me,' her nephew answered drily.

'Well, I can see that for meself!' his aunt snapped her impatience with his cheekiness. 'I wonder what they're doin' here?'

Giles had felt Lily's tension as Judah had remarked on her beauty, but he was now aware of Lily's dismay at the realisation that her bonnet and gloves had been discovered on the grassy bank where she had left them in their haste to duck beneath the willow.

'What does it matter what they's doing 'ere?' Judah had obviously reached the end of his patience. 'Take the bonnet and gloves wi' ye, if you're that worried about 'em, and let's get on to the village!'

'If'n your poor mother were alive she'd turn over in her grave to listen to the way you speak to your elders and betters.'

'If'n she were alive she wouldn't be in her grave.'

'I believe it is safe now, Lily,' Giles murmured reassuringly several minutes later as the Lovells' voices became fainter and then faded away entirely. He finally heard the closing of the gate going into the churchyard as evidence that they had indeed gone on their way to the village.

Only Giles immediately realised, as he looked

down at the pale oval of Lily's beautiful face in the cool darkness, that he now faced a much more serious—and immediate!—danger than discovery by the Lovells.

Chapter Thirteen

'I fail to understand what you find so amusing?' It had taken Giles some seconds to realise that Lily was not trembling with fear as he had originally surmised, but was instead laughing, her eyes now glowing with amusement in the strange half-light beneath the branches of the willow.

That laughter still trembled on her lips as she shook her head. 'I was only thinking of how all your misconceptions of my behaviour must now be shattered.'

'Oh?'

She nodded. 'In one morning you have accepted that I loved Edward only as a brother, learnt that I would not consider taking Sir Nathan Samuelson as a husband if he were the last man on earth and that the only time I chanced to meet Judah Lovell was yesterday, when you happened to see him escorting me to Mrs Lovell's campsite.'

Yes, Giles had indeed come to a realisation of all those things. 'Which would seem to leave me as the only man in your life....'

Lily's amusement faded as she became aware of how very alone they now were beneath the silence of the willow's thick branches, and that Giles's arms still circled the slenderness of her waist. 'You?'

His eyes glowed down at her in the darkness. 'You must know that I desire you, Lily. How could you not?' he added. The evidence of that desire was all too evident to them both.

She moistened her lips with the tip of her tongue, suddenly very aware of the pulsing heat of Giles's desire as it pressed against her soft abdomen.

Urgently.

Temptingly!

'Dare I hope you feel that same desire for me, Lily?'

She breathed shallowly. 'I—'

'Please tell me the truth of it, Lily,' Giles urged huskily, his arms tightening about her waist. 'For I will not frighten or disgust you with the depth of my...my arousal, a second time.'

Lily stared up at him in the gloom, able to see the fierce glitter of Giles's gaze upon her, and the sharp blades of his cheekbones, the firmness of his jaw clenched so tightly beneath the sensuality of his sculptured lips.

Did she desire Giles?

It seemed now as if Lily could not remember a time when she had not.

Their conversation today meant she could no longer see him as Edward's cold and arrogant older brother. Or as the man who had insulted and reviled her because he believed her guilty of trying to ensnare his besotted younger brother into matrimony. Neither could she any longer believe him to be coldly callous about the estate or his father's health.

Lily had now seen him as a man who loved his family deeply, and in such a way that he was willing to do anything, say anything, in order that he might protect them from all that he thought might harm or threaten them. He was a man who had given up his life in the army, a life he was so suited to and a career which he had loved, in order to take his place here at Castonbury as his father's heir.

He was, in fact, all that Lily admired in a man.

And the man that she knew she desired with every particle of her being.

And as surely as Giles's doubts had been dispelled, in regard to her intentions towards Edward, Sir Nathan Samuelson and even Judah Lovell, so had Lily accepted she would, by necessity, one day become that old maid she had imagined.

Despite being adopted by Mr and Mrs Seagrove, she was, and would always be, a foundling, her only choice to marry someone like Sir Nathan, an unpleasant man whom no other woman wished to take for her husband, or to become the plaything of a man like Judah Lovell, a good-natured wastrel, who would take and use her body and emotions before discarding them.

If that truly was to be her fate, then Lily would rather choose the man who might one day discard her.

She now took a determined breath. 'I was not frightened or disgusted the other day, Giles.'

'No?' He looked down at her searchingly.

'No. I—I thought it beautiful,' she admitted softly. 'I thought *you* beautiful.'

Giles stilled, momentarily stunned into silence by Lily's words, by the unmistakable sincerity of her husky tone. 'Men are not beautiful, Lily.' He finally regained his own voice ruefully. 'We are brutal, selfish creatures, more often than not led by our—' His harsh words ceased abruptly as Lily placed her fingertips against his lips.

'Giles, if your intention is to succeed in shocking me into running away from you, from this, then do not even try.' She pulled out of his arms to step away from him, her gaze meeting his unwaveringly as she reached behind her.

Her intention of unbuttoning the back of her gown was so achingly obvious that Giles could only watch in mute fascination as she finished unfastening the buttons before the bodice of her gown slid down the slender length of her arms and she allowed the gown to fall to the ground, leaving her dressed only in a thin chemise and white stockings secured in place by two pretty blue garters about her thighs, the heavy length of her ebony hair flowing seductively over her bare shoulders and down the slender length of her spine.

Giles sucked a gasp of air into his lungs as he gazed at the full plumpness of her breasts beneath her chemise, the tips hard and red as berries, her waist slender, with a dark triangle of curls visible between the gentle curve of her thighs.

She looked, in fact, so beautiful, so like Giles had thought of her so many times in his tortured nights, that he felt a moment of light-headedness as all the blood in his body seemed to rush to one single location. 'You are so very lovely, Lily,' he groaned, his hands clenched and trembling at his sides.

'As are you,' she assured softly as she stepped forward to slide his jacket from his shoulders before her fingers moved to the buttons of his waistcoat.

'No.' Giles placed one of his hands over hers to still those questing fingers. 'Before you do that you must know that I have— That I have many scars from battle...'

'And, if I am not mistaken, many that are not visible to the eye,' she guessed huskily.

'Perhaps,' he allowed gruffly.

'Then, if you allow it, I shall kiss each and every one of the scars that I do see.' She looked up at him in mute appeal.

It was a plea Giles was unable to resist, groaning his acquiescence even as his hand dropped back to his side and he stood tense and shaking as Lily removed his waistcoat, before untying and discarding his neck cloth, the slow unfastening of the buttons of his shirt revealing the first of those scars.

Giles drew in a ragged breath as he felt the softness of Lily's lips against his hot and sensitised flesh as she gently kissed the length of the first scar, the silky curtain of her hair as warm against his skin as he had imagined it might be.

He offered no further resistance as Lily freed his shirt from his breeches before lifting the garment over his head, her gaze darkening as she viewed the half-dozen or so scars that criss-crossed his chest before her fingers traced caressingly the lines and planes of his torso.

'You must have been very brave—'

'I am not brave, Lily, I am—was…merely a soldier,' he corrected gruffly.

Lily's hands were warm against his flesh as she glanced up at him in gentle rebuke. 'Can you never return to that life?'

'It would be better for my own peace of mind if I were to accept that this, being heir to the Castonbury estate, is now my fate.' His voice sounded harsh in the silence.

She looked up at him as her fingers once again began to lightly trace the scars upon his chest. 'It is not all bad, surely?'

'Not all, no.' Giles drew in a sharp breath even as he forced the tension from his shoulders and felt the pleasure of those caresses. 'Indeed, I am slowly learning it has unexpected…compensations.'

She chuckled huskily. 'And are those compensations to your liking, my lord?' Her lips were once again light as a butterfly as she kissed the long scar on his belly that he had received some four years ago and which had put him on his back in the hospital for months following the battle.

'Oh, yes.' Lily was to his liking! Her hands and lips

traced that scar down to where his long, hot length tented the front of his breeches. 'Not yet!' Giles reached out to clasp the tops of her arms as she would have unfastened the buttons which would release that hardness to the caress of her lips and tongue. 'I wish to kiss and touch you first, Lily.' He wanted to worship at her feet. To touch and kiss every inch of her silken body before claiming her as his own.

For he intended to claim every part of her. Would make love to Lily in such a way she would never be able to forget how it felt to have him touching her, or dispel the taste of him from her lips and tongue, and the feel of him moving inside her hot and silken sheath.

His eyes were fully accustomed to the half-light now, allowing him to step back slightly and gaze his fill of Lily's pale ivory skin. He slipped the straps of her chemise from her shoulders before it fell softly to her waist, leaving bare her full, pert breasts tipped with those ripe buds on which he had long ached to feast.

Lily gasped softly, her hands moving up to rest on Giles's shoulders for balance as one of his hands lightly cupped her breast, his gaze continuing to hold hers as his head lowered and he began to lick and tease that full and sensitive tip. Long, arousing sweeps of his tongue swept against aching flesh, teeth gently biting, tasting, before he finally parted his lips and pulled her nipple deeply, hungrily, into the moist and encompassing fire of his mouth.

She felt the rush of heat between her thighs as Giles moved his other hand up to cup her other breast before rolling the sensitive peak between thumb and fore-finger, setting a rhythm that caused a point between her thighs to swell and moisten. To ache with need. To burn.

Lily's hands rose from Giles's broad shoulders to become entwined in the heavy silkiness of his hair. 'Please…! Oh, please!' She felt the heat of the increasing moisture between her legs as she moved restlessly, groaning softly, trembling uncontrollably, as Giles's other hand stroked between her thighs and pressed gently against the sensitive throbbing bud there.

She felt cool air brushing against the dampness of her nipple as Giles released her before dropping down onto his knees in front of her to slowly slide her chemise down over her hips and allow it to fall to the ground beside her gown, her stockings and gar-ters now her only adornment. 'Have you touched and caressed yourself since we were last together, Lily?' His fingers lightly parted the dark curls between her thighs, the warmth of his breath a teasing caress against her skin.

Lily felt the burn of colour in her cheeks. 'I—'

'There must be truth between us from now on, Lily.'

The truth. The truth was that until four days ago, until Giles had touched her so intimately, Lily had known nothing of the pleasures of her own body. Had never dreamt…imagined—

'Did you touch your breasts, Lily? Did you caress your breasts until you ached with need?' he pressured huskily.

'I cannot—'

'You can!'

'I— Yes, yes, I did that!' she admitted breathlessly.

'And did you touch yourself here, where you ached the most?'

Giles swept his tongue across the aching place between her thighs, causing Lily's legs to tremble so much she would have fallen if not for her hands gripping Giles's warm shoulders. 'Lily?' His tongue rasped against her a second time.

'Yes!' She shuddered uncontrollably as the pleasure became almost unbearable.

'And here?' That marauding tongue swept lower, caressing, building the need until she thought she could take it no longer.

'Yes…'

'And did you put your fingers here?' He gently nudged her legs apart before moving closer, his fingers taking Lily to the edge of that plateau of hot and overwhelming pleasure. 'Lily, answer me,' he urged fiercely.

She felt bereft, empty, without Giles's mouth on her. 'Yes!' she groaned achingly. 'Yes. Oh, yes! I did all of those things. All of them!' And she had. Every night since Giles had made love to her she had moved restlessly in her bed, until, with a groan, she had had no choice but to give in to the temptation to caress her breasts, to rub the throbbing ache between her thighs, her own fingers in place of him.

'And did you climax, Lily? Did you rub and caress yourself until you reached completion?'

'Yes!'

'And did you think of me when the pleasure came, Lily? Did you imagine it was me touching you?' he pressed urgently.

'Yes…' she sobbed.

'I have thought of you too, Lily,' he admitted gruffly. 'Each and every time I have brought myself to the same point, I have closed my eyes and imagined it was your hands touching and caressing me.' He smiled ruefully as she looked down at him in surprise. 'Oh, yes, Lily, I have needed to find a release for my desire for you too. Many times over. But none of my imaginings measured up to the reality of touching your silken skin, to tasting you, and holding you.' He buried his face between her thighs once more.

She gave a low cry of rapture as Giles sent her over the edge of that plateau and into the deep and overwhelming sea of wave after wave of uncontrollable pleasure.

Again, and yet again, he took her to that plateau and then over its edge, until Lily answered only to the relentless caress of Giles's mouth and hands. 'Please! No more!' she finally begged as she swayed weakly. 'I cannot again, Giles. Please, no more.'

He ran his tongue lazily over the sensitivity of her inner thigh. 'Do you want me, Lily? All of me?'

She was mindless with that need. She knew that a hundred Mrs Lovells, and a dozen Judah Lovells, could now be outside on the riverbank, and she would not care. Only Giles existed for her at this moment in time.

'Lily?'

Her knees buckled as another wave of pleasure overwhelmed her, and she knew she would have fallen if Giles had not held her so tightly. 'Yes, I want you,' she gasped, her voice raw.

'Then you shall have me.' His eyes glittered in the gloom of the weeping willow as he moved to smooth his jacket on the ground before lowering her onto it. 'But first I have to kiss you,' he groaned before his mouth claimed hers.

Minutes, hours, days could have passed as Giles kissed her, lingering to play and stroke once that first hunger had been assuaged, the heat of his tongue seeking out every sweet curve of her lips and mouth, the smooth column of her throat, the slope of her breasts, allowing her the time to recover from his earlier onslaught, when he had been unwilling to give her respite as he brought her again and again to climax just so that he might hear her gasps of pleasure and mewling cries as she shuddered and trembled to completion.

Giles had never before known a woman who responded so readily, so completely, or gave that response so honestly. So much so that he ached to be inside her just so that he might hear those groans again as she reached orgasm.

'Will you help me take off the rest of my things?' He sat up to begin pulling off his boots, for once cursing his boot-maker for having made them such a perfect fit.

Lily chuckled huskily as she moved up on her haunches to aid him, completely unconcerned with her near-nakedness, and rendering Giles temporarily still as he gazed hungrily at the gentle sway of her bared breasts as she pulled off one boot after the other before her deft fingers moved to the fastening of his breeches.

She gasped slightly as she saw that last scar etched deep into his muscled thigh, her lips as soft and tender as butterfly wings against his puckered flesh.

Giles reached up to touch either side of her face. 'You truly are a wonder to me, Lily.' He kissed her again hungrily, only to break off that kiss as he felt her cool fingers close about him. His hands closed about those caressing fingers. 'Not this time, Lily. I—I am too far beyond control to hold,' he acknowledged gruffly as he gently pushed her back onto his jacket before moving over and between her parted thighs.

He rested on his arms as he paused to look down at her in the dappled darkness. He saw her dark curls, wild and wanton, about her bare shoulders. Her eyes were languid with longing. Her lips were full and swollen from his kisses. The dark triangle of her curls was a sharp contrast to the long length of him as he shifted to slowly guide himself into her.

'You will not get me with child as my father did my mother?'

Giles drew in a harsh and rasping breath at the

sound of her husky plea. 'No, I—I will be careful,' he assured her gruffly as he began to enter her inch by slow inch, the pleasure of it so overwhelming that Giles began to doubt his ability to control himself. 'Lily?' He looked down at her as he heard her sharply indrawn breath, very aware that there was still an equal amount not yet inside her. 'I do not want to hurt you—'

'I do not want you to stop!' She reached down to clasp his buttocks as he would have pulled back. 'It is only—' She shook her head. 'You feel so silky and smooth and yet so hard and big at the same time.'

It took every ounce of Giles's self-control to raise his head from looking down at their two joined bodies to instead look at Lily's face in an effort not to give in to the need he felt to thrust fully inside her, until he was totally surrounded by her moist heat. 'I am not hurting you?'

'No,' Lily assured, never having imagined that having a man inside her would feel like this, so full, so much pressure, the long length of him seeming like wood encased in velvet as he slowly entered her. 'Well, perhaps it feels a little…strange,' she conceded as he continued to look down at her. 'But I do not want you to stop.'

'Then we will go slowly. Very slowly,' he promised

gruffly. 'And if it becomes too much for you, then you must tell me and I will stop immediately.'

Lily was not sure that going slowly would ease the pressure building inside her; in fact, she was sure it would not. She knew only that she needed—wanted—something, and it only increased, intensified, at his slow and tortuous entry.

She gasped as she raised her legs and wrapped them about Giles's waist, lifting, bringing him fully into her and resulting in a momentary pain, a ripping, as that long and velvet length surged fully inside her, filling her completely. With a groan, Giles drove forward, touching something deep inside her, a place that had never been touched before, and which once again sent her spiralling up to that plateau of pleasure.

His eyes glittered in the darkness as he raised his head sharply. 'God, Lily!'

'Do not stop, Giles,' she pleaded, and her legs tightened about him as she began to move, working herself along his pulsing length and causing herself to quiver and contract. 'Please do not stop!'

Giles knew he would not have been able to stop if his life had depended upon it, groaning even as he lowered his head to take one tight nipple into his mouth as he plunged into her, again and again, not even the shock of knowing he had pierced Lily's innocence enough to bring him to his senses as she undulated rhythmically beneath him.

Only the remembrance of her earlier plea made him pull out as he felt her pulsing in orgasm at the same time as his own climax began to explode.

He let out a roar of ecstasy as his release burst from him, until he knew himself completely spent, and could only collapse against the heat of her breasts.

And only just in time, as the faint sound of voices—Mrs Lovell and her nephew returning from the village?—could once again be heard heading towards the river!

Chapter Fourteen

'And I thought I told ye not to mess with the lasses about here.' Mrs Lovell could be heard scolding her nephew as the voices drew closer. 'I'll have ye know that Mrs Hall is a respectable widow.'

'It's usually the respectable ones as is most grateful for a bit of attention!' Judah came back cheekily. ''Specially when they's as pretty as Mrs Hall.'

His aunt gave a disgusted snort. 'You'll meet your match one day, Judah-me-lad, mark my words, and it can't come soon enough for me. Now hold on to this here basket whilst I go and see if there's any mushrooms beneath this willow.'

Which was the only warning Lily and Giles had of Mrs Lovell pushing aside the willow branches and poking her head inside where they still lay together in a naked tangle!

Lily's eyes were wide with shock as she hurriedly reached out to pull Giles's discarded shirt over their nakedness before looking pleadingly across at the Gypsy woman.

Mrs Lovell seemed completely at a loss for words for several long seconds as she took in the scene before her, her expression one of open-mouthed incredulity. Then she clamped her lips together noisily before speaking weakly. 'No, it seems as if someone has been here before me....' She ducked quickly back out of the branches—hopefully before her nephew could catch a glimpse of Lily and Giles entwined together. 'Let's get along, boy, I has things to do back at the yag. And I reckon some young lady might be along later to collect her bonnet and gloves,' she added pointedly, followed by the sound of them both making their way along the riverbank.

Lily was unsure if she had even remembered to breathe, for what had seemed to last for hours could in reality have only been a few brief seconds. She was now absolutely mortified that Mrs Lovell should have found her and Giles in such a compromising position.

'What are you doing?' Giles could only stare up at Lily in confusion as she slipped quickly out of his arms before standing to begin hurriedly collecting up her clothes.

She pulled her chemise on over her head before releasing the long cascade of her hair from the neckline. 'Surely it is obvious?'

Giles sat up to rest his arm on one bent knee. 'You cannot just dress and leave as if nothing has happened!'

'I must leave now if I am to go and retrieve my bonnet and gloves from Mrs Lovell before returning to the vicarage in time for luncheon.' She shook out her gown before stepping into it and pulling it up over her arms to settle it on her shoulders before reaching back to refasten the buttons. 'And now that she has—has discovered the two of us together, I feel that I really should go and offer her at least some sort of explanation for—for what she has just witnessed.' Her face was very pale in the sun-dappled gloom.

'Would you like me to come with you?'

'Certainly not!' She turned to protest forcefully. 'It will be…awkward enough, without having you present too!'

Giles stood up abruptly. 'We need to talk before you leave—'

'Did you not hear me just say that I have to go immediately if I am to visit Mrs Lovell and return home in time to eat luncheon with my father?' Lily avoided meeting Giles's gaze as she stepped away to smooth her crumpled gown in preparation for emerging from what she had thought to be the privacy of the willow branches.

'I heard you.' His hands reached out to grasp her shoulders as she would have turned to leave. 'Look at me, Lily,' he instructed firmly. 'I said look at me!' He shook her slightly as she instead kept her gaze levelled on the silky dark hair covering his scarred and naked chest. A naked chest which Lily had so enjoyed kissing and caressing only minutes ago....

But to raise her gaze to look at Giles's face would, she knew, be to see the condemnation of his expression, and to look down lower, to where his shaft was still visibly semi-aroused against his body, would be even more embarrassing.

How did one usually go about bringing an end to an encounter such as theirs had been? Lily had no experience upon which to base her actions; she only knew she found the aftermath of their spent passion to be awkward in the extreme.

Her closest friends were Lady Kate and Lady Phaedra, the three women often confiding in one another, but once again Lily knew she absolutely could not discuss this with either of them!

She shook her head. 'As I am sure Mrs Lovell is only too well aware, it would only give rise to speculation if I were to return home without my bonnet and gloves. Surely we can talk another time, if you really feel we must.'

His fingers tightened painfully on her shoulders. 'Oh, I definitely feel that we must!' he grated forcefully. 'What on earth did you think you were doing?' he added exasperatedly as he gave her another shake. 'Damn it, Lily, did you not think it might be important to inform me that…that I would be your first lover?'

'And why should I have told you that?' Lily did look up at him now, her gaze wary.

'Because I could have hurt you. More than I obviously did,' he added.

'I am not hurt, Giles,' she assured softly. 'You were…extremely considerate with me.' Once again she could not meet his gaze. 'I…enjoyed the experience very much.' She had more than enjoyed it; for her, it had been a life-changing experience. But in such a way that she could not even bear to think about it now, let alone discuss it with this angrily impatient Giles.

'You enjoyed—!' Giles stared down at her in exasperation, still reeling from the shock of knowing that minutes ago he had taken Lily's innocence. He had thought— Had assumed— Her enthusiastic response to his lovemaking, four days ago as well as today, had led him to believe…

What had it led him to believe? That he had been right about her character all along, and that Lily had taken other lovers before him?

Their actions today had shown him that those thoughts, beliefs and assumptions had been mistaken.

He should have known, should have guessed the truth, when their conversation earlier today had succeeded in eliminating each and every one of the men living locally with whom Lily might possibly have been intimately involved in the past. His brother Edward. Sir Nathan. Even that rascal Judah Lovell.

Yes, Giles should have realised the truth of Lily's innocence, but he had not, and now she—

'I have no idea what you are thinking behind that fierce scowl.' Lily looked up at him warily in the dappled darkness. 'But I trust that whatever it is, you do not intend to make any more foul or false accusations…?'

Giles could feel the tension in her shoulders, as if she were preparing for a verbal blow. A blow she obviously expected him to deliver. 'Why?' he groaned huskily instead.

She blinked long dark lashes. 'Why what?'

He frowned. 'Why me?'

She breathed softly. 'I do not understand.'

'You must!' Giles could feel the rapid beat of her

pulse beneath his fingertips as he looked search-ingly into her eyes. 'You are young and beautiful. Desirable—'

'And totally unsuited to being anything more than wife to a man such as Sir Nathan Samuelson, or mis-tress to a man of my own choosing,' she finished bluntly. 'I chose you.'

'You wish to take up the offer of becoming my mis-tress?' Giles echoed incredulously.

In truth, Lily had not thought beyond the here and now, beneath this willow with Giles. And, her own emotions aside—and the awkwardness of being dis-covered by Mrs Lovell—she could not in truth feel regret for the choice she had made.

Well…she could perhaps have wished the embar-rassment of their present conversation had not oc-curred.

Her own emotions were something Lily would have plenty of time—hours, days, weeks, months ahead!—in which she might consider the folly of not having come to a realisation of those feelings earlier.

For Giles's part, she had no cause for complaint; as she had already stated, he had proven to be consider-ate as well as passionate in his attentions towards her. Everything and more, in fact, that any woman might wish for in a lover.

As the pleasurable ache between Lily's thighs surely testified!

She straightened. 'Could we not just agree that we both...enjoyed our time together, and leave it at that?'

'No, we damn well—!' Giles broke off his ferocious outburst as he saw the way Lily flinched at his vehemence. 'Lily—' he deliberately gentled his tone '—surely you cannot expect to...to give me your innocence, and then just walk away as if nothing has occurred?'

'Why can I not?'

'Because—' Once again Giles had to make a deliberate effort to bite back his frustration with Lily's calm composure. A composure he found all the more baffling because of his own lack of it! 'I cannot talk to you when I am not even dressed!' He moved to gather up his drawers, cursing under his breath as he pulled them on. 'Damn it, Lily, can you not see that we at least must discuss what will happen now!' He straightened impatiently.

'I have told you of my intention to go and collect my bonnet and gloves from Mrs Lovell—'

'I did not mean literally!' Giles glared.

Lily knew that, of course; she would just rather the two of them did not have this conversation, particularly now. Facing the curious Mrs Lovell already promised to be embarrassing enough! She also felt a little discomforted and damp between her thighs, and her legs were feeling decidedly unsteady.

There was also, she realised, a heaviness where her heart should be....

None of which she wished to reveal to this impatiently angry man who was the cause of that discomfort! 'I do not have time for this now, Giles.'

'When do you expect you will have time for it?' he cut in harshly.

Never, if Lily had her way. 'Do you regret what happened?'

His face darkened. 'Of course I regret it!'

Lily flinched at his vehemence. 'Then there is nothing more to be said.' She held her shoulders stiffly.

His expression softened. 'Lily—'

'If you will excuse me?' She avoided the hand he lifted with the obvious intention of grasping her arm. 'I have Mrs Lovell to visit, and lunch to eat with my father.' In her present mood, it would probably choke her! 'And this afternoon I still have several things to do ahead of the well-dressing celebrations.' Her back was straight and uninviting as she moved the branches of the willow aside.

Giles's expression was pained as he stood bare-chested beneath the shadows of the willow, knowing the evidence of their lovemaking was unmistakable for any who cared to look at Lily; her ebony curls fell in a loose tangle down the length of her spine, there was a slightly dreamy look to her eyes, and her lips looked full and a little swollen. There was also a slight redness to the skin visible above the scooped neck-line of her gown, no doubt caused by the stubble upon Giles's chin. 'Lily, please—'

'Goodbye, Giles.' She spared him a last cursory glance before setting out along the riverbank, no doubt in the direction of Mrs Lovell's campsite.

Giles cursed the fact that he could not follow her without causing a scandal if he were seen by anyone dressed only in his breeches and with his own hair no doubt in disarray.

Instead he returned to collect the rest of his clothes, only to bestow instead a frustrated punch of his fist into the trunk of the tree, uncaring—welcoming, even—the pain of the cuts and grazes he received to his knuckles for his trouble.

If Lily seriously thought this was an end to their conversation then she was in for a sharp awakening!

Lily did not, as she had said she would, go straight to Mrs Lovell's campsite. The tears that fell hotly down her cheeks prevented her from being in anyone's company for some time after she had left Giles. Instead she managed to stumble blindly a safe distance away from the willow tree, making sure she was off the main path and collapsing beneath a tall oak, before allowing the deep sobs to rack her body.

Giles was quite correct to ask her what on earth she had thought she was doing!

Had she really thought that she might behave as so many gentlemen did, by taking her pleasure with Giles, without consequence? Oh, not the consequence of an unwanted pregnancy; she believed Giles when he assured her there would be no consequences of that nature. But had she really believed that she could make love with him and her emotions would remain unengaged?

Had she not realised that her emotions must already be engaged for her to wish to make love with Giles in the first place?

If she had not, then she was a fool. A blind, stupid fool.

Because now she knew beyond a shadow of doubt that she had fallen in love with Giles Montague!

No girlish infatuation—she was far too old for that—but a deep and abiding love.

In these past few hours she had come to admire everything about him: his deep love for his family; his obvious bravery as a soldier; his caring and consideration for the people who lived and worked on the Castonbury estate, despite his earlier reluctance to assume his role as heir, even including the comfort and well-being of the transitory Mrs Lovell. And as for his looks…!

Lily had only to gaze upon Giles's harshly chiselled features and firmly muscled body for her pulse to race and her skin to feel hot and fevered!

What must he think of her now?

Did Giles hate and despise her for being the temptress he had thought her to be a year ago? More so, perhaps, because she had ultimately displayed that wantonness with him?

How would she ever be able to face him again knowing how he must now despise her?

She could not.

She would not!

She must find a way to leave Castonbury in the near future, and it must be in such a way that her father would find acceptable. For Lily would not, could not, remain in Castonbury and suffer the pain of seeing on a daily basis how Giles must now feel towards her.

Mrs Lovell looked up from poking her fire as Lily silently entered the campsite some minutes later, her sharp gaze roving critically over Lily's dishevelled appearance. 'Sit ye down, lass, an' I'll brew some tea.'

Lily cast a wary look at Judah as he lazed on the other side of the fire. 'I really cannot stop—'

'I said sit ye down, lass. You, boy.' She turned to her nephew. 'Take the pail and go and collect some fresh water for the tea.'

He rose languidly to his feet, his dark gaze fixed questioningly on Lily. 'You look just like—'

'And is it for you to comment on how a lady does or doesn't look?' His aunt gave him a disapproving glare.

His handsome face flushed resentfully. 'I was only saying—'

'Well, don't.' Mrs Lovell thrust the bucket at him.

Judah seemed distracted as he slowly took the bucket, his narrowed gaze still fixed on Lily as she stood at the edge of the campsite. 'She looks different with her 'air down like that. Almost as if she might be one of u—'

'Will you just go and get the water, Judah Lovell, afore I clip yer ear for the second time today!' his aunt rounded on him fiercely.

Judah shot his aunt a resentful glare. 'I'm going, ain't I?'

'Not as quick as I'd like, no.' Mrs Lovell watched her nephew until he had sauntered well out of earshot.

'Sit ye down, lass.' She turned to Lily. 'Before ye fall down,' she added firmly as she straightened to collect up mugs for the tea.

Lily sat. Or rather, she collapsed weakly onto one of the logs upended beside the fireside, but unable to feel any of the warmth emitted by its flames. It caused her to wonder if the ice about her heart was not taking over her whole body. She moistened dry lips before speaking. 'I am sorry for being the cause of discord between you and your nephew—'

'Ye ain't,' the old lady assured her bluntly. 'I hadn't set eyes on him for twenty years until he turned up here again—nor wanted to—and the sooner he goes off again about his own business the better I shall like it.' Her expression was grim as she picked up a cloth to lift the kettle from over the fire.

Lily blinked as the elderly lady poured the boiling water into the waiting teapot. 'But I thought you sent Judah for more water?'

'Menfolk has no place in our conversation. 'Specially ones as nosey as Judah.' Mrs Lovell frowned her disapproval in the direction her nephew had taken to the riverside.

Lily chewed on her bottom lip. 'I am sorry for—for what you saw earlier.'

'Here's your bonnet, gloves and hairpins.' Mrs

Lovell placed them beside Lily as she handed her a steaming mug of the hastily brewed tea. 'Drink that down ye, lass, and maybe you'll feel a little better.'

Lily gave a choked and humourless laugh. 'I somehow doubt that, Mrs Lovell.'

'Nothing's ever as bad as ye think it is.' The elderly lady made herself comfortable on the stool facing Lily across the fire, her sharp gaze fixed on Lily's face.

'I believe this might possibly be worse, so much worse, than I think it is!' she assured emotionally, but sipped her tea obediently anyway. But she could not taste the brew, nor did she feel any melting of that inner ice.

Mrs Lovell eyed her curiously. 'Do ye love him?'

Lily glanced up and then as quickly looked away again as she saw the speculation in the other woman's curiously sharp gaze. 'Would a more pertinent question not be what Lord Giles's feelings might now be towards me?' She would not insult the elderly lady by even attempting to pretend she did not know exactly to whom Mrs Lovell was referring.

'It's obvious to anyone with eyes in their head that he's fond of ye.' The older woman gave a dismissive snort. 'And that you're fond of him. You'd have to be stupid as well as blind not to see the way the two of

ye were looking at each other when ye were here together a couple of days past.'

'No—'

'Oh, yes,' the older woman confirmed with satisfaction. 'So what's got you so upset about it all that
you're as white as a ghost?'

Lily gave a rueful shake of her head. 'Do you really
need to ask me that?'

'Well, as long as there'll be no chivvy as a result—'

'There will not,' Lily assured hastily.

Mrs Lovell nodded. 'Then I would say that the two
of you were only doing what comes naturally.'

Lily gave a slightly bitter laugh. 'My behaviour
today has been shocking, Mrs Lovell. Absolutely scandalous.' She trembled slightly as she avoided meeting
that shrewd hazel-coloured gaze. 'I do not suppose
you would care for a travelling companion when you
leave Castonbury? No, I do not suppose you would.'
She answered her own question dully as the elderly
woman looked taken aback by the request. 'I am afraid
I have been extremely stupid, Mrs Lovell, and must
now find some way in which to salvage a scrap of my
pride, at least.'

'Well, you won't succeed in doing that by running
away.' The older woman tutted disapprovingly. 'And

for what it's worth, whatever you did ye weren't alone when ye did it.'

No, Lily certainly had not been alone when she had behaved so shamelessly. If she had been alone, then it would not have been so shameless! 'I am afraid that sort of—of behaviour may be acceptable for a gentleman, but it is certainly not the case for a single lady.'

'I got no time for such nonsense,' Mrs Lovell scorned.

Lily, unfortunately, did not have that same freedom of choice. Something she should surely have thought of before making love with Giles! Maybe she had thought of it, but at the time had just not cared? However, it had been a rash moment she would no doubt have plenty of time to regret during the coming days and weeks!

Her more immediate problem was to find some way—although goodness knew how it was to be found—of getting through the next few days at least, without finding herself alone again in Giles's company. Something which, Lily knew, with the well-dressing celebrations to take place at Castonbury Park in two days' time, was going to be extremely difficult to achieve.

'Would you like me to help ye rearrange your pretty hair?'

Lily gave a pained wince at the kindness she heard

in Mrs Lovell's gentle tone. 'I would, thank you.' She distractedly gathered up her hair and coiled it up onto her crown.

The older woman moved round the fire to begin putting in the pins to hold it in place. 'I can't believe— Lord Giles is a good man. An honourable man…'

'Oh, he is,' Lily assured hastily, having seen the genuine fondness between Giles and the elderly Romany on her previous visit here.

'Then I don't see what the problem is.' Mrs Lovell moved back to her seat on the opposite side of the fire.

Lily imagined that life must be so much simpler for Mrs Lovell, stopping to camp when and where she liked, travelling on when she became bored or restless, eating and sleeping to no other clock but her own.

Unfortunately Lily's life was not the same, the stigma of her birth having already given her a precarious position socially, as well as having attached preconceived expectations to her character. Expectations which she had surely only confirmed with her behaviour today with Giles.

'I am sure you are right, and I am worrying unnecessarily.' She stood up dismissively. 'I really must go now, my dear Mrs Lovell. But I will see you at Castonbury Park for the well-dressing?'

'Ye will. But—'

'I really must make haste.' Lily secured her bonnet about her now-tidy hair. 'Father will be expecting me.' She hurried off before Mrs Lovell had a chance to say anything further.

With any luck, by the time she returned to the vicarage Giles would already have been back to collect Genghis and would by now be safely on his way to Castonbury Park.

Chapter Fifteen

It did not take a glance into Mrs Lovell's crystal ball—if indeed she possessed one—for Giles to realise that Lily was deliberately avoiding him. That she had been successfully avoiding him for the whole of the two days since they had made love together beneath the willow.

Not that Giles had too many hours to spend brooding over the reasons for that. He had found the time to visit the vicarage yesterday, only to learn that Lily was not at home, and so he had spent an hour talking with Mr Seagrove instead. Otherwise Giles's attentions had been completely taken up by the problem of the increasingly pressing financial situation now besetting the whole of the Montague family. A problem his father seemed to have chosen to ignore by once again withdrawing to his rooms and retreating into silence.

Giles had paid another visit to the lawyers on the day following his lovemaking with Lily, after which he had been forced to once again send word to his man in London to advance more of his personal funds.

But the letter which had been delivered to him earlier this morning, if it should prove to be genuine, made all of those other problems pale into insignificance!

None of which Giles could allow, or would allow, to be seen during the well-dressing celebrations. His instructions to Mrs Stratton, as well as Monsieur André, were that all arrangements for those celebrations were to proceed with the Duke of Rothermere's usual largesse.

But beneath all of those other problems was still the knowledge that Lily was deliberately avoiding him.

Even now, on the day of the well-dressing, she had managed to stay away from him by keeping herself busy outside in the garden, helping to put up the tables and chairs, as well as preparing the numerous stalls necessary for the celebrations later today.

It did not please Giles in the least that when he did finally chance to meet up with her it was in the company of that charming rascal Judah Lovell!

The two of them appeared to be arranging the covers over the poles for the tent where Mrs Lovell was to do her fortune-telling; Lily was laughing softly at something the young, handsome and—damn him— flirtatious Romany had just said to her.

That humour faded the moment she looked up and saw Giles standing several feet away watching the two of them. 'Lord Montague.' Her curtsey was as formal as her words, her gaze lowered demurely.

His mouth tightened as he nodded in curt acknowledgement of her greeting. 'Lily.' His gaze was icy as he turned to the younger man. 'I wonder if you would mind leaving us for a few moments so that I might talk privately to Miss Seagrove?'

'Sure an' that's up to Lily 'erself, don't ye think?' Judah's expression bordered on the insolent as he met Giles's gaze in open challenge.

Giles's eyes narrowed upon hearing Judah refer to Lily by her Christian name, his voice dangerously soft. 'Whether you choose to go or stay is your own decision, surely.' The threat in his tone was unmistakable.

Judah held his gaze for several seconds longer before he turned to look down at Lily. 'What do you think, Lily?'

What Lily thought was that the tension between the two men was palpable, so much so that she was forced to repress a shiver of apprehension as she looked from one to the other and saw the unspoken challenge as their gazes met and clashed.

Having managed to avoid seeing Giles for the past two days, she had no wish to speak with him now, either privately or in the company of others, but the contest for her attention was such that she was sure only her acquiescence to Giles's request would succeed in putting an end to it without the possibility of blood being shed. 'Perhaps, if Mr Lovell does not mind continuing on alone for a few minutes, the two of us might stroll about the garden together, Lord Montague.' She gave a gracious bow of her head as she preceded Giles in the direction of one of the rose beds.

She was so aware of Giles, as he first walked behind her and then at her side as he easily caught up with her, his strides being so much longer than her own.

The past two days had been nothing short of purgatory for Lily.

Not only had she gone out of her way to avoid any situation in which she might find herself face to face with Giles, but as he had also warned, her father had spoken to her concerning Sir Nathan's interest. An interest she had no hesitation in assuring her father she did not, and would not ever, return. That her father had been relieved by her answer she had no doubt, but he had also felt duty bound to point out the advantages of such a marriage.

And all the time he had done so Lily had been aware of the fact that not only was such an alliance wholly repugnant to her, but coming so soon after her lovemaking with Giles, it was now also totally out of the question for her to accept a proposal of marriage from any gentleman, repugnant or otherwise.

Leading her to question whether she had not consciously known that all along, and if it had not contributed to her recklessness that day.... Certainly she could no longer offer herself to any decent man as an innocent bride.

'Are you well?'

She glanced sideways at Giles upon hearing his softly spoken query, but was unable to read any of his thoughts from the remoteness of his expression.

This did not stop Lily from being wholly appreciative of his handsome ensemble. He wore a dark grey superfine over a paler waistcoat and white linen, with dove-grey breeches and black Hessians, his dark hair having been blown across his brow by the warmth of the light breeze.

She turned away from that breathtaking handsomeness. 'I am very well, thank you, Lord Montague. And you?'

'As well as can be expected when my lover calls me "Lord Montague" in that cold tone and has been avoiding my company for two days!'

Lily gasped softly at the directness of Giles's attack, colour burning her cheeks as she came to an abrupt halt in order to glare up at him. 'How dare you speak to me of such things here?' she hissed fiercely, very aware of the dozens of other people milling around the gardens and grounds of Castonbury Park, all helping to prepare for this afternoon's celebrations.

'Where else should I speak of them, when I have not so much as managed to set eyes upon you?' he came back unapologetically.

Lily turned to glare at him, the warmth of her embarrassment still high in her cheeks. 'I believe it would be best for all concerned if you did not speak of it at all, but rather tried to forget it ever happened!'

'And is that what you have been attempting to do?'

'We were not talking about my feelings on the matter!'

'Oh, no, Lily, this avoidance really will not do at all.' Giles shook his head, more than pleased to have her full attention, no matter what the reason.

She had looked pale when he had approached her earlier, the grey of her gown doing little to add to that colour, but the angry blush now in her cheeks, and the glitter in those clear green eyes as she glared up at him, made her appear more like the beautiful woman he had made love to beneath the willow.

'Do you really imagine that I could ever forget— ever want to forget—our lovemaking, Lily?' he prompted huskily.

Her hands were clasped tightly together in front of her. 'I wish that you would try!'

Giles gave a pained wince at her vehemence. 'Why?'

'Because—' She gave a disbelieving shake of her head. 'You said that you regretted what had happened.'

His eyes narrowed. 'Are you saying you now regret it too?'

She glared her exasperation. 'Has my avoidance of you since not indicated as much?'

Giles looked down searchingly into the beauty of her face—dark lashes surrounding those extraordinary green eyes, her small nose, those wide, lush lips above a small and determined chin. It was a face which had haunted Giles's days as well as his nights since they had last met. 'I regret very much taking your innocence, Lily,' he told her softly. 'But it is only the timing I regret, not the deed itself.'

'You talk in riddles!'

'Do I?'

Lily gave an agitated shake of her head. 'I do

not have the time to deal with your mockery today, Giles—'

'And if it is not mockery?' he prompted huskily. 'If my reason for wanting to see you again was so that I might ask if you would consider becoming my wife?'

Lily's gaze flew to his face, her expression startled. She saw only that same wide forehead, dark brows over grey eyes, high cheekbones either side of the arrogant slash of a nose, his lips sculptured perfection above a stubbornly relentless jaw.

Except…

There was something different about his eyes. A softness? An uncertainty, perhaps?

If that was so, then it was a softness and uncertainty which did not in the least detract from the fact that he must once again be mocking her!

She shook her head. 'The silly cat may look at a king, my lord, may perhaps even make love with him, but never any more than that.' She turned away with the intention of returning to her previous task.

Only to have her arm firmly grasped by Giles's fingers as he halted that departure. 'You are referring to yourself as a silly cat?'

'What else?' She sighed her impatience with his persistence. 'You are Lord Montague, and heir to the Duke of Rothermere, and I am merely the vicar's adopted daughter, an abandoned child of questionable parentage at best.'

'And the heir to the Duke of Rothermere may marry where and with whom he wishes!'

'And a sensible heir would never wish to find himself married to the penniless adopted daughter of the parish vicar!'

Giles mouth twisted as he thought of the state of his family's finances, and the letter he had received earlier that morning. 'We may be more equal in that than you can ever imagine, Lily.'

'Somehow I doubt it very much!'

He frowned. 'Does that mean you would not even consider me if I were to offer you marriage?'

'So that you might once again accuse me of plotting and planning such an outcome? I think not, Giles!' Lily eyed him scathingly.

'I offer no such accusations—'

'Then perhaps that will come later!' She gave an impatient shake of her head. 'Now if you are quite finished playing with the cat, my lord, she is wishful of returning to help prepare for the celebrations later today.' She gave his restraining fingers about her arm a pointed look.

If Giles had needed any further confirmation of Lily's lack of deception in regard to her reasons for making love with him—which he did not—then her refusal to even take seriously his offer of marriage left him in no doubt as to her innocence; the designing and scheming woman he had once believed her to be would have had no hesitation in greedily accepting even the suggestion of a proposal of marriage from the future Duke of Rothermere!

He drew in a harsh breath. 'Mr Seagrove informed me, when I called at the vicarage yesterday, that you have refused any suggestion of a marriage between yourself and Sir Nathan Samuelson.'

Her chin rose. 'And is that why you have chosen to hint at an offer of marriage yourself today? Because you wished to bedevil and taunt me with the possibility of it?'

Giles searched the proud beauty of her face. 'Does the possibility bedevil and taunt you, Lily?'

It did, more than Lily would ever allow Giles to see, when she knew an offer of marriage from him was much like an elusive and beautiful butterfly, fluttering just beyond her reach, beguiling and tempting her to scoop it up in her hands and hold it tightly to her, only to find when she opened up her fingers that her hands were empty.

'No, it does not,' she answered him flatly. 'I have not now, nor will I ever, have any desire to receive a marriage proposal from you, let alone trouble myself giving an answer to it. Now, if you will excuse me?' She looked at him haughtily. 'As I have said, I still have much work to do.'

Giles slowly uncurled his fingers from about her arm, remaining beside the rose bed as Lily instantly turned and walked back in the direction of where she had been working earlier with Judah Lovell.

He had not dared to imagine what Lily's reaction might be to the suggestion of marriage between the two of them, but he had hoped—he had certainly hoped—that it might be favourable. To have the first proposal of marriage he had ever made in his life thrown back in his face without thought or consideration would have been humiliating if Giles did not find it so amusing at the same time.

A burst of laughter overtook him as he gave in to that amusement; Lily was, without a shadow of a doubt, the most unpredictable, beautiful and enchanting woman he had ever met. Or ever hoped to meet....

And if she believed their conversation over in regard to a marriage between the two of them, then she was very much mistaken.

'—cannot imagine what has happened to Mrs Lovell, can you?' Mrs Stratton frowned as she looked pointedly towards the line of people from the village already gathered outside the tent where the elderly Romany should have been waiting to begin telling their fortunes.

Should have been waiting, because as Lily and the housekeeper of Castonbury Park could clearly see, Mrs Lovell had not as yet arrived at the celebrations. Lily had not expected her to attend the well-dressing ceremonies—she never had in the past—but she never missed the party afterwards. 'She assured me that she would be here in time....' Lily voiced her own concern. 'I wonder what can have happened to delay her?'

Hannah Stratton shook her head. 'Shall I send one of the maids over to check, do you think?'

Lily placed a reassuring hand on the older woman's arm. 'I will go myself.' In truth, she would welcome the time such a task might enable her to spend away from the crowd of people milling about the gardens of the estate. And from the overwhelming presence of Giles Montague, especially....

She had assisted her father earlier during the ceremonies at the three wells in the village, murmured polite approval to Mrs Crutchley as to the splendour of the floral arrangements at each of the wells, invented amusement for some of the village children when they had become a little restless—and all of that time been completely aware of Giles as he stood attentively at her father's other side in representation of the Montague family.

Indeed, his appearance, in blue velvet and grey silk, had been of such magnificence that Lily challenged any woman, in love with him or otherwise, not to be affected by such a proud display of male elegance!

Certainly Lily had been far from immune to such splendour, her gaze returning again and again to the arresting handsomeness of Giles's face, as she looked at him from beneath the brim of her cream bonnet which she had prettied up with the same dark green ribbon which adorned the high waist of the new moss-green gown she had made especially for the occasion.

At the time of choosing the material and ribbon for the new gown—a mere two weeks ago, although it seemed so much longer!—Lily knew she had done so in the hopes of impressing Giles. A forlorn hope now, if ever there was one!

Nevertheless, Lily had chosen to wear her new gown anyway, aware that she was in need of all the self-confidence she possessed if she were to get through the rest of the day.

She could see him across the garden even now, as he talked with his father, who had decided to make a brief appearance in order to welcome everyone to his home. Giles looked so handsome and aristocratic next to his much frailer father. A breathtaking and disturbing handsomeness which Lily would indeed welcome escaping from, if only for the short time it took her to find and bring back Mrs Lovell.

'I will not be long.' She smiled reassuringly at Mrs Stratton now. 'With any luck, I may meet Mrs Lovell coming along the towpath.'

'Let us hope so.' The housekeeper nodded distractedly as she obviously spotted something occurring in the tea tent not to her liking or satisfaction.

Lily took advantage of that distraction to hurry away, slipping quietly from the throng of people towards the direction of Mrs Lovell's campsite.

'Have you seen Miss Seagrove?' Giles frowned his displeasure as he stood beside Mrs Stratton, having spent the past hour escorting his father about the garden, then returning the exhausted duke to his rooms and the attentions of Smithins. He now found himself free to seek out and speak to Lily, only to discover she was nowhere to be found in the gardens or the kitchens, and no one he had questioned had seen her either.

Giles had been fully aware of Lily's efforts to avoid conversation with him during the well-dressing ceremonies this afternoon—indeed, each time he had so much as dared a glance at her, she had quickly turned away in an effort not to meet his gaze. And if she had now decided to absent herself from the celebrations at Castonbury Park as another means of avoiding him, then Giles very much feared he would have to go to the vicarage and bring her back here by force, if necessary!

Everyone he and his father had spoken to as the two of them moved slowly amongst their guests had only complimentary words to describe how capably Lily had organised today's event, and the last thing Giles wanted was to deprive her of the enjoyment of all her hard work because she felt such a pressing need to avoid his own company.

'She went to look for Mrs Lovell—' Mrs Stratton glanced down at the fob watch pinned on the white collar lapel of her black gown. 'Oh, dear, I had not noticed how the time had flown by, but I believe it is now more than an hour since Lily left to seek out the Gypsy woman. What do you think could have happened to delay them both?' She frowned.

Giles had no idea, but he certainly intended on finding out. Especially after a narrow-eyed glance about the milling crowds showed that Judah Lovell was not currently present amongst the guests either! 'Do not concern yourself, my dear Mrs Stratton.' He smiled reassuringly at the housekeeper. 'I am sure that all will be well.'

'Perhaps Mrs Lovell has fallen ill? Do you think perhaps I ought to accompany you?' She looked flustered at the mere idea of abandoning her duties here.

Giles patted her arm reassuringly. 'I am sure you have quite enough to do, Mrs Stratton, without concerning yourself about this matter too,' he assured dismissively.

'Well…I do still have to oversee the entrance of Monsieur André's delicious cakes and delicacies.'

'Then do not let me delay you, Mrs Stratton.' Giles nodded approvingly, keeping his smile firmly fixed in place until the housekeeper had hurried away to cluck over the French chef's confectionaries, his expression only becoming grim as he turned to stride off in the direction of Mrs Lovell's campsite.

The whole way there he knew that if he discovered that rascal Judah Lovell anywhere within Lily's vicinity, he was like to turn violent with jealousy!

The scene that met Giles's gaze when he reached Mrs Lovell's campsite seemed to imply that someone had already beaten him to those feelings of violence.

Mrs Lovell's belongings were scattered haphazardly about the clearing—furniture and utensils thrown from the brightly coloured caravan and lying broken, clothes and other fabrics ripped into unrecognisable rags; even the fire, which Giles knew was never allowed to go out, lay in a heap of cold ashes in the centre of all the other chaos.

But he could see no sign of Lily, or Mrs Lovell or even Judah Lovell.

It took Giles some minutes more to realise that Judah's much shabbier caravan and horse were no longer parked alongside his aunt's....

Chapter Sixteen

Lily lay with her hands and feet tied, a dirty handkerchief stuffed in her mouth. She had been bundled into the back of a not very clean Gypsy caravan, and the lurching movement of that vehicle only seconds later gave testament to it being driven away from the campsite at great speed. What was happening to her?

One minute she had been standing looking in astonishment at the shambles that was Mrs Lovell's campsite, and wondering where on earth that elderly lady could be, and the next Lily had found herself grabbed from behind, a rope quickly tied about her wrists, before she was turned to face her captor.

Judah Lovell!

'What—'

'There's no time for talking now.' His expression had been grimly determined as he'd pulled a filthy handkerchief from the pocket of his baggy trousers and pushed it into her mouth.

Lily gagged at the taste and smell of that ragged piece of material, her eyes starting to water, but whether from the smell or shocked tears, she was unsure.

Cruel humour glittered in those dark eyes as the young Romany saw her response. 'Not what you're used to, is it, missy? Never mind, we'll soon 'ave plenty of gold for ye to buy a dozen new silk 'andkerchiefs if ye want 'em! In the meantime—' he turned Lily roughly and pushed her towards the back of his caravan '—we'd best be away from 'ere smartish, afore someone—probably that snooty Lord as keeps sniffing about your drawers—decides to come looking for you.'

Giles? He was referring in that derogatory way to Lord Giles Montague? The man that Lily loved with all her heart....

'Thought I didn't notice how cosy the two of you were, aye?' Judah had eyed her tauntingly as he bundled her inside his caravan and tied her feet together with another piece of rope. 'Never mind, you'll forget 'im soon as you 'ave me between your legs, and then we'll see who's the better man!'

Lily had no doubt as to who was the better man as

she kicked out with furious indignation, but Judah only pushed her the rest of the way inside his caravan.

He laughed cruelly as he saw how easily he managed to suppress that show of anger. 'Don't you worry, lass, I likes 'em feisty!' The door had been closed, shutting Lily into complete darkness.

And here she had remained, being bounced uncomfortably against the bare wooden floor for what seemed like hours, but was in all probability only half an hour or so, all the time hoping that snooty lord would indeed realise she had gone missing and come looking for her.

'Well, don't just stand there looking, lad, untie me!' Mrs Lovell glared up.

Giles had no idea how long he had been standing lost in shocked disbelief at the destruction all around him, when he heard the sound of a groan coming from the other side of Mrs Lovell's brightly coloured caravan, his years of battle instantly telling him that it was a moan of pain. Striding hurriedly about the caravan he had come across Mrs Lovell, seated on the ground, her wrists tied to the huge wooden wheel of the caravan, the blood and bruising about her face indicative of the violence she had suffered.

He moved quickly down onto one knee now, to

begin untying the bonds about her wrists, his expression coldly grim as the elderly lady gave another groan of pain. 'Who did this to you? Whoever it was I will see that they are—'

'Never you mind about me.' Mrs Lovell winced as she slowly lowered her hands, the unnatural position of two of the fingers on her left hand indicating that they might be broken. The split on her swollen bottom lip made her words slightly slurred. 'He's taken Lily—'

'Who has taken Lily?' Giles sat abruptly back on his haunches, his eyes turning glacial.

'Who do you think has taken her?' The elderly woman got awkwardly to her feet with Giles's hand beneath her elbow—the only part of her that did not seem to be bruised or broken! 'That black-hearted, no good, thieving, son of a murdering—'

'Your nephew?' Giles removed his handkerchief from his pocket and moved hastily to the bucket of water, dampening the silk material before wiping away the worst of the blood on Mrs Lovell's face. 'Are you saying that Lily has gone with Judah Lovell?'

The old lady looked up at him with eyes as sharp and dark as a bird's. 'Lily wouldn't go anywhere willingly with that evil—'

Giles stilled. 'You are saying that Lily has been kidnapped by your nephew?'

'Tied up and bundled into the back of his vardo is what she's been!' Mrs Lovell, obviously tired of his careful dabbing at her cuts and bruises, grabbed the handkerchief from his hand and impatiently wiped the blood away herself.

Giles eyes narrowed as he saw the amount of swelling and bruising the elderly lady had suffered. 'Those look like the result of someone's fists.'

Her mouth set determinedly. 'Oh, don't you worry, laddie, he'll be made to pay for every one o' these hurts when I next sees him. In the meantime, you'd best go after him. Now. Afore any real harm befalls Lily.'

'Explain, if you please.' The years Giles had spent as an officer in the army were the only thing preventing him from reaching out and shaking Mrs Lovell within an inch of her life, and if she did not soon explain to him when and for what reason Judah had tied Lily up and taken her away with him, then he would forget those years of training and give in to his instincts.

'There's no time for that now,' the elderly woman snapped her impatience. 'It's enough for you to know he's taken Lily against her will, heading Buxton way, and that he means to marry her as soon as possible.'

Giles staggered a step back. 'Marry her!'

'Thought that might get your attention.' Mrs Lovell

eyed him knowingly. 'Yes, he means to marry her. But she don't want to marry him. So if you want to put a stop to it you'd best follow on pretty smartish. 'Cos once he's made her his wife there'll be no stopping him. Now go and get that big horse of your'n and get after him. Now!' she added grimly.

Giles still had absolutely no idea why Judah Lovell should have taken Lily, or why he meant to marry her; it was enough for now to know that she had not gone willingly. 'You will be all right alone here whilst I am gone?'

Mrs Lovell gave a grimace. 'I don't know of anyone else as wants to punch and kick me, if that's what you mean!'

For beating up a lone elderly lady, Judah Lovell deserved to be thrashed. For daring to tie up and take an unwilling Lily, he deserved, and would receive, so much more!

Bounced and jostled, every inch of her battered and bruised, Lily had no idea how much longer she could bear to suffer the darkness and discomfort of the caravan, along with the worry about Mrs Lovell's condition, let alone not knowing the reason for any of it.

Surely Giles—someone—would have noticed by

now that she was missing, and attempt to seek her out? To find Mrs Lovell too....

Surely Judah was not so low, so base, as to have harmed his own aunt? The state of that dear lady's belongings, broken and ripped, along with the fact that she was nowhere to be seen, would seem to indicate that he had.

As he meant to harm Lily?

But why?

What possible reason could Judah Lovell have for kidnapping her? Was it possible that he was somehow mentally deranged? Lily could think of no other reason—

All thoughts ceased as Lily heard the sound of shouting outside, accompanied by the caravan surging forward as the horse was encouraged to speed up, several painful splinters going into her bare arms as she was once again thrown across the rough wooden floor, only to be tossed back in the other direction as the caravan came to a lurching stop.

There was the sound of more shouting—could one of those voices possibly be Giles's or was that just wishful thinking on Lily's part?—followed by a brief silence, before the door at the back of the caravan was wrenched open and the blinding sunlight streamed inside to where she lay.

* * *

Giles's earlier anger was as nothing compared to the blinding rage that consumed him as he wrenched open the door at the back of Judah's caravan and saw Lily lying on the dirty floor, her hands and feet tied, a dirty gag filling her pretty mouth, all making Giles wish that he had inflicted mortal damage on Judah Lovell rather than just landing a blow which had rendered him unconscious.

His fury abated slightly—but only slightly—as he saw the way Lily's eyes lit up at the sight of him, before those green eyes instantly became awash with tears. Hopefully ones of relief at being rescued, rather than from physical pain, else Giles really would be pushed into committing an act of violence from which Judah Lovell might not recover!

'Lily!' Giles climbed into the caravan to lift her quickly up into his arms and cradle her against him as he untied the rope from her wrists and removed the gag from her mouth. 'You— I— Thank God I found you in time!' His arms tightened about her and he buried his face against her throat once he had discarded the rope and filthy rag, no longer sure whose tears were dampening her skin, her own or his. He rocked her backwards and forwards in his arms as if he never wanted to let her go again.

In time for what, Lily was unsure; she only knew she was so glad to see Giles, to be held safely in his arms. She no longer cared if she revealed her feelings for him as she threw her arms about his neck and clung to him as if she never wished to let him go.

'Do you feel up to receiving a visitor?'

Lily looked over to where Giles stood in the doorway of one of the guest bedchambers at Castonbury Park.

In truth she was still slightly disorientated at having been brought here at all, once Giles had issued orders for the grooms who had accompanied him to follow on behind and bring the unconscious Judah Lovell back with them to the house, before then sitting astride Genghis with Lily cradled gently in his arms.

They had entered Castonbury Park along the front driveway rather than the back, well away from the curious eyes of the people attending the well-dressing celebrations in the gardens. Giles had refused to relinquish her even once he had slid down from Genghis's back, but instead carried her into the house and up the stairs to this magnificent bedchamber, all the time issuing orders to the servants for hot water to be brought up for a bath, and soothing lotions, all to be delivered immediately if not sooner. Indeed, Lily felt sure Giles would have remained in the bedchamber whilst she took her much-needed bath—and that Lily would have let him—if Mrs Stratton had not shooed him out of the room!

An hour later, freshly bathed, with her hair washed and still damp about her shoulders, she was dressed in one of Phaedra's night-rails. Mrs Stratton tucked her into the warm bed before disappearing along with the bathwater, and Lily now felt as if being tied up and carried away by Judah Lovell must have been a dream. Or a nightmare.

At least, she might have thought that, if not for the soreness of her wrists and ankles where the ropes had chaffed her skin, and the aches and pains in her body from being thrown uncomfortably about the floor of the dirty caravan.

She felt a little shy now as she faced Giles across the width of the bedchamber. 'Of course you must come in, Giles.' Her voice was huskily inviting. 'I have yet to thank you for rescuing me, and—'

'I am not in need of thanks,' he assured her gruffly as he entered, closing the door behind him but making no effort to cross the bedchamber to her bedside.

Lily drank in her fill of him, noting that he had changed out of the clothing he had worn earlier—no doubt it was as filthy as Lily's gown had been. He appeared to Lily now as every dear and beloved inch the aristocratically handsome Lord Giles Montague.

'Nevertheless, I do thank you.' Lily looked down at the gold-coloured brocade coverlet under which she lay. 'I do not know why Mr Lovell behaved in the way that he did, but I am grateful for your rescue. If not for you, I am sure I would have suffered a much worse fate.' She repressed a shiver of revulsion as she recalled the physical threat the golden-haired Romany had made to her before he closed her inside the confines of his caravan.

'Do not think of that now, Lily!' Giles crossed the room in three long strides until he reached her bedside, and was able to take one of her hands firmly within his grasp as he looked down at how tiny and fragile she looked as she sat propped up against the pile of lace pillows.

Tears once again flooded those moss-green eyes. 'I could not find Mrs Lovell earlier. Do you think it possible—?'

'She is safe in the bedchamber next to this one,' Giles assured quickly.

A look of relief instantly came over her pale features. 'I was so worried. I saw the destruction of her home and belongings, and feared that—' She gave a pained frown. 'He did not harm her?'

Giles's expression was grim. 'He beat and kicked her cruelly, and deliberately broke two of her fingers, but the doctor has seen her and says she will recover in time.' He would not soften the blow by lying to Lily after all that she had already suffered.

She gasped. 'I must go to her—'

'And so you shall.' Giles released her hand to firmly grasp her shoulders instead as he looked down into the pale beauty of her face.

'Lily, I thought I had lost you earlier today!'

Her throat moved convulsively as she swallowed before speaking softly. 'I, too, thought I was lost.'

Giles looked down at her searchingly. 'It must not be allowed to happen again.'

'No.' After the ordeal Lily had suffered today, of believing herself to have been taken away from Giles for ever, of that wicked young man carrying out his threat to claim her for his own, she no longer cared in what capacity she might remain in Giles's life, lover or mistress, only that she should never be parted from him again.

'Heavens, how I love you, Lily!' Giles gathered her up into his arms. 'I love you so very much that I will not allow anyone or anything to take you from me ever again!'

Giles loved her?

He *loved* her?

He raised his head to look down at her as he sensed how she had stilled with shock. 'You did not listen to me properly earlier today, Lily, when I spoke of marriage between the two of us. I love you, I am in love with you and I wish—above and beyond all else—to have you for my wife!'

Lily stared up at him, not sure she could have heard him correctly. Had Giles really just said—? Had he just stated—?

His laugh was husky—and slightly uncertain? 'Is there any hope for me, Lily? After all that I have said and done, my abominable treatment of you, is there any chance you might possibly one day come to return my feelings for you?'

It was uncertainty, Lily realised dazedly. The haughtily self-confident Lord Giles Montague was uncertain of *her*. Of her feelings for him!

How could it be possible? What had she ever done to deserve that a man like Giles, a man she now knew to be honourable and true, should fall in love with her and wish to make her his wife?

The latter was impossible, of course, given the differences in their stations, but the fact that he loved her, that he wanted—that he had asked—her to be his wife, was so incredible to Lily that she could only stare up at him with all the love she felt for him glowing in her overbright eyes.

'Lily?'

She melted at the uncertainty she still heard in his dear strong voice. 'Oh, Giles, do you not know how much I—' She broke off as a knock sounded softly on the door of the bedchamber before it was opened and Lumsden stood stiffly in the doorway.

The butler swiftly averted his gaze from where Lily, wearing only the borrowed night-rail, was still held firmly in Giles's grasp. 'Mrs Lovell is becoming agitated at your delay, Lord Giles.'

'I had forgotten all about Mrs Lovell!' Giles shook his head. 'Please assure her that Miss Seagrove and I will be with her immediately, Lumsden.'

'Certainly, my lord.' The butler bowed stiffly before his downcast gaze was once again raised to look at Lily. 'I am pleased to see you feeling so much better, Miss Seagrove.'

'Thank you, Lumsden.' She smiled at him warmly. 'I am pleased to be so!'

He nodded stiffly. 'I will tell Mrs Lovell that you will be with her shortly, my lord.'

'Oh, dear.' Lily chuckled softly once the butler had left, closing the door quietly behind him. 'He is no doubt scandalised to find the two of us alone together and so close in this bedchamber, and me in a borrowed shift.'

They weren't close enough, as far as Giles was concerned, nor would they be until he had Lily as his wife, safely sharing his own bed. 'You were about to say, "Giles, do you not know how much I…"' he prompted huskily.

She avoided meeting his gaze. 'Should we not go to Mrs Lovell?'

Yes, they should. And they would. As soon as Lily had completed that sentence. No matter what it might be! 'Please, Lily?' he groaned achingly.

After all that the two of them had shared, the intimacy of their relationship, it did not seem possible that Lily should once again feel shy in Giles's company. And yet she did.

'Lily, please!'

She could not bear it, could not bear to see the suffering upon his dear and handsome face a moment longer! 'I am already in love with you, Giles.' Her voice was husky but firm. 'I could not have made love with you if I had not already been in love with you, my darling Giles!' she assured him when he seemed able only to stare down at her in stunned disbelief.

'You— I—' He turned to scowl at the door as there was a second knock upon it in as many minutes. 'What is it, Mrs Stratton?' he prompted impatiently as it was she who this time entered the bedchamber uninvited.

The housekeeper looked uncomfortable. 'Mrs Lovell is threatening to get out of bed and come to see Lily for herself if you do not both go to her in the next few seconds.'

'We are coming right now, dear Mrs Stratton.' Lily laughed as she climbed out of bed to pull on the robe which matched her night-rail.

Giles reached out to grasp her hand before she could follow the housekeeper from the bedchamber. 'This conversation is not over, Lily,' he warned determinedly.

'I hope not, Giles.' She stood up on her tiptoes to kiss him lightly on the lips. 'Oh, I do so hope not!' Lily could feel the warmth in her cheeks as she continued to hold his hand as they left the bedchamber together.

Her good humour faded the instant she saw Mrs Lovell looking frail and every inch her seventy-six years as she sat propped up against the pillows in the adjoining bedchamber, her long dark hair shown to be liberally sprinkled with grey as it lay loosely across her narrow shoulders, her poor face battered and bruised. 'Oh, my dear!' Lily released Giles's hand to run across the room, hesitating only as she reached the bed, unwilling to take the elderly woman in her arms, as she so longed to do, for fear she might some-how increase her suffering. 'Judah Lovell is a foul and unfeeling monster!' she cried.

The last time Lily had seen Judah Lovell he had been unconscious, thrown across the saddle of one of the grooms' horses. But looking down at the many bruises and cuts that young man had inflicted upon his own aunt—with his fists?—and the splints support-ing her two broken fingers, Lily wished vehemently that he had not merely been knocked unconscious but dead!

Mrs Lovell gave a wan smile as she reached out with her uninjured hand and grasped one of Lily's. 'He has truly been revealed as the "dark and danger-ous man" that the tea leaves warned us of, my love. He may have the face and hair of an angel, but his heart is as black as the deepest night,' she added in answer to Lily's puzzled frown.

And Lily had feared—fleetingly—that it might be Giles who was that 'dark and dangerous man' who wished to harm her.

How ridiculous that fear now seemed, when he had become the dearest person in the world to her, and the truest friend. Indeed, he was so dear to her, so much a man that she had come to admire as well as love, that it seemed impossible now to think she had ever thought of him in any other way.

'I do not understand why—why your nephew behaved in this way.' She shook her head. 'What could he possibly hope to gain by injuring you and carrying me off in that way?'

She gave another shudder at the thought of what her fate might have been if Giles had not rescued her.

A shiver which Giles saw and responded to by putting his arm about her waist and drawing her near.

'So it's like that, is it?' Mrs Lovell looked pleased by the possessive gesture. 'I had hoped that it might be, but ye never can be sure.'

'You may be very sure, Mrs Lovell.' Giles spoke quietly but firmly. 'I intend to make Lily my wife and ensure that no harm will come to her ever again.'

The elderly woman nodded. 'In that case, there's a tale I must tell the both of you.'

'You really must not trouble yourself with this now—'

'Oh, yes, my chivvy, I must.' Mrs Lovell assured Lily gruffly. 'Today has shown it's a tale that's long overdue.'

'But—'

'Sit ye down, lass, and listen to what I has to say,' the elderly woman instructed firmly.

Giles released Lily only long enough to fetch the stool from in front of the dressing table, and a chair from beside the window, waiting until Lily was seated in the chair before perching on the stool beside her and taking her hand back into his; if he had his way he would never allow Lily out of his sight or out of reach of his touch ever again!

He turned to look at Mrs Lovell, his expression one of gentle enquiry. 'Unless I am very mistaken, one of the things you wish to tell us is that Lily is your granddaughter?'

Chapter Seventeen

'What—?' Lily gasped breathlessly, her eyes wide and shocked as she stared down at the sunken figure in the bed.

'Ah.' Mrs Lovell gave Giles an appreciative glance. 'So you've guessed that, have you?'

'Not until a few minutes ago,' Giles conceded. 'But the likeness between the two of you, now that I see you together with your hair loose about your shoulders, is unmistakable to someone who cares to look.'

'Hard to believe I was once as beautiful as Lily, hmm?' The old lady cackled at her own joke before sobering. 'Judah Lovell saw that same likeness when Lily arrived at the yag with her hair down two days ago!' Her gaze had hardened.

'You—'

'Could the two of you please, please, be silent for

just a moment?' Lily regained her breath enough to be able to gasp. 'I am really your granddaughter, Mrs Lovell?' She looked down at the other woman uncertainly.

The elderly woman's expression softened as she steadily returned that gaze. 'You really are.'

'But I— You had only a son, I thought.' Lily was still too stunned to be able to make any sense out of Giles's statement and Mrs Lovell's confirmation of it.

'Matthew,' the elderly lady confirmed gruffly.

Lily nodded abruptly. 'And when I asked you several years ago, you said that I was not the daughter of one of the young ladies in your tribe.'

'And I didn't lie to you.' The older woman nodded. 'It was my son, Matthew, who was your father.'

Lily's throat moved convulsively, and she barely breathed. 'And my mother?'

Mrs Lovell smiled emotionally. 'Thea. Dorothea. Matthew's wife, and my own daughter-in-law.'

Lily blinked. 'But— Then I am not— The two of them were married when I was born?'

'For a year or more.' The old lady nodded as she gave Lily's hand a squeeze with her uninjured one.

Lily turned dazedly to Giles. 'I am not illegitimate, after all….'

'No, my love.' He smiled at her reassuringly. 'And

it would not have mattered to me if you were. I love you, and would still have wanted you for my wife, no matter who your parents were.'

Lily smiled at him lovingly through her tears. Tears of happiness. Not only did Giles love her and want to marry her, but she was the daughter of Matthew and Dorothea Lovell, the granddaughter of Rosa Lovell. She had a family. She belonged!

She had loved Mr and Mrs Seagrove all of her life, and always would. They were, and always would be, the mother and father of her heart, who had loved and cherished Lily as their own.

But ever since she had been called 'Gypsy' as a child, and Mrs Seagrove had explained when and how she had been left to them as a gift to their childless marriage, Lily had felt a certain sense of displacement, of not quite belonging anywhere. To finally learn who her real parents were, who her grandmother was, meant more to her than she had ever realised. It was—

Lily turned quickly back to Mrs Lovell. 'Where is my mother now?'

'Ah, my chivvy.' Tears filled the elderly lady's eyes. 'She died long ago. It was—'

'No!' Lily groaned achingly. 'When did she die? How did she die?'

It was impossible for Giles to miss the silent plea

for help in Mrs Lovell's eyes as she turned to him. 'Shall we let Mrs Lovell—your grandmother—tell us all in her own way, my love?' he urged Lily gently, wishing there was some way he might spare her any more anguish, but knowing that she needed to learn the truth of her parents and her birth. The strong and determined Lily whom he had come to love would accept nothing less!

She seemed to mentally shake herself. 'Of course. I am sorry, Mrs— Grandmother,' she corrected shyly.

Tears glistened in those wily hazel eyes. 'Ah, and it does my old heart good to hear you call me that at last!'

'I will call you nothing else from this moment on.' Lily nodded firmly.

Mrs Lovell settled herself further up the pillows. 'Then I must begin at the beginning of this tale and not the end.' She nodded decisively. 'Your mother's name was Dorothea Sutherland. She was the daughter of Sir Thomas Sutherland, from Yorkshire. He was a very wealthy and widowed gentleman who had arranged for his only daughter, Dorothea, to marry a lord or an earl or some such—I forgets now. Anyway.' She drew in a deep breath. 'Dorothea, being an independent young lady of twenty-three, and with a definite mind of her own, weren't having none of it.' Mrs Lovell turned to smile affectionately at Lily. 'It's obvious where your own stubborn nature comes from!'

Giles chuckled softly at the slight indignation in Lily's expression. 'You are very stubborn, my love. And I am thankful for it,' he added gruffly. 'I believe I might have continued to wallow in my own arrogant assumptions if not for your determination to convince me otherwise.'

'Very nicely done, Lord Giles.' Mrs Lovell shot him a mischievous glance.

'I thought so.' He nodded ruefully.

'Well, as I say, Thea were a stubborn one. And besides, she already had her eye set on the handsome young Gypsy that was visiting the village with his tribe.' She chuckled wryly. 'My Matthew didn't stand a chance against such a determined young woman, and afore any of us knew about it the two of them had run off together and were married.'

'Were they very much in love?' Lily prompted huskily.

'Very,' Mrs Lovell had no hesitation in confirming firmly. 'Thea's father were none too pleased, o' course, and refused to have any more to do with her once he knew of the marriage. But Thea weren't bothered one little bit. She and Matthew were happy, and she took to the travelling life like one born to it.' Her eyes glowed with pride for the young lady who had been her daughter-in-law. 'Some o' the tribe were none too happy about bringing in an outsider either. Black Jack Lovell, Judah's da, were one o' them.' Her mouth tightened. 'Until he ferreted out that Thea had an inheritance, that is, and decided he might like a bit o' that for himself.'

'An inheritance?' Lily looked puzzled. 'I thought you said her father had disowned her?'

'He did.' Mrs Lovell nodded abruptly. 'But her ma, being a forward-thinking lady, had left some money when she died for Thea to inherit when she turned twenty-one. Once Black Jack found out about it my Matthew and Thea were doomed,' she added heavily.

Lily swallowed down the nausea that had risen suddenly to her throat. 'The shooting accident in the woods?'

'Weren't no accident.' Her grandmother snorted. 'Nor were it the gamekeeper as done it neither.' She scowled. 'I were never able to prove it, but Black Jack Lovell killed my Matthew, your father, as sure as I'm laying here!'

Lily gave a dazed shake of her head. 'But why? What could he possibly have hoped to gain by doing such a thing?'

'Ten thousand pounds.'

'Ten thousand pounds?' Lily gasped.

Her grandmother nodded. 'That were the sum of Thea's inheritance.'

Lily looked stunned. 'But I do not see how? How did your brother-in-law intend to take possession of my mother's money?'

'Could he possibly have intended to marry Matthew's widow?' Giles prompted softly.

'Aye.' Mrs Lovell scowled darkly. 'Thea, being a woman of sense, saw through him. Besides being well along with you, Lily, she were heartbroken at Matthew's death.' She sighed deeply. 'We both were.'

Lily fell back against her chair, so bombarded with information—with emotions—that she could only cling tightly to Giles's hand as her world shifted and settled, before as suddenly shifting again.

Her father had been Mrs Lovell's son, Matthew, her mother Dorothea, a lady, and the daughter of Sir Thomas Sutherland.

Except that was not the end of the story. It seemed that Mrs Lovell—her grandmother—believed that Matthew had been murdered by her own brother-in-law, for the sole purpose of marrying Thea himself and taking possession of her inheritance.

She swallowed hard. 'And is—is my grandfather, Sir Thomas, still alive?'

'No, my chivvy.' Her grandmother looked regretful. 'I found out shortly after Thea died that he'd been killed in a hunting accident six months after Thea ran off with my Matthew.'

Lily looked searchingly at the elderly lady. 'You discovered this shortly after my mother died?'

Mrs Lovell winced. 'You're far too clever fer your own good! Yes, it were after Thea died. I—I had the idea that perhaps your grandfather might be willing to take in his newborn granddaughter and bring her up as his own. But it weren't to be.' She sighed heavily. 'Sir Thomas had been dead almost a year by that time, and wi'out any sign of forgiveness for his only daughter.'

Lily drew in a ragged breath. 'My mother died giving birth to me.' It was a statement rather than a question, and was the only explanation Lily could think of for Mrs Lovell hoping that her maternal grandfather might take in a newborn baby.

'Aye, she did,' her grandmother confirmed quietly. 'But not afore she had named you Lily Rosa, after her own mother and Matthew's.' She smiled tearfully. 'You were such a beauty, Lily, and Thea was so proud o' you.'

Lily gave a pained frown. 'You did not consider keeping me yourself?'

'O' course I considered it.' The old lady bristled. 'I would have liked nothing better. But I daren't.'

'Black Jack?' Giles frowned darkly.

Mrs Lovell nodded. 'As I said, I had no proof that he'd killed my Matthew, but I let him know that I knew, and advised that he take himself off to other climes, and never come back if'n he didn't want me to go to the authorities and leave them to decide what had really happened that day. I told the duke o' my suspicions too, as to who had really slain Matthew—I couldn't let some poor innocent take the blame.' She looked at Giles. 'Your da saw my predicament, and instead of dismissing the gamekeeper he moved him to another o' the Montague estates.'

Giles shook his head. 'I never knew that....'

'No reason why anyone else should know,' the elderly lady dismissed briskly. 'It was between your da and me.'

'It was indeed.' He nodded. 'Black Jack would appear to have confirmed your suspicions by taking his son and going to Ireland.'

The elderly lady sighed. 'But even that weren't far enough away for me. Not when there was a vulnerable babe to consider. The tribe moved on at the end of the summer as usual, but Thea was near her time, so we stayed a few miles from Castonbury until the babe was born. When Thea died giving birth to Lily I knew I had to protect her in some way.'

'By leaving her with the Seagroves once you had discovered that her grandfather was dead, and then returning to your tribe and telling them that both Thea and the baby had died.' Giles looked anxiously at Lily as he spoke, heartsick on her behalf for having learnt who her real parents were, only to as quickly find that they were both lost to her for ever.

'Yes.' Mrs Lovell's voice quavered with emotion. 'I didn't want to give you up, Lily,' She clutched anxiously at her granddaughter's hand. 'I just didn't know how else to protect ye. If Black Jack ever found out that ye were alive, none of my threats would have made an happerth of difference to his one day coming back and claiming ye for himself, or his son.'

Lily still felt completely overwhelmed by all that Mrs Lovell had told her. 'But why? I do not understand. And what possible reason could Judah have had for carrying me off in that way today? Why did he attack you so viciously? Break up your beautiful home and destroy all your things?'

The elderly lady grimaced. 'Because he was looking for something.'

Lily blinked. 'But what? And what can it possibly have to do with me?'

Her grandmother smiled. 'Can you have forgotten your mother's ten thousand pounds?'

'I—' She gave a confused shake of her head.

'I was going to tell you all afore I left Castonbury this summer.' The elderly woman nodded. 'You'll be twenty-one come October, Lily. And on the day of your twenty-first birthday, or the day ye marry, you'll inherit Thea's fortune.'

Lily looked stunned once again. 'I will?'

'Judah couldn't know it, o' course, but your inheritance is all nice and safe in the bank waiting for you, exactly where Thea left it.' Mrs Lovell nodded with satisfaction.

Giles drew in a sharp breath as he realised his worst fear had just become realised. Lily was to be an heiress, whereas he—he was nothing more than the precarious heir of a dukedom which was almost bankrupt!

'Judah told me his da were rambling in his fever when he died a year ago—and may his soul rot in hell!' Mrs Lovell added hardly. 'He told Judah the real reason they went to Ireland, of Thea and Matthew, and the fortune he had lost when Thea and the babe died. It were our misfortune that there were nothing to hold Judah in Ireland once his da were dead, and that he decided to look up his old aunt in Castonbury.' She shook her head impatiently.

'When he recognised the likeness between us the other day, and realised the truth of it, Judah decided to take your fortune for himself.' She gave another disgusted snort. 'That boy's as stupid as his da. Thought I carried the money about with me in my varda. As if!'

'And that is why he beat you?'

'Yes, my chivvy. But he didn't get nothing out o' me.' Her grandmother squeezed her hand reassuringly. 'I told him your money was in a bank where he couldn't get his dirty hands on it.' Her face darkened. 'That's when he decided to carry ye off and marry ye.'

Lily now understood only too well those remarks Judah Lovell had made to her concerning silk handkerchiefs.

Just as she now realised that not only did she have a grandmother, but a fortune too. A fortune which would make her more Giles's equal, and as such able to accept his proposal of marriage....

'Giles?'

He looked up from where he had once again been reading the letter delivered to him only this morning, his expression softening as he saw Lily standing in the doorway of his father's study, and still wearing the borrowed robe and night-rail. 'Is all now settled between you and your grandmother?' Giles had excused himself from the ladies' company shortly after the revelation about Lily's fortune, needing to be alone with his thoughts for a while.

With the knowledge that he was no longer in a position to ask Lily to become his wife.

'For now.' She nodded, smiling as she entered the room and closed the door softly behind her. 'I have left my grandmother and my father to speak privately together.' Her smile widened. 'I believe a considerable amount of that conversation will be memories of what a little hellion I was as a child!'

Giles chuckled huskily. 'I remember you being an enchanting hellion.'

Her eyes widened as she moved to stand in front of the desk where he sat. 'You do?'

He nodded. 'Very much so.'

'And I always believed you never even noticed that I was alive!'

'You were far too impishly entertaining to ignore,' Giles assured softly.

Lily tilted her head as she studied him quizzically. 'You seemed to…leave us rather abruptly, earlier.'

Giles's gaze could no longer meet her probing one. 'Sir Rufus had arrived to deal with Mr Lovell.' He referred to the local magistrate. 'And I thought to allow you and Mrs Lovell some time alone together.'

Her eyes glowed. 'Is it not wonderful news, Giles?' She clasped her hands together. 'Not only do I have a grandmother, but a fortune too!'

'Wonderful news,' he echoed softly.

She frowned. 'You do not seem particularly pleased?'

Perhaps because he was not. Which was totally selfish of him!

And he did not mean to be selfish; it was only that Lily's change in circumstances, when placed beside the now-dire ones of all the Montague family, made it impossible for him to repeat his proposal of marriage to her. 'I am very pleased for you, Lily. I can only imagine how relieved you must be to know the truth after all these years.'

'But...?'

He gave a pained frown at her intuitiveness. 'What makes you think there is a "but"?'

Lily looked down at him searchingly. She had come to know this man very well in the past two weeks—to love him—and although Giles had not returned to that haughtily arrogant gentleman she had known previously, neither was he the loving man he had been but a few hours ago.

'There is a "but," Giles.' She deliberately moved about the desk as she spoke, standing so close to him now that her thigh touched his, and knowing that he was affected by her proximity as a flush darkened his cheeks and his gaze burned hotly as he looked up at her. 'Tell me what is wrong?'

He drew in a ragged breath. 'Could you perhaps return to the other side of the desk?'

'No.' She smiled confidently, knowing that whatever was wrong it had nothing to do with Giles falling out of love with her.

That flush deepened in his cheeks. 'I cannot think logically when you are standing next to me, Lily!'

'And if I have no wish for you to "think logically"?' Lily looked at him teasingly.

'I must!' He stood up abruptly to stand some distance away in front of the window, his hands clasped tightly together behind his back. 'Lily, I— There is a letter atop the desk. I think you should read it.'

Lily looked down curiously at the desktop. 'This letter?' She picked up a single sheet of white notepaper.

Giles glanced back at her. 'Yes.'

'But it is addressed to the Duke of Rothermere.'

He grimaced. 'And my father would have a heart attack and die if he had been allowed to read it before I did!'

'And yet you wish *me* to read it?'

Giles smiled grimly. 'You will see why once you have done so.'

Lily frowned as she turned her attention to the letter, quickly reading the words written there, and the signature of Alicia Montague at the bottom of the sheet of paper. 'This lady says that she is your brother Jamie's widow? And that there is a child!' Lily raised a hand to her throat.

'A boy of eighteen months.' Giles nodded abruptly. 'Named Crispin for my father.'

Lily blinked. 'You had no knowledge of your brother having married before the receipt of this letter?'

Giles shook his head. 'None.'

Lily allowed the letter to flutter back to the desktop before moving quickly to Giles's side. 'She states the marriage took place in Spain some two years ago, shortly before Lord James's death.'

'She states that, yes.'

'But would Lord James not have told his family, told you, if that had been the case?'

'I would like to think so, yes.' His expression was grim. 'I find it...curious indeed, that this woman has waited all this time to declare herself my brother's widow, and her son his heir.'

Lily looked at him searchingly. 'What do you intend to do about it?'

'I had thought to go down to London immediately and speak with this lady myself— What is it?' Giles prompted softly as she gasped.

She chewed on her bottom lip. 'I had not imagined the two of us would be parted so soon after our betrothal?'

Giles drew in a sharp breath. 'There can be no betrothal between us now, Lily.'

'What?' She stared up at him dazedly, her face having gone pale. 'I do not understand, Giles. Earlier today you said— You asked— You do not for one moment think—? Giles, it makes no difference to my love for you whether you are heir to the dukedom or not.'

He shook his head. 'I did not for one moment think that it would.'

She looked uncertain. 'You no longer wish to marry me?'

Giles groaned as he saw the pain in her green eyes, awash with unshed tears. 'Of course I wish to marry you, Lily.' He grasped both her hands tightly in his. 'There is nothing I want more! But— There are several other things you are as yet unaware of.'

'What things?' Her expression was distraught. 'Do you have a secret wife hidden away somewhere too? A son of your own your family is unaware of?'

'No, of course I do not,' he dismissed impatiently.

'Lily, last year my father—' He shook his head. 'All you need know of that is that because of an unwise decision he made a year ago, the Montague family is all but bankrupt.'

She stilled. 'And this is the reason that the estate was allowed to become run-down? And why you personally paid for several of the refreshments at today's celebrations?'

Giles nodded. 'And why my father and I visited the lawyers together last week—on the occasion you believed I was endangering his health by taking him out for a carriage ride,' he added drily. 'And why I have myself called upon them again earlier this week.' His expression was grim. 'All to no avail. The family coffers are all but empty, and Jamie's inheritance from our mother is caught up in the same legality as the naming of the heir to the Duke of Rothermere. Although the latter may not be quite so urgent now that it seems a child who is only eighteen months old may eventually become that legal heir.'

Lily gave a slow shake of her head. 'I am sorry for all of that, of course. I can appreciate how worrying it must have been for you. But I do not see why it should affect our own plans to marry. In fact—' her expression brightened '—once I am in possession of my own inheritance I will be able to—'

'No, Lily!' Giles's hands tightened painfully on hers, his eyes glittering with intent. 'I will not hear of you putting a single penny of your inheritance towards saving the Montague family!'

'And I will not hear of you being so noble as to renege on our betrothal because your family's finances are unsettled and my own are suddenly changed!' Her eyes glittered just as intently.

Giles's expression softened slightly as he saw that determination in her expression. 'You truly are magnificent when you are angry, Lily.'

'Do not attempt to flatter me out of my present mood, Giles.' She glared up at him. 'If you so much as attempt to back out of our betrothal, out of a false sense of pride, then I shall be forced to visit lawyers of my own with a view to suing you for breech of promise!'

He smiled. 'It is not false pride, Lily. Nor, if you recall, did you ever formally accept my marriage proposal.'

'I am accepting now!' There were two bright spots of angry colour in her cheeks as she continued to glare up at him. 'I love you, Giles, and I have every intention of marrying you!'

Giles's heart had leapt at her declaration, only to

sink again as he thought of all the reasons he should refuse. If Lily were to marry him, then she would be marrying a man whose position in life was no longer secure; Giles's personal fortune was dwindling by the day in an effort to keep the Montague family in the luxury to which they were accustomed, and if Alicia Montague's claim should prove true, then he was no longer the future Duke of Rothermere either. It might mean that he could eventually rejoin the army, of course, but would Lily really want that sort of life for herself now that she had the money to do whatever she wished?

'I can imagine nothing I would enjoy more!' Lily's reply was the first indication Giles had that he had asked that last question out loud. 'Mrs Lo— My grandmother—' her face flushed with pleasure '—was quite correct when she predicted that I have always wished to see more of the world. It must be my Romany blood, but I am sure I should enjoy nothing more than accompanying my husband, Lord Giles Montague, when he travels with his regiment.'

Giles felt his earlier resolve weakening in the face of Lily's enthusiasm. In the face of the love for him that shone in the clear green brilliance of her eyes....

'Oh, my darling Giles.' Lily clasped his hands

tightly as she glowed up at him. 'Can you not see how wonderful it will be? The two of us married and together always?'

Giles could see. And how he hungered for it. Hungered for Lily! 'You are an heiress now, Lily, a very wealthy young lady, and may have your choice of husbands—'

'Then I choose you.' Her mouth was set stubbornly. 'If you will have me?'

'If I will have you!' He released her hands to crush her tightly in his arms. 'How can I possibly resist you?' He groaned.

'It is my hope that you cannot.' She smiled confidently.

He sighed his defeat in the face of her determination and his deep love for her. 'Then we shall only be married on two conditions.'

She eyed him quizzically. 'Which are?'

'Firstly, that we will not marry until the identity of the heir to the Duke of Rothermere has been decided upon.'

'But does that mean you will not make love to me again either, until after that matter has been settled?'

How could Giles possibly be with Lily, be in love with Lily and know that love was returned, without making love with her? 'I will make love to you again in but a few minutes if you agree to my second condition!' Giles assured vehemently.

'Very well, I agree.' She grinned up at him impishly.

He shook his head. 'Secondly, that when you come into your inheritance in a few months' time, not a penny of it is to be put at the disposal of the Montague family. That condition is more important to me than the first, Lily,' he insisted as she would have protested.

Lily gazed up at him searchingly, noting the pride in Giles's expression, the determination in his gaze and the stubborn set of his jaw. 'Very well, I agree to your second condition, also. For now,' she added warningly. 'If circumstances should change, then I also reserve the right to change my mind and help in any way that I can.'

'Just knowing that you love me and intend on becoming my wife will be enough to help me to get through this,' he assured huskily.

She reached up and cupped either side of his face as she gazed up at him with all the love she felt for him shining in her eyes. 'I will love you always, Giles. Always.'

'As I will always love you, my darling, darling Lily!' Having believed such a short time ago that he must, in honour, let Lily go, Giles now found himself totally lost to the warmth of her love.

A love for each other that he had no doubt would last a lifetime.

* * * * *

Read on to find out more about
Carole Mortimer
and the

CASTONBURY
PARK
A Regency Upstairs Downstairs

series…

Carole Mortimer was born in England, the youngest of three children. She began writing in 1978, and has now written over one hundred and fifty books for Mills & Boon®. Carole has six sons: Matthew, Joshua, Timothy, Michael, David and Peter. She says, 'I'm happily married to Peter senior; we're best friends as well as lovers, which is probably the best recipe for a successful relationship. We live in a lovely part of England.'

Previous novels by the same author:

THE DUKE'S CINDERELLA BRIDE*
THE RAKE'S INDECENT PROPOSAL*
THE ROGUE'S DISGRACED LADY*
LADY ARABELLA'S SCANDALOUS MARRIAGE*
THE LADY GAMBLES**
THE LADY FORFEITS **
THE LADY CONFESSES **
JORDAN ST CLAIRE: DARK AND DANGEROUS ***
THE RELUCTANT DUKE **
TAMING THE LAST ST CLAIRE **

*The Notorious St Claires
** The Copeland Sisters
*** The Scandalous St Claires

Did you know that some of these novels are
also available as eBooks?
Visit www.millsandboon.co.uk

AUTHOR Q&A

Where did you find the inspiration for Giles and Lily?

Giles is exactly the kind of strong and aristocratically arrogant Regency hero that I love! He also possesses a strong affection and allegiance to his family, as well as an inner determination of will which has seen him survive years of battling against Napoleon's armies as well as the death of two of his beloved brothers. His seriousness of nature hides a deep sensuality, which instantly responds to the exotic and lovely Lily.

Lily was just a wonderful character to write about: independent, capable, and more than a match in will for the arrogant Giles. Her own birth and heritage are something of a mystery until the very end of the book, although I do give tantalising hints as to that heritage throughout the story.

Bringing this unlikely hero and heroine together was tremendous fun.

What are you researching for your upcoming novel?

I am in the middle of writing a Regency duo at the moment, titled *The Daring Duchesses* and due to be published later in the year. A Mills & Boon® Historical *Undone!* e-Book, an introduction to the duo, has already been written, and I have almost finished the first of the duo.

The three heroes are named Dante, Devil and Lucifer, which should give readers some insight into the nature of the three men my three feisty duchesses fall in love and lust with!

What would you most like to have been doing in Regency times?

Well…falling in love with one of my own Regency titled heroes would be a wonderful start! I like my Regency heroines to be not only feisty but independent and strong, so I wouldn't have been one of those women who were content to sit back and do embroidery and manage the household and children while their husbands made all the important decisions. I would probably have been something of a rebel—and loved every moment of it!

AUTHOR NOTE

Through a series of e-mails passing back and forth between the eight authors involved in this Regency continuity, we came up with the idea of an overarching story that would, and does, affect the whole of the Montague family. Sounds straightforward, doesn't it? Except we are eight individual authors, living in different parts of the world, and when for some of us it might be daytime, for others it's night-time—and vice versa! One thing is for certain: we all got to know each other very well through e-mail during six weeks of thrashing out the plotline and then our own individual stories with regard to how they would affect the other seven. That being said, it was tremendous fun, and it has forged a wonderful feeling of friendship between all of us!

My hero, Giles, is the second son of the Montague family. The original heir to the Dukedom, Jamie, was lost in battle against Napoleon's army over a year ago. The family, especially Giles, were devastated by his death, and Giles is now a somewhat reluctant heir. Except, because Jamie's body was never recovered, the law of the time states that Giles cannot officially be declared the heir, and nor can he inherit Jamie's personal fortune, left to him by their mother. All of this leaves the family in a state of flux. Their father, the present Duke of Rothermere, is in precarious health and funds, which only adds to those feelings of confusion and unrest.

Adding to Giles's own disquiet is his realised and unwanted attraction to Lily Seagrove, the adopted daughter of the local vicar—a man Giles has long respected, who is a friend of his own father, the Duke of Rothermere. Lily was left on the doorstep of Mr and Mrs Seagrove's vicarage as a newborn baby, meaning that her real parentage is shrouded in a mystery—although many in the village of Castonbury believe that because of her black curling hair and exotic beauty she is somehow related to the tribe of Romani, who for many years have stayed in the village every harvest time. To Giles, future heir to a dukedom, she is forbidden fruit—both as Mr Seagrove's adopted daughter, and more specifically as the illegitimate daughter of one of the roving Romani. But she is a forbidden fruit he finds it more and more difficult to refuse...

Don't miss the next instalment of Castonbury Park—
THE HOUSEMAID'S SCANDALOUS SECRET
by Helen Dickson

**'Your discretion and good behaviour would be
most appreciated…'**

Returning to Castonbury Park is just another job for
Colonel Ross Montague. With his family in disarray, he
promises to do his utmost to see order and decorum
restored once more. That is until he's sidetracked by the
beguiling eyes of Castonbury's newest maid—Lisette.

An affair would be most improper…but when neither can
deny their blazing desire, all society's rules are discarded.

So, in a house where gossip is rife, Lisette must try her
best to keep her passionate liaison a secret…!

THE HOUSEMAID'S
SCANDALOUS SECRET

Helen Dickson

He raised the stakes higher.

'There is nothing wrong in sharing a kiss,' he stated, now in a more assured tone. 'A mere kiss,' he said, his voice sounding low and husky, 'can be far more tempting than you realise. In fact, I think we might get to know each other better, Miss Napier. So long as we resolve to be discreet,' he said, having no wish to create a scandal by forming a relationship with his sister's maid.' I don't think either of us would enjoy all the attention we would receive at Castonbury Park.'

Lisette stared at him in disbelief at what he was suggesting. Though her stomach clenched with fear she slowly smiled, for she could not deny to herself that she liked the way he touched her. But to become closer would be a dangerous game to play, one that she would not willingly choose to become involved in. Not because it would be distasteful—for she found Ross Montague desirable in every way—but because she could never be anything to him other than his mistress, and she had too much self-respect for that.

'I think that what you are suggesting is an illicit attachment, sir—in which I shall be judged to be a scheming hoyden. I would despise myself—and you. I have done nothing to invite your attentions or encourage the feelings that have taken root.' She stepped away and turned from him. 'Excuse me. I must go back.'

Ross's burst of laughter halted the flow of words abruptly and Lisette spun round, her eyes flashing with indignant sparks.

'How quickly you rebuke me. And there you are, all soft and tempting. And then you chasten me for looking at you and kissing you. Fickle woman,' he teased.

'You deserve to be rebuked,' she was quick to add.

'You think so?' Ross took her in his arms once more. He knew he was playing with fire, but it was the risk that made a game exciting. He did not want to give up the tormenting delight of being alone with her. It was like an addiction—an addiction to the game of testing his desire for her against his resolve. And so he kissed her again—her hair, her cheek, caressing her lips with his own. He pressed her back against a tree, and his mouth travelled downward to where her neck disappeared into the collar of her dress. Lisette held her breath, and the fires of passion and wild, wanton sensations again began to flare within. A touch, a kiss, a look and he could rouse her. What madness.

'Your heart beats much too quickly for you to claim no interest, Miss Lisette Napier...'